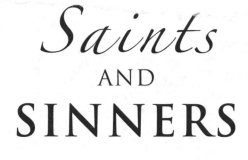

# Saints
## AND
# SINNERS

# PAUL CUDDIHY

# *Saints* AND SINNERS

BLACK & WHITE PUBLISHING

First published 2010
by Black & White Publishing Ltd
29 Ocean Drive, Edinburgh EH6 6JL

1 3 5 7 9 10 8 6 4 2    10 11 12 13

ISBN: 978 1 84502 301 0

**FT
Pbk**

Scottish
**Arts** Council

Typeset by RefineCatch Limited, Bungay, Suffolk
Printed and bound by MPG Books Limited, Bodmin, Cornwall

# ACKNOWLEDGEMENTS

It might have taken me almost forty-four years to get here but it's been worth the wait. I've not been on my own, however, and there are people who, in their own way, have helped shape me and this book. I might be getting all the glory but they're getting my heartfelt thanks, which isn't much but it's the best I can offer!

To Karen, who has made me the person I am and without whom I would be absolutely lost. Like everything else I do, this book is for you, and also for our children, Louise, Rebecca and Andrew, our three greatest achievements in life.

To my Mum & Dad, who gave me a love of books and who always encouraged me to write. And to John and Helen Quail, for everything.

To Stephen Maule, who has had faith in my ability as a writer for almost thirty years, and who will now be shamelessly name-dropping me in every conversation!

To Nichola Fullerton, who inspired me to try and finally achieve my ambition. I couldn't have done it without you and no matter how many people read this book, I will always be glad you were the first.

To Chris Dolan who, as well as being a friend, is one of the most generous and helpful writers I know, and Professor Willy Maley, who has brought some great names to the literary game.

To Lynne Hamilton, who read the book and gave me positive feedback, and Tony Hamilton, who read the last page, which was an achievement in itself. Thanks also to Allan Dougall, John McLaughlin and Craig Dunbar.

To everyone at Black & White Publishing for believing in my novel and giving me this wonderful opportunity.

I thank God every day for the life I have and count my blessings for everyone in it.

TO
KAREN
*Everything I have and everything I am is all because of you.*


TO
LOUISE, REBECCA AND ANDREW
*You make us proud parents every single day.*

# I

# GUARDIAN ANGEL

It might have been the braying of a restless horse or the snap of a branch, like a chicken's neck being wrung, but when Mick Costello recalled it later, he swore it was a hand that shook his body awake, though when he opened his eyes there was no one there. Whatever it had been, Mick sprung out of bed, alert and on edge. He crept across the room and gently edged the latch up before inching the door open. Clouds of mist silently buffeted each other as they rolled towards the cottage, ready to devour it.

Mick stared hard at the mist – he didn't know why – because there was nothing to see, just a wall of soft, white tufts that moved and shifted shape as they got closer to him. It wasn't even like night-time, when his eyes would adjust to the darkness as he walked across the fields from Doogan's, navigating a precarious path home. He had to admit he'd often owed more to good fortune than good sense, especially when he'd had one too many for the road, and there were times when his mother demanded to know who he'd been scrapping with when she saw the state of him in the morning.

'You'll not tell me you fell this time, Michael Costello,' she'd say, peering closely at his battered face. 'There's an angry fist to blame for that eye and no mistake.'

'I swear to God, mammy,' he'd reply, blessing himself. 'It was an accident.'

She would shake her head as she shuffled away from him towards the steaming stove, Mick's nose sensing breakfast wasn't too far away.

'But you should see the state of the wall that did it.'

'You're an awful boy, Michael Costello. Just like your father and no mistake. He was fond of the drink, too, and that's what done for him, God rest his soul.'

Mick would groan and bury his head under his jacket, though it never drowned out his mother's voice or the clatter of pots and kettles on the stove.

'Now get yourself up out of that bed,' she'd snap. 'Everyone else is already out working and there'll be no breakfast for those that don't pull their weight in this house.'

Now Mick could hear his mother's gentle snoring and he glanced over to where she slept, his youngest sister, Margaret, wrapped across her stomach. The other girls – Bridget and Mary – slept back-to-back in the far corner of the room while Patrick had rolled himself into a ball on the bed where Mick had been lying, his sleeping body suddenly cold with the departure of a warm companion.

Mick sighed, his shoulders relaxing, and he pushed on the door, glancing out one final time before he'd let it close over again. Something caught his eye; a glint of light, just for the briefest of moments before it disappeared in the mist, but it was enough to put him on edge again. His heart was thumping and he checked to make sure it hadn't wakened anyone else in the cottage.

Leaving the door unlocked, Mick scurried back to bed and grabbed his clothes, his head almost diving through the hole in his jumper in its eagerness to help him dress quickly. He waited till he was back at the door before he stepped into his damp boots, like standing in a cold pool, but he knew his feet would soon heat up once he was on the move. Slipping his jacket on, his hand automatically reached into the pocket and retrieved a black, woolly hat his mother had knitted him. It would keep his ears warm, he thought, as he edged his way out of the cottage, closing the door over as gently as he could from the outside, all the while desperate not to wake the rest of the family.

Once outside, facing the mist like he was standing guard against its inevitable onslaught, Mick wasn't sure what to do next. The noise of a horse made up his mind. He scurried round the side of the cottage and across the sodden turf until the outline of a wall became visible. He leapt over it effortlessly and immediately crouched down behind its solid form, hoping the chickens wouldn't betray him.

His eyes remained focused on the place where he had seen . . . what? Nothing now but the white clouds and Mick began to wonder if his eyes and ears had been playing tricks on him, but he'd had no more to drink the night before than on any other occasion, and his head didn't feel at all fuzzy.

The sound of a horse again.

Mick tensed and lowered himself until his eyes were staring across the top of the wall. Out of the mist they appeared, men and beasts, ghostly apparitions that he still wasn't sure were real or not. He quickly counted them. Twelve, as far as he could see, including two on horse-back, all wearing red jackets – the Queen's men – except for one rider.

When he dismounted, Mick noticed he was all in black, like an undertaker, but he didn't think the man was there with news of a relative's demise, though he suspected he was here to measure someone for the drop. The man took off his hat, wiped the front of it on the sleeve of his long jacket and then slipped it back on, where it perched perfectly on his head. Mick could have blown it off without too much effort if he'd been close enough, but he wasn't for trying it now.

The man in black stood a few paces from the cottage door. He nodded towards the red jackets, four of whom ran forward and disappeared inside the cottage. Mick cursed the fact he'd left the door off the latch. The rest of the soldiers stood alert, rifles pointed at the door. Their comrades quickly re-emerged into the cold.

'He's not there,' one of them reported to the man in black.

'That's impossible,' he said, signalling to the rest of the men. Seven of them disappeared into the cottage while the original four stood awkwardly outside. This time Mick could hear noises coming from inside, raised voices from his family and the soldiers. Then the seven red jackets came out to report the same thing as their four companions.

'So who is in there?' asked the man in black.

'The mother and some children,' one of the soldiers said. 'Four of them. Three girls and a boy.'

'Well, bring them out then.'

Mick gripped the edge of the wall, digging his fingertips into the hard surface until it hurt and turned his knuckles white.

His mother was pushed out first, with Margaret's thin, bare arms wrapped round her waist. As the older woman stumbled, one of the soldiers instinctively grabbed her arm to steady her. The man in black stepped forward and punched him.

'This isn't a mercy mission,' he said as the soldier staggered back, holding his hand to his face.

Then Patrick and his other sisters appeared beside his mother. The five of them clung to each other for comfort and warmth. The soldiers spread out until they formed a semi-circle round the shivering group. The man in black produced a parchment from his jacket which he unrolled and began reading.

'By the power invested in me by her gracious majesty, Queen Victoria, Sovereign of the United Kingdom and of the Dominions, in this year of our Lord, eighteen hundred and ninety-one, I hereby serve notice of a warrant for the arrest of Michael Costello, in relation to crimes, specified herein, against said Crown. He is to surrender his person to the authority of the Crown, in this instance being myself as the legitimately appointed magistrate of the county of Galway . . . Where is he?'

There was no reply.

'I am here for Michael Costello and I will not ask you again. Where is he?'

None of them know where I am, Mick wanted to shout out but he didn't. He glanced at his fingers, still digging angrily at the wall as tiny traces of blood began to creep out from under them.

'Get the woman,' Mick heard the man in black say and he saw two red jackets grab his mother. He wanted to jump over the wall as the soldiers got involved in a tug-of-war with his brother and sisters over his mother, but it felt like an invisible hand held him back.

The children's collective strength was no match for the soldiers and his mother stood between the two men while his siblings howled into the cold morning, kept back by the rifle butts of the other men.

'If you want to defy the Queen's law, then Ireland will have another few orphans this very morning,' the man in black said.

'I don't know where he is,' she said, 'and even if I did I wouldn't tell you.'

'So be it.'

The man in black nodded to one of the soldiers, who stepped out to face Mick's mother, no more than six paces from her. Now was the moment when Mick had to give himself up, but still he couldn't. His eyes searched the ground around him until they stopped on a rock nestling comfortably in the soggy grass. His bloody fingers started digging at the turf, easily unearthing the rock. It more than covered his hand but he knew he'd be able to throw it as far as he wanted, from here to Doogan's if necessary.

As he stood up his knees cracked and he paused, though no one would have heard it above the wails of his brother and sisters, which were loud enough even to wake his father, and he'd been dead over five years since. Out the corner of his eye, Mick saw a mound of cow dung and quickly immersed the rock in it before launching it towards his mother. He watched as it sailed effortlessly through the air, piercing the rolling clouds of mist and gliding like an eagle towards its target. He muttered a prayer to Saint Jude, knowing that it would be a miracle if he was successful. And then like a silent bullet, it smacked the soldier pointing a rifle at his mother straight in the face and laid him flat out on the ground.

There was a split second of silence as his comrades tried to comprehend what had happened but before anything else could fill that space, Mick began whooping, giant screams of delight that filled every inch of the air. He was dancing, jumping about like he'd won first prize at the Tuam Fair. Then the first bullet whizzed by his ear and slammed into the chicken coup. He heard a muffled squawk and knew it had found a target. Not waiting to be next, he turned and ran, vaulting over the wall at the other side of the pen and sprinting across the field, stumbling and falling and picking himself up and running again.

He could hear voices and more gunshots trying to hit shadows and still his legs kept moving. The voices weren't getting any further away and he knew he'd have to reach the river to have any chance of escape before the horses caught up with him.

His throat was burning, his chest ready to burst but still he kept going, pushing one heavy leg in front of the other. He'd never been much of a runner but now he felt he could run to the end of Ireland if needs be. His life depended on it, after all. Still the voices pursued him, though they'd obviously decided to save their bullets until they were sure what they were shooting at. That thought gave him a moment of relief but it didn't slow him down.

Then he heard the gurgle of water and felt he was almost safe, though in almost the same instant came a thunderous rumble as hooves closed in on him. He pushed himself even faster, struggling for breath as the dawn cold rushed into his mouth every time he tried gulping for much-needed air. And then he was on his back. He lay flat on the wet turf, dazed. He knew whatever he'd hit hadn't been solid enough to be a wall – he couldn't think of any man-made obstacle in the field anyway – and he'd bounced backwards. A snort told him it was a cow. He'd kill that bloody Edward Ryan when he saw him. He was forever letting his herd have the run of the field at all times of day or night.

Mick pushed himself up on his elbow, aware that the thunder was closer than ever, and came face-to-face with a bull. Shit! He staggered back to his feet, not sure whether to sprint or try to creep apologetically past the beast. He rubbed his head, aware of a dull pain that would surely produce a great bump before too long, but now was not the time to feel sorry for himself. He stared at the bull, which stared back unblinking. It snorted, rolls of condensed breath escaping from its square nose and mingling with the mist. Mick didn't need a second invitation to start running again.

The bull was right behind him and Mick knew he couldn't run in a straight line. He swerved to the right and then to the left, all the time the beast's heavy breathing following him. Where was the river? He could hear the water, even louder than before, but just as it emerged from the mist he heard a crack, like the angry spit of a log on the fire, and his left shoulder jerked forward, seared by a hot poker. He stumbled on through the reeds and plunged, head first, into the water.

Mick could never decide what hurt more – the ice-cold river as it welcomed his body, or his flesh, burning from the callous brand of a bullet. He flapped and flailed in the water, trying to get back to the surface and at the same time, pushing himself away from the edge. The bull wouldn't pursue him any further but he knew the others would be less reluctant.

'I think I got him,' a voice said above the clatter of hooves on the ground. 'He's in the water.'

Other voices were getting nearer as the soldiers caught up.

'Spread out along the bank and shoot on sight,' one said. 'And someone do something about that bloody bull.'

A single gunshot rang out in the cold morning, followed swiftly by the crash of the dead beast to the ground. Mick swam with even more determination.

The pub was now enthralled, even those who'd heard the story many times before. Mick Costello could tell a good tale, that's what they all said, and he knew it himself. He sat back and folded his arms with a knowing smile.

'It's thirsty work, this story-telling,' he said.

There were a few groans but within minutes another pint and a glass of whiskey appeared in front of him. He took a long gulp of beer, burping gratefully before sipping the golden liquid and running his tongue across his lips to clear up any stray drops. There were other tales, each one worth a pint or two, and he wasn't slow to produce them on occasion, but this was his favourite. It was also where his story – the reason why he was sitting talking to familiar faces and complete strangers on a cold December Wednesday night in a Glasgow pub – began, so it was well worth the telling, and not just for the drink that wet his whistle and refreshed his memory.

He stood up and stretched, provoking a few groans, and noticed the face of the man who'd supplied the latest drink.

'Don't worry, lads, I just need to make some room for this,' Mick said, lifting up his pint, and the supplier's face relaxed. 'I'll be back in a minute.'

He staggered through the men who'd crowded round the small wooden table and headed towards the back of the pub, the clouds of smoke hovering just below the ceiling reminding him of the mist that morning and a wave of homesickness washed over him. It took him by surprise and he was glad of the fresh air that slapped his face as he stepped outside.

An old man stood at the wall, one hand holding it up while he swayed and sprayed at the same time. Mick stood at the opposite end and stared down at the gutter as he emptied his bladder. A match was struck on the wall behind him and Mick turned his head while trying to make sure he didn't wet himself. Someone lit a cigarette and blew a ball of smoke towards Mick, but the figure stayed hidden in the shadows.

'*God save Ireland, said the heroes . . .*'

The old man in the corner started to sing. Mick thought he recognised the tune and he was sure the old man heard, in his own mind, the right words, but no one else would know what he was saying.

'*God save Ireland, said they all . . .*'

A cough from the shadows and another ball of smoke. Mick finished and turned round.

'You're a grand man for the stories,' the smoking man said.

'Not a word of it a lie and that's the truth,' Mick said.

'No doubt, Mick. No doubt.'

Mick stared at the orange glow in the darkness.

*'Whether on the scaffold high . . .'*

'Who are you then?'

'Just call me your guardian angel.'

Mick took a step forward.

'This is not the time for jokes,' he said. 'You know my name so I'll have yours.'

*'Or the battlefield we die . . .'*

The smoking man took a deep draw on his cigarette and stepped out of the shadows.

'You don't know me,' he said and it was true. Mick didn't recognise him at all. The brow of his cap hid his eyes and cast a shadow over half his face every time the cigarette lit up.

*'Oh, what matter when for Erin dear we fall.'*

'Meath?' Mick said.

'Close. Westmeath.'

Mick nodded. It was a gift he had and it had won him many a drink and more than a few shillings over time. 'Two guesses is all I need,' was always his bet to identify the county of the speaker. If he needed a third go, then the drink was on him and there weren't many times he had to dip his hand in his pocket.

'So what do you want with me?' Mick said.

'There's someone been asking after you,' the man said, taking a final suck on his cigarette before flicking the tiny end in the direction of the old man who was staggering back and forth trying to fix his trousers.

'Who?'

'Short fella. Thin. Nose all bent out of shape.'

'Are you joking me?'

'Dresses all in black. Do you know him?'

Mick nodded.

'He's been offering a tidy sum for any information and it won't take much to persuade someone. You know what it's like yourself.'

'So he's here then,' Mick said, more to himself than the smoking man, but he still got a grunt of agreement in reply. The news shouldn't really have surprised him, yet he shivered like someone had walked over his grave. Part of him was surprised that it had taken so long, yet there was a nagging question at the back of his mind as to how the man in black had found him at all. Even as it pushed its way to the front of his mind, Mick already knew the answer.

It didn't take too much thought to figure out he was hiding somewhere in Britain. He'd fled without a penny in his pocket so America was out of the question. Then it was just a process of elimination. That it had taken almost two months told Mick the search had begun in England – Liverpool probably, then Manchester, and maybe down to London, before heading up to Glasgow.

'Just watch your back, Mick,' the smoking man said. 'That's the message I was sent with.'

'Who sent you?'

The smoking man laughed, a gruff sound that quickly became a heavy cough.

'Your guardian angel . . . and that's no joke.'

Mick nodded and slipped back inside the pub, wishing he could make his excuses and leave, but there was a fresh pint and a whiskey waiting for him along with an eager audience which would quickly turn nasty if he didn't finish what he had started.

He sat back down and clutched his pint, taking a long gulp. His eyes remained on the door at the back of the pub that led out to the toilet but when it opened it was only the old man who staggered in, crashing straight into the back of a heavy, red-haired drinker who spilt the contents of his jug over the floor. He spun round, ready to flatten the culprit, but when he saw who it was he merely shook his head and turned back to his company.

Still the smoking man didn't appear and Mick realised he'd slipped away as discreetly as he'd appeared. Someone slapped Mick's shoulder, eager for the rest of the story, and a pain shot down his left arm, reminding him where he'd stopped his tale.

# 2

## GALWAY KISS

Mick knew he'd been shot but he wasn't giving up without a fight. He managed to push himself about thirty yards downstream, thankful of the mist that aided his escape. There were many voices now at the river as Mick had reached the other side. The first time he tried pushing himself out of the water a pain like a hot branding iron on tender flesh fired through his torso and he let out a scream as he fell back into the water. The soldiers immediately raced towards the source of the noise, one or two of them letting off indiscriminate shots that disappeared into the mist.

He tried again to get out, this time biting down on his tongue as the pressure of his emerging body put almost intolerable strain on his shoulder, but Mick knew it was now or never. Falling onto dry land, he staggered to his feet and stumbled until he collapsed and rolled forward, disappearing from the flat land into a ditch that was invisible to the naked eye. Mick started grabbing at the grass and shrubbery, ripping it up and dropping it on top of his body. It was a pathetic attempt at disguise which would probably be spotted right away but he didn't know what else to do. He only knew that he couldn't run any further.

The soldiers were still on the far bank of the river, though he heard a voice ordering someone to search the other side, quickly followed by the splash of a body entering the water. Mick tried to regain control of his breathing but it didn't help that he was shivering as well now. He lay flat on his back and wished the mist would clear so that he could catch one last glimpse of the blue sky before they found him.

The waiting was the worst part. Waiting to be captured, executed or worse. Tortured. He clenched his fists, ready to throw at least one punch. It would never be said that Mick Costello went down without a fight.

He tensed at the clattering of a rifle on wet boots. Footsteps grew closer and were almost on top of him. He was tempted to hold his breath but knew he'd give himself away when he eventually had to exhale, so he tried breathing softly through his nose. Mick glanced to his right and saw a black, leather boot, so close he could just about kiss it. One step backwards and the boot would crush his face, but it didn't move.

'Any sign of him?' a voice asked out of the mist.

'What do you think?' the soldier muttered before shouting, 'Not yet.'

Mick could hear another horse approaching on the other side of the river and he grabbed hold of the boot, taking its owner by surprise, knocking him off balance and toppling him to the ground. He was upon the soldier in an instant, his thick fingers embracing the man's neck and squeezing as hard as he could, no longer caring that his left arm felt like it was going to fall off.

The neck was scrawny and under-fed but still the soldier thrashed and kicked and fought like a drowning man. Mick knelt on the man's arms and kept squeezing, trying to push the life out of him. He knew it was just a matter of time but he still had to be quick. It was the legs that seemed to die first, seconds before the rest of the body caught up, and when Mick released his grip the soldier sank limply to the ground.

Mick blessed himself as he took a quick glance at the purple face, tongue sticking out like a drunken man, but he was already unbuttoning the red jacket. He wouldn't say a prayer now. He'd save it for the morning after.

'Riley. What's going on over there?'

Mick pushed his foot into the first black boot, which was too small. He curled up his toes and pushed again. It would have to do.

He snatched the rifle up and began to walk away when he realised he'd forgotten the hat. Without that he was wasting his time. It fitted snugly on his head and he tipped it forward to hide as much of his face as possible. He nudged the lifeless body with the toe of the black boot and it rolled into the ditch. Mick took a few steps back and realised that it was almost completely hidden from view.

'RILEY!'

'Sir?'

'Any sign of him?'

'Nothing, sir,' Mick said in a near perfect Cork accent. It was another one of his gifts.

'Well, get back over here. We'll spread out and wait till the mist clears. Then there'll be no hiding place for him.'

Mick inched himself into the water, holding the rifle aloft with his right hand and swimming with his left, though he quickly changed. The pain in his left shoulder was marginally more bearable holding the weapon than trying to push through the water. When he got to the other side he clambered onto the grass, stifling a groan as he accidentally put his full body weight on his injured shoulder. Standing up, he bowed his head and shuffled back towards the rest of the soldiers.

'No sign of him then?' said a voice in the crowd.

'No, sir. Nothing,' he said, finger poised on the rifle's trigger, ready to swing into action at a moment's notice. If he was going down he was going to take as many of them with him as possible. He stopped and waited but no one said anything. A cigarette tin was thrust under his nose and his fingers scrambled among the tobacco to rescue one of the white sticks. He grunted thanks and stuck it in his trembling lips. A flame drew closer to his face, its outer glow offering comforting warmth to his skin and he moved the cigarette closer, drawing deeply on it and nodding.

Most of the soldiers rested lazily on their rifles. One or two had sat down but the ground was still damp. Mick knew he was too wet to bother about the cold seeping through his body but opted to remain on his feet. Whatever might happen, he wanted to give himself a standing start.

He was glad no one wanted to talk to him. It wasn't that he couldn't maintain the Cork accent but he didn't know anything about the recently departed Riley and knew he risked exposing himself as soon as he opened his mouth. It was still early in the morning. These men had probably been awake at least an hour or two before they'd arrived at his cottage and were thankful of the temporary respite.

The rumble of hooves approaching out of the rapidly thinning mist seemed to act like an invisible jolt and men sprang to attention while those on the ground quickly scrambled to their feet. The man in black appeared before them, drawing up his horse a few feet from the assembled group. One of them – the sergeant, Mick guessed – stepped forward with a shake of his head.

'He can't have got far,' the man in black said.

'His body might have sunk, sir,' the sergeant said. 'Devlin said he definitely hit him.'

'Well then, I want a body. Get your men in that water and start searching.'

'Yes, sir.'

The sergeant spun round as the soldiers looked every which way but at him, the appeal of a dip in the icy water lost on all of them. Mick guessed he'd be chosen. He was already wet, after all.

'I want two men to come back with me to the cottage,' the man in black said. 'We're taking his family in. If he's still alive that should flush him out.

The sergeant nodded and suddenly every pair of eyes was eagerly trying to catch his.

'Murphy and Riley . . . RILEY!'

Mick looked up, then immediately down again, mumbling 'Sir,' and shuffling forward till he stood shoulder to shoulder with another soldier he presumed was Murphy. He'd been too busy thinking about his family. What would this incident do to them, his mother in particular? His teeth crunched together angrily and his finger twitched on the trigger, but he managed to fight the urge to lift the rifle and strike down the man in black.

But he was being sent back up to his cottage. The man in black had already brusquely steered his horse around and was galloping away up the field, so he began running just off the left shoulder of Murphy, who led the way. Mick glanced round at the rest of the soldiers who shrunk with every step he put between him and them until they vanished. Ahead of him and Murphy were only fields and random clumps of mist, now isolated like lost sheep searching for the flock.

He kept his eyes on his companion, who was concentrating on running across the heavy ground, his irregular breathing a sign of the physical struggle. Mick slipped in behind him and smashed the rifle butt down on the man's skull. He fell forward, his face sinking into the turf and Mick had spun his rifle round and thrust the bayonet into Murphy's back before he'd a chance to even register the first blow. He pulled and tugged until the flabby flesh released the silver blade, now dripping with blood, and he stood, poised to repeat the motion, but Murphy didn't move. Mick blessed himself and then moved on towards the cottage with a surer and quieter step.

He heard the sobs before the cottage came into view, but when he saw his home, he almost charged at it with a blind rage. The peat roof was already ablaze, beyond the point of any rescue even if the whole of Galway had turned up with a bucket of water each.

The man in black stood back from the burning cottage, hands on hips, admiring his handiwork. Mick's family cowered at the side. His sisters clung to each other and wailed, though the cackling flames had dulled the sound, while his mother was on her knees tending to Patrick who was lying flat on his back in the mud. His brother was a fiery character and the fact he was only eleven wouldn't have stopped him trying to protect the family and their home.

Mick strode past the fire as it devoured all the memories of his life thus far, happy and sad. The man in black, wearing a satisfied smirk, looked at him.

'Keep an eye on them,' he said, nodding towards Mick's family. 'I had to sort the boy but the women shouldn't be too much trouble.'

15

Mick grabbed his hat, throwing it at the man in black, and raised his rifle. The man's eyes opened wide at the same time as his mouth, which no doubt wanted to cry out some plea for help or clemency, but a tiny noise like a creaking door was all that escaped. Mick pulled the trigger and the rifle jammed.

Like a slap on the face it seemed to force the man in black into action and he snatched at the pistol in its holster, but it was barely in his hand when Mick swung the rifle wildly, knocking the weapon out of the man's hand. In the same motion he stepped forward and crashed his forehead off the bridge of the man's nose, flattening him.

He raced over to where his family remained, silent and stunned at what they had just witnessed. Bridget still couldn't quite recognise her brother in a soldier's uniform until he started speaking.

'Mammy, you need to go. Now! They'll kill us all if they find us.'

His mother nodded but her eyes strayed to the prone figure of Patrick. Mick knelt down beside his brother, sliding his good arm under the young boy's back and levering him up.

'Patrick, listen to me. You need to get mammy and the girls away from here.'

Patrick nodded groggily as a dribble of blood trickled down the side of his face from the wound on his temple.

'You're the man of the family now. I'm counting on you. Can you do it?'

Patrick nodded again, this time trying to inject more vigour into the action.

'Come on, let's be getting you on your feet,' Mick said, helping the injured boy up and keeping a tight grip round his waist even after doing so.

'You need to go to John McDonagh's place,' Mick said, looking at his mother. 'Tell him what happened. He'll help you out. You'll be safe there, but you need to go now.'

Mick glanced back at the man in black who still writhed on the ground like a snake. Saint Patrick was meant to have got rid of all of them, Mick thought with a grim smile. He turned round and stared at his sisters.

'You three need to help mammy. No more crying until you get to McDonagh's. Okay?'

The three terrified girls nodded.

'Go! Now!'

Mick ushered them away and they began to stagger off like wounded beasts. There was no time for goodbyes. Mick didn't look back at them as he strode across towards the man in black, his eyes searching the ground for the rifle, though when he heard voices floating into earshot about the noise of the fire which was now hungrily devouring the cottage, he glanced round. His family was almost out of sight now and he knew it wasn't them.

He stopped and listened again. It was the rest of the soldiers. They'd found Murphy or Riley, or both, and he knew they'd be upon the cottage in minutes. He had to delay them long enough to let his family get as far from here as possible and give them a chance of reaching McDonagh's safely.

His feet crunched on the rifle as he scurried about and he grabbed it up, breaking into a jog round the side of the burning building, stopping to go back and claim the man in black's pistol. Taking up a position against the wall where he'd hidden earlier in the morning when the soldiers first arrived, he cocked the pistol. When the first shadowy figure appeared on the brow of the horizon he fired. The shot missed its target but still forced the soldier to throw himself hastily to the ground, no doubt followed by the rest of his comrades.

Slowly, Mick could see heads and bodies appearing, though they stopped beside the foremost soldier. Mick breathed deeply and waited. The soldiers must have known it was only one man they were facing but who wanted to be the one who took the bullet so the rest might overpower the shooter?

It was a few minutes before the red jackets began to move forward. Mick grabbed the rifle, closing his left eye and staring through the sight with his right eye. If the thing hadn't jammed, he'd have a much better chance of hitting someone, he thought, training the sight on the bobbing head of the sergeant and pressing the trigger in frustration. A roar burst out of the weapon and Mick spun back, tumbling across the grass and dropping the rifle. He heard screams and shouts and knew instinctively that the sergeant was dead. Another sign of the cross, more than he'd ever do in a month of Sundays.

The man in black's horse stared at him as he got to his feet. Mick smiled and raced over to the massive beast. It reared as he leapt on top of it, nearly sliding over the other side as he battled for a few moments to get it under control. He knew his family would get to John McDonagh's and he also knew they'd be safe there. Now he needed to look after himself. He steered the horse away from the burning cottage and it was then that he heard the sobs. He looked down at the man in black who remained head down in the mud, face buried in his hands, and he was crying like a baby. Mick shook his head and dug his heels into the beast, gripping the reins as it galloped away.

There was silence in the pub for a few seconds, maybe even as long as a minute. A few voices that hadn't been listening, or who'd heard the story before, could be heard muttering in the corner and the occasional shout or burst of laughter flew across the room.

'You're saying the man was crying?' somebody eventually asked.

'Sobbing like a baby so he was,' Mick said. 'I couldn't believe my ears.'

He could see his audience struggling with the image. Who ever heard of a man crying? He was no man at all is what they thought.

'Well seeing he was an Englishman,' someone said to murmurs of agreement but Mick shook his head.

'Here's the thing,' he said. 'He was a Mayo man and that's the honest to God truth.'

A few heads shook furiously. Voices expressed disbelief. What self-respecting Irishman ever cried after a fight? It was almost beyond belief and one or two eyed Mick suspiciously, beginning to doubt the truth of his tale. He was thankful there were no Mayo men in his audience. In the past they'd felt forced to defend the honour of their county and that ensured a messy end to the night. Mick found that a pocketful of pepper was a great advantage. Throw some of that in the challenger's face and follow up with a couple of punches or a bottle cracked over the skull and, more often than not, the fight would be over before it even started.

'Jesus, Mick, God was looking after you that day,' another voice eventually said.

One or two others agreed. Mick just nodded and then leant forward to snatch up his pint and drain it dry, slamming it none too subtly back down on the wooden table. Hopefully someone would take the hint. The news about the man in black's arrival in Glasgow wouldn't leave his mind, however, and it was probably better if he could get away from the pub and have a clear head to think with.

'So did that all really happen?' It was a quiet voice at the edge of the crowd, a female voice, and everyone looked round.

Her hair, tied back, was as black as coal, but a few strands had broken free and dangled down the side of her face. She returned his smile but it was clear to Mick that she was expecting an answer. He hadn't noticed her before and could only presume she'd hidden behind one of the burly men who'd stood at the front. That wouldn't have been too hard, given that she was half their size.

'What do you think?' Mick asked, folding his arms. She mimicked the action and he grinned.

'I think maybe it was a bit of the drink talking,' she said.

'Is that right then?'

'Aye.'

Mick guessed she was about the same age as him, certainly no older than twenty at most, but she was sure of herself amidst this sea of men.

'Well, maybe you're right and maybe you're not,' he said, 'but do you think I could make this up?'

Mick slipped out of his jacket, pulled down his braces and quickly unbuttoned his shirt to expose his bare, left shoulder.

'Now tell me if you think the drink did that?'

'Jesus, Mary and Joseph,' someone said as the girl shrugged, and it seemed like everyone else blessed themselves. It still made Mick smile, even after having seen it happen so many times before.

'That looks like a map of Ireland.'

# 3

## WHAT KATE DID NEXT

Her tongue started down in Cork, caressing its rugged borders with a tenderness that would melt the hardest Irish heart. She retraced her steps a few times until it felt like she'd completely devoured the county before she slid onto Wexford and then up to Wicklow, whispering each county in turn with a grasp of geography that impressed Mick. She planted her first kiss on Dublin that seemed to cover Louth as well and seemed content to smother the capital with her lips. Mick wasn't complaining, even after she decided to move onto Down.

By the time she'd got up as far as Antrim, Mick groaned and she remained there for a few moments, evidently pleased with his response, though she barely touched Derry before landing at Donegal.

'Home at last,' she whispered with a giggle while Mick, face down and eyes closed, grinned.

He could feel her body-heat seeping into his, her legs straddling his waist and he sighed deeply, almost relaxed enough to fall asleep but knowing why he would much rather stay awake.

Her fingers threaded their way through his coarse hair, stopping on their aimless journey to untangle the barriers they came up against, and still she remained in Donegal. There was Sligo to come, Mayo, his own county of Galway, Clare and Kerry to navigate before she returned to Bantry Bay, but she'd travelled enough of Ireland for one night, thought Mick.

He stretched and roughly nudged her off his body, spinning round in the same movement so that his arm was under her back to cushion the tumble and he was on top of her. Her legs wrapped themselves round his waist again like they were a permanent attachment and her arms pulled his head down till their lips met and their tongues jostled for space.

Her heels were pressing on his back, demanding his body and he thrust forward. She groaned and gripped his hair as he moved back and forth with the urgency of a newly-released prisoner, beads of sweat dropping onto her breasts, immediately bonding with her own moisture. God, he loved Ireland.

Mick lit a cigarette and watched her as she slept, face buried in the pillow. He'd made sure the blanket covered her waist and he gently flicked her hair back so that he could study her profile. As he stood over her, he studied the scar she wore on her back, though it didn't resemble any country he had ever seen on a map. His fingertips hovered above it but he knew their coarseness would waken her if he touched her flesh.

Someone had taken a belt or a whip to her and not too long ago either. It was a fresh wound, still red raw, the skin yet to form a protective scab over it, but he knew he wouldn't ask her about it when she woke up. He knew her name – Kate – and that was as intimate as he sensed she would allow it to be. If truth be told, he was happy enough with that as well.

He'd hoped, even as he'd put his shirt back on in the pub, never once looking away from her warm, brown eyes, that he was not going home alone, though he guessed she'd have something to say about it. She hadn't been afraid to speak up already, bold words in the company of men, so he didn't imagine it would just be as easy as buying her a drink, settling her on his knee where she'd been able to feel his intentions and it wouldn't matter if he forgot her name or even bothered to ask for it in the first place. No, he realised there would be a bit of work involved with this girl.

Most of Mick's audience had drifted away like a cloud of

cigarette smoke, some to the bar, others tagging onto the edges of other conversations, while one or two staggered out the door, ready to navigate the dark and unsteady road home.

'What's a girl got to do to get a drink around here?' Kate shouted out.

'You want to know, darling?' said a drinker at Mick's table, licking his lips hungrily to much laughter. Even Mick was smiling.

'I'm not that thirsty,' she said, hands thrust on hips.

'She got you there, Teddy.'

Teddy shrugged, standing up and gripping his bollocks.

'There's many a woman would be happy for a bit of prime Kilkenny meat.'

'So that's why they're all so hungry in Kilkenny then,' she said, waving her pinkie at him.

'You cheeky whore,' Teddy said, moving towards her.

Mick stood up. 'Take it easy, Teddy. Sit yourself back down. Come on now.'

Teddy reluctantly dropped back onto the seat, helped by Mick's firm hand on his shoulder, nervous snickering from other drinkers ringing in his ears.

'If you were my woman with a mouth like that, I'd soon knock it out of you.'

'If I was your woman – '

'And you,' said Mick, turning to the girl. 'Learn to know when to shut up.'

She made to speak again but Mick grabbed her arm.

'You can help me with the drinks,' he said.

Mick stood leaning against the bar as the pints appeared before him. The offer of a drink had calmed Teddy down and he was talking with someone else, the girl already forgotten.

'You can thank me later,' Mick said as she stood, arms folded, glaring at him.

'If he can't take it, he shouldn't give it out.'

'That's true, but you're talking about a pub and an Irishman and drink. You were just about to get your face rearranged for your sharp tongue.'

She glanced over at Teddy and then back at Mick, her face softer, almost shocked.

'Don't mind Teddy,' said Mick. 'He's a good man.'

She raised her eyebrows.

'There's plenty in here who wouldn't have backed down, and there's a few who would do a lot worse than bury their fist in your face.'

She leant on the bar, not bothering that her elbows were swimming in a puddle of ale. Mick watched her out the corner of his eye. He wanted to stare at her. No, in truth he wanted to rip her clothes off, cover her naked body with a thousand kisses and then ride her till his cock was ready to fall off. He could feel it getting hard just thinking about her and he knew he'd have to think of something else before anyone noticed.

He thought it was her black hair, long and wild, like she'd just battled her way through a Galway storm, the Atlantic winds doing their very worst. Then he caught sight of her eyes again and his heart started beating faster. He watched as her tongue caressed her bottom lip and he had to stifle a groan. At this rate he'd have to stand at the bar for the remainder of the night with his back to the rest of the pub.

'So have you had a good enough look then?'

She smiled as Mick reddened and looked away, stuttering a few sounds that constituted his best effort at a reply. Her glass was placed on the bar, dwarfed by the bulky pints, and Mick picked it up, offering it to her.

'Thanks,' she said, their fingers touching as she took the glass. She smiled again and this time so did Mick. Now he knew for sure he wasn't going home alone.

Kate groaned and rolled onto her side but she didn't wake up. Mick had nearly finished his cigarette, each draw now almost burning his lips and fingers but he was determined to suck as much life out of it as possible before he had to kill it.

It was only now, in the silence of early morning, that he thought again about the man in black. A tiny flash of the weak dawn light had managed to push in beyond the flimsy blanket covering the window and it crossed Mick's foot, warming it as he continued to watch Kate. He was tempted to get back in beside her and wake her so she could continue her tour round Ireland, but he was also thirsty, hungry and desperate to empty his bladder.

Throwing on his shirt and stepping into his boots he shuffled across the wooden floor and unlocked the door, holding his breath as it groaned when he opened it. He glanced over his shoulder but Kate never stirred and he stepped outside, closing it silently behind him. He climbed down three flights, keeping his right shoulder pressed to the wall to guide his way in the gloomy darkness of the staircase. When he got to the bottom he followed the pale, grey light that hovered in the back court, lazily shining through into the close.

Eyes shut, he listened to the trickle of water splashing off the outside wall. He looked down at his target but the bricks were so dark and dirty it was hard to see where he'd soaked them. He felt like it went on forever and he had to shuffle back so that his feet didn't end up swimming in the frothy liquid.

There wasn't absolute silence but it was near enough for this place; a baby crying – hungry or dying, he couldn't tell the difference – in one of the rooms in the building behind him; a cough here, a shout there, but nothing in anger. The clatter of hooves on the cobbled street, getting closer, louder, and then just as quickly fading away. And high above, a bird serenaded him, an unlikely song of beauty amidst the stony sadness. It must have lost its way, he thought, for who would stay here if they had the wings to fly away?

He stepped back into the close, clearing his throat and spitting the contents out onto the grass just as a loud crash of water landed where he'd stood seconds before. It was a lucky escape. A shower of piss was enough to wake any man. He'd done the same many a time, but he'd come outside so as not to disturb Kate. Thanking God for his good fortune, Mick made his way upstairs more confidently, his eyes having adjusted to the bleakness.

As he approached the room, resolved to wake Kate and let her warmth seep through him once again, a crack of light escaping from under the door caught his eye. He stopped and carefully stepped out of his boots, leaving them on the floor as he crept towards the room, praying that his feet wouldn't find a loose floorboard. He pressed his ear close to the door. There was a voice, deep and confident, questioning her, though he couldn't recognise its origins. Occasionally, Kate would answer with a word or two.

Mick glanced back at his boots and then down at his body. He could make good his escape but he'd have to find trousers quickly or he'd be locked up in no time at all. And what would happen to Kate?

He knew her name and what would make her scream with delight when he was on top of her but beyond that, nothing. So what was he risking his life for? His right foot was almost in the boot again when he stopped. He knew he couldn't leave her. He sighed angrily and slid back to the door.

The man was pacing up and down the room, his heavy soles clumping on the wooden floor. Mick pictured Kate cowering in bed, the blanket hastily clasped to hide her nakedness. The element of surprise was his only weapon, he realised, as he took a step back and battered open the door with his right shoulder, shouting wild, Gaelic curses as he did so.

Kate screamed and buried her head under the cover. Mick stumbled into the room and looked round, searching for the man who stood by the window, arms folded and wearing a grin as wide as the Clyde, displaying a full set of teeth the same dirty yellow shade as the dog collar round his neck, which had lost its pure sparkle, worn down by years of sweat, along with the incense that clung to it with smoky relish.

'I see you're still as big an eejit as ever, Michael Costello.'

Mick stared from the man to Kate and back again, his mouth unable to produce the sounds his brain was frantically trying to send it. Kate's black hair slowly reappeared from under the blanket, followed by her puzzled face, which glanced at both men in turn.

'It's not like you to be lost for words, Michael, but I don't suppose you'll have been expecting me,' the man said with a nod towards Kate.

'Thomas . . . Thomas, it's good to see you.'

The two men moved towards each other, throwing arms over shoulders and hugging warmly. They broke the embrace after a few seconds and stood back.

'You're looking good, Mick, if a little under-dressed.'

'Well, you did catch me with my trousers down,' Mick laughed with a glance at his bare legs.

Kate coughed.

'Sorry . . . Kate, this is my brother, Thomas . . . Thomas, Kate.'

'Nice to meet you, Father, I mean, Thomas, I mean . . .'

'Thomas'll do. I mean, we're nearly family now,' he said with a wink that made Kate blush.

'Maybe you and I can catch a spot of fresh air and let this young lady get herself together now,' Thomas said, throwing a pair of trousers at Mick and nodding at the door.

'Aye . . . We'll be downstairs,' Mick said to Kate, whose eyes were urging him to get out as soon as possible. When the brothers were outside the door, Mick popped his head back inside the room.

'Lock the door after us, now,' he said. 'I'll give you three knocks when I get back so you'll know it's me.'

She slammed the door in his face without reply, though he heard the key being turned and he relaxed as he pulled on his trousers, reclaiming his boots on the way out.

'Let's go for a walk,' Thomas said when they popped out of the close-mouth. He turned left and began striding down the street, Mick almost having to break into a jog to keep up with his brother. They passed few people on their aimless journey that seemed to involve taking every left turn, though everyone who did scuttle past doffed their cap with a bow or quickly curtsied.

'They don't usually do that to me,' said Mick. 'They must be trying to make me look good.'

Thomas just frowned.

'Can we not stop or at least walk a bit slower? I'm gasping here.'

Thomas stopped and turned to his brother.

'Did our mother drop you on your head as a baby?'

'What?'

'What's in there?' Thomas said, knocking the side of Mick's head with his knuckles.

Mick pushed the hand away. 'Behave yourself now.'

Thomas shook his head and started walking again, though at a more agreeable pace for Mick, who was also trying to light a cigarette at the same time. He stopped to let the tip of the flame caress the tobacco, inhaling deeply to get it lit. Thomas stopped a few feet away and was lighting his own cigarette, which looked thicker and healthier than Mick's scrawny effort. Collections must be good these days, Mick thought, but he just nodded at his brother through the haze of their intermingled smoke. The cigarette seemed to slow Thomas down and they continued at a more leisurely pace, still turning left at each corner.

'Did you get my message?' Thomas asked after a few minutes.

'What message?'

'My warning. Last night.'

'So that was you then? I should have guessed.'

'So what are you playing at, Mick?'

'I don't know what you're talking about.'

'Going home with some . . . some harlot you barely know.'

'Now wait a minute, Thomas. I'll not have you speak like that about her.'

'What's her name then?'

'Kate.'

'Kate who?'

Mick shrugged. 'She's a good girl,' he muttered.

'You're a bloody eejit,' Thomas said, this time with no accompanying grin. 'This isn't a game, Mick. After what happened back home, you're a wanted man. When someone's offering six guineas just for an address, then it's serious business.'

'Six guineas?'

'I'm just surprised you're still here. I'd be tempted myself with a sum as fine as that.'

Mick whistled as his brother flicked his cigarette stub away.

'Now will you take a telling, Mick?'

Mick shrugged.

'It's maybe better that you get out of Glasgow for a while.'

'But where will I go? I've already run away here and he's found me.'

Thomas stopped and plunged his hands into his pockets. He glanced up and down the street.

'I've got a friend in Liverpool. I'm sure he would help.'

'But he'll find me there, Thomas. He's not stupid. I'd rather stay here and take my chances.'

Thomas shook his head and started walking away. Mick watched him for a few seconds but knew he'd catch his brother up soon enough. He ran along the street until they were shoulder to shoulder, and they continued walking in silence.

Mick understood Thomas meant well. Hadn't he helped him when he'd first arrived in Glasgow, giving him a bed and some food for a few days until he'd managed to find work that would pay for a room of his own? Mick suspected his brother's influence even there. A priest's recommendation was a powerful incentive and if he'd also let it be known that Mick was his brother it would have set the seal on Mick's success. Mind you, he still had to turn up every morning and wait to be picked out as one of the chosen few from the hundreds who scurried to the gates of whatever building site or factory was hiring that day, pushing his way past resentful mutterings when the foreman's finger pointed to him.

He wasn't afraid of hard work, which was just as well, since most of the time it was working on the roads. With a shovel in hand, they dug every day, shovelling dirt from one spot to another without ever seeming to get very far, but he could see from what others had done before them that progress would be made, that someone, somewhere, was in control, in possession of the plan they were all apparently following. Not that any of them particularly cared. As long as there were five shillings in a dirty brown envelope with his name scrawled on the front waiting for him every Friday lunchtime, then he'd dig from here to Timbuktu if necessary.

'Mammy's fine, if you're thinking of asking,' Thomas said.

'You've heard from her?'

'I got a letter from John McDonagh.'

'So they're safe?'

'He wouldn't say where, didn't even mention their names, just in case the letter fell into the wrong hands, but they're fine.'

'He's a good man.'

'He is that.'

Thomas stopped at a corner and Mick realised they were back at his own street.

'I need to be getting back,' Thomas said, holding out his hand. Mick took it and the brothers shook firmly but affectionately.

'So why did they come for you in the first place?' Thomas asked. Mick smiled.

'I knew it was killing you, wanting to ask again.'

'Well, God loves a trier.'

'It's best you don't know, Thomas.'

'You keep saying that, but maybe I could help?'

Mick shook his head and pulled his hand away.

'Look after yourself, Thomas.'

'You, too. I mean it.'

Mick watched his brother cross the road, taking the deferential salute from a driver guiding his horse and cart along the road towards Glasgow Cross, and then he broke into a run towards the close, suddenly remembering Kate and hoping that, even if she was now dressed, her mind wouldn't be fixed on staying that way.

A cluster of people huddled just inside the close, their murmurings instantly silenced when they saw Mick. Something was wrong. He bounded up the stairs two at a time until he was on the third-floor landing and then sprinted to his room where he saw that the door had been knocked clean off its hinges. The room was empty, the blanket sprawled across the floor. Mick picked it up and threw it back on the bed, then snatched it up again and tossed it over his shoulder as he noticed the stain on the mattress.

He dabbed his fingertip on it and held it up to his eye. It was blood. He spun round at the creak of a floorboard from the doorway. A woman stood, gripping her shawl tightly across her chest and peering nervously into the room.

'There was a racket fit to wake the dead,' she said. 'Poor girl was screaming like a lunatic . . . well, until he knocked her sense-less.'

'Who? Did you see him?'

'I kept my door locked, mister. I've got children. They were terrified. But I heard him. A voice like the devil himself,' she said, making the sign of the cross.

Mick slumped down onto the bed and buried his head in his hands.

'Kate,' he muttered.

# 4

## DOUBTING THOMAS

Thomas Costello traced a familiar route back towards the chapel house but it was not with the same purposeful stride that he had set out with an hour earlier. It made him smile to think of Mick still up to no good, though he could feel his face tingling with guilt as he thought of the naked woman in his brother's bed. He was glad the darkness of the room had concealed his embarrassment, and he avoided the candlelight for much the same reason.

If truth be told, and he knew it would have to be when he made a full confession to Monsignor Dolan later in the day, he'd had to suppress the feeling of curiosity which surged through his body. No, it wasn't curiosity, but he could hardly bring himself to acknowledge the truth. He was a priest, after all, a man of God, and impure thoughts were the sins of mere mortals.

He was never sure whether he ever really believed that, even back at seminary in Maynooth, when they had been warned of the temptations of the flesh. 'The ways of the evil one are many and varied,' Canon Barclay, their theology master had hissed. 'He is a cunning adversary and you will have to be on your guard at all times.'

The old man would peer over the top of his spectacles, looking to catch the eye of the curious or spot the disinterested, the latter quickly brought back into line by a silver crucifix he always kept on his desk that would be thrown venomously and accurately at the temple. Blood was often spilt in his classroom.

'A woman's body is the vessel of the devil,' Canon Barclay would declare in a harsh Cork brogue, running his tongue hungrily across coarse lips like he was remembering the taste of female flesh from the distant past, though Thomas would immediately ask God silently to forgive him for having doubted such an esteemed priest as Canon Barclay.

Thomas thought of his own mother. She was a good woman, devoted to the Church and her children, while enduring the penance of an alcoholic husband. He knew in his heart, even if it could not be said of any other woman in the world, that she was not the vessel of the devil. He knew better than to say it aloud, however. If there was one thing that vexed Canon Barclay more than a lack of concentration, it was dissent, disagreement or even curiosity.

They were there to become good priests of Holy Mother Church and that meant listening to him, not questioning him. Doubt was not a Catholic virtue, Canon Barclay believed. Obedience was, and that's what he demanded of his students.

He thought of his former teacher again as he pulled his jacket lapels tightly together to shield against the early morning chill. God rest his angry soul, he thought, shuddering as he pictured the old man looking down on him with a shake of the head and a sharp admonition for the impure thoughts he no doubt knew Thomas was harbouring. Or maybe he is looking up at me, Thomas thought. 'God forgive me,' he muttered, but he still allowed a tiny smile to escape from the edges of his mouth.

He knew his eyes betrayed his true feelings back in the bedroom. He avoided looking directly at the woman, fearing she would guess right away. Perhaps she did anyway, but as he paced up and down the room, asking questions that he felt his position entitled him to, he'd snatch surreptitious glances at her bare shoulders that peeked out provocatively from underneath the blanket. He imagined what the rest of her looked like. If she simply dropped the cover or if he was so bold as to snatch it from her grasp he could have satisfied his curiosity. More likely, he would have struck a match to his simmering desire.

Thomas guessed Mick would have done just that, but he was not his brother. He fingered the collar round his neck, reminding himself of what he was, and always would be. The poor girl would probably have died of shock, he thought, and God knows what Mick would have done if he'd burst in on such a scene.

He had sought out his brother for a reason and the girl had merely been a distraction. O'Connor informed him about her last night. Thomas had hoped Mick would at least have shown a little bit more care and sense of self-preservation especially after the warning, but after O'Connor, who'd waited in the shadows until closing time at Haggerty's, reported back to him that Michael hadn't left the pub alone, Thomas realised he needed to speak to his brother face-to-face.

O'Connor could be an intimidating presence when he wanted to be. Certainly, Thomas was always uneasy when he met him although he'd never shown anything but the utmost respect for the priest, but whatever talents he had in that particular field were lost on Mick.

Thomas still wasn't sure, even after his early morning visit to his brother, whether it had left the desired impact. He had exaggerated the sum being offered for information on Mick. The real amount had only been told to him second-hand in any case, but he guessed the larger figure might appeal to his brother's vanity. And while he still didn't know what had brought the soldiers to their mother's cottage, Thomas knew from what Mick had told him that he'd made powerful enemies that day. His brother would be safer away from Glasgow. Hiding in a city as small as this, and with a fondness – or a weakness – for drink and women, was a recipe for disaster.

Thomas shook his head despairingly. He'd visit Mick again, maybe even as soon as this afternoon, though he realised it was probably better to let the younger man sober up a bit. The message might have a bit more resonance to a clear mind.

Up ahead a crowd of people, five or six-strong, huddled round the front of a building. Thomas started to cross the road to avoid them but one man noticed his presence, nudging another bystander who turned round. Someone else shouted, 'Father! Father! Over here!' and he had no choice but to continue on his path until he reached them. As he did so, they parted like the Red Sea to reveal an old man slumped against the tenement wall. He was rocking side to side but somehow managed to retain enough balance to avoid toppling over completely. A walking stick cut a lonely figure on the pavement, just out of reach of the old man, whose trousers wore the dark stain of an overflowing bladder. Thomas screwed his face up at the stench seeping from the frail body.

The old man coughed and spat out a mouthful of blood that turned the ground black. A wayward trail of red liquid that hadn't managed to escape trickled down the side of his mouth but he appeared oblivious to its presence. Thomas crouched down, swallowing hard to settle his stomach, suddenly thrown into turmoil by the old man's odour. He removed a snowy white handkerchief and ran it gently down the side of the old man's face.

Thomas couldn't help glancing at the hankie and then wished he hadn't. He looked round, wanting to throw it away, but the old man coughed again and Thomas sprung to his feet, stepping back to avoid being hit by any of the debris. He leant over and thrust the small piece of cloth into the old man's hand. He clutched it, moving his fingers over its surface like a blind man and the faintest flicker of gratefulness broke out across his lips. Either that or it was simply another glimpse of his pain.

He obviously realised what was in his palm as he moved his shaky hand up to his face and dragged the stained hankie across his mouth. Thomas noticed the old man's hands were pale and bony, like death had already set in. He'd probably been lying in the street all night, though any sympathy was tempered by the smell of alcohol, which cloaked the old man like a dirty rag.

'Bless me, Father . . .' the old man mumbled and Thomas leant in closer to try and decipher what was being said. Another deathly cough escaped as the priest rummaged in his jacket pocket for his stole, draping the regal purple sash round his neck.

'In nomine Patris, et Filii, et Spiritus Sancti. Amen,' he said, making the sign of the cross over the old man, to which everyone else followed suit, with some going down on one knee beside him. As he muttered the prayers of the confessional, Thomas was aware of shuffling feet behind him and glancing over his shoulder he saw that the crowd had expanded. It was mostly men who had stopped on their way to work. Many of them had removed their caps and they stood, heads bowed; a few lips moved in silent prayer.

'Is he dead?' one man near the back of the crowd asked.

'Not yet,' another said, blessing himself, an action automatically imitated by those standing either side of him.

Thomas frowned and turned back to the old man, his wizened face now the same colour as his hands. The priest grasped one of those hands, surprised by the strength of the grip in response, but it was a short-lived burst of spirit and Thomas could feel the life draining out of the old man until his hand rested limply in his palm while the other still held the stained handkerchief.

'Pater noster, qui es in caelis, sanctificetur nomen tuum,' Thomas began praying and the crowd, suddenly transformed into dawn mourners, silently listened as the mysterious Latin words which they would hear at Mass every Sunday without knowing what they meant, floated out across the cold Glasgow street.

'Adveniat regnum tuum,' murmured Thomas. 'Fiat voluntas tua, sicut in caelo et in terra. Panem nostrum quotidianum da nobis hodie, et dimitte nobis debita nostra sicut et nos dimittimus debitoribus nostris. Et ne nos inducas in tentationem, sed libera nos a malo. Amen.'

With a final sign of the cross over the old man's body, Thomas stood up, his knees cracking in the sombre silence, a hand at his elbow to steady him. Thomas accepted the nods of the crowd as he slowly walked through them. His work was done here now, for what it was worth. If there was a soul to have been saved there, then he had done all he could have. Now the practicalities of death would take over and someone would be along with a horse and cart to scoop the old man off the street and away to a pauper's grave unless a relative appeared to claim him, in which case Thomas might well get a knock on the chapel house door later, enquiring as to the availability of his professional services. He suspected, however, that the man had died unknown and all alone.

Now he was aware of a hunger rumbling in his stomach and he hastened his stride until the tip of St Alphonsus' Church could be seen, licking his lips as he thought of the breakfast Mrs Breslin would prepare for him.

He sat nursing a mug of tea in his hands, staring into the dancing flames of the fire that Mrs Breslin had built up on his return. She had fussed like a devoted mother when he'd stepped back into the house, offering promises of food and warmth in one breath and then words of chastisement in the next for having been out on such a cold morning without his heavy coat.

Thomas could only smile and allow the housekeeper her say. She'd hung up his hat and jacket for him, insisting that he put on a jumper which she retrieved from his room, before ushering him into the front room and setting him down in the armchair nearest the fire, which was soon sparked into life.

As Mrs Breslin bent over the fire lighting the coals, Thomas had sneaked out to the bathroom without a word. He wanted to scrub the stench of death from his hands but even as he held them in the bowl he wasn't convinced that the cold water was doing the job. He'd ask Mrs Breslin for some hot water later on, though he'd tell her it was to heat his flesh. The mention of death would arouse her curiosity and she'd plague him for details that she'd carry back to her own house later on. She might even know the old man and he didn't want to take the chance in case she insisted on talking about it longer than would feel comfortable for him.

Mrs Breslin had a husband and several children of her own – five, he thought – yet she was at the chapel house every morning before seven and sometimes it felt like she never left. It was a labour of love for the church, he knew, but the wage redeemed from the weekly collection, meagre as it was, was probably just as appealing.

'Are you looking for answers in the flames, Thomas?'

Thomas looked up as Monsignor Dolan stood in the doorway.

'I was dreaming, Peter. I think I'd have been sleeping in another five minutes.'

'Well, I'm sorry to have disturbed you then,' Monsignor Dolan said, sitting down on the armchair opposite Thomas's and holding his hands out in front of the fire, rubbing them together appreciatively.

'Quite the early bird today?'

'It's been a rough morning,' Thomas said. He explained about the old man, but mentioned nothing of his brother, while in the back of his mind he wondered how he could possibly unburden the sin of his impure thoughts to his fellow priest. He knew that the seal of secrecy in the confessional box would not be broken but he couldn't see how it would do anything other than alter their relationship. What would the older man think of him? He couldn't bear the thought of disdain or disgust creeping into the building, an unwelcome houseguest.

Peter was his boss, in this house and chapel at any rate. He was the parish priest of St Alphonsus', as well as having the elevated title of 'Monsignor', so a modicum of deference was required. Thomas didn't mind. He'd served under fiercer priests than Peter and, though never admitting it out loud, he actually liked his colleague.

Peter was in his sixties, he guessed. They never spoke about such specifics as age, but Thomas has made an educated guess from what the parish priest had said regarding his studies, his contemporaries and when he arrived in Glasgow. He was a Wexford man, though he was just as fiercely proud of his adopted city as he was of his homeland. He'd been at St Alphonsus' for as long as anyone could remember and though he could be a fierce orator, particularly when attacking the scourge of alcohol – despite his fondness for a late-night dram himself – and the evils of Protestantism, his parishioners had a fondness for the priest that Thomas envied.

The older man sat back in his chair and crossed his legs, slipping a hand inside his jacket to retrieve a long, white envelope.

'So what have you been up to?' he asked as he handed the letter over. Thomas studied it, turning it back and forth, reading his own name on the front of it above the name of the church. When he flipped it over, he recognised the seal immediately. He stared up at Peter.

'I know,' said the parish priest. 'And I'm not moving until I know what's in that envelope.'

Thomas studied the envelope nestling in his palm. He wasn't sure if the handwriting was Archbishop Eyre's. Probably not, he thought. It was more likely to be one of his staff, who would also have sealed it. He ran his fingertips over the seal, half expecting it to burn his flesh and then smiling at his own stupidity.

'Are you not going to open it then?' Peter asked impatiently.

Thomas tugged at the envelope but, realising it needed a bit more coaxing to open, went over to the writing table in the corner and retrieved a paper knife. Its sharp blade slid effortlessly through the paper, leaving the seal intact. He took the letter out, discarding the envelope, and scanned it quickly. Peter sat where he was, ostensibly calm and disinterested, but Thomas knew that curiosity had gripped the older priest.

To receive any correspondence from the Archbishop of Glasgow was rare and when it did arrive, it was always addressed to the parish priest. Indeed, there were times when Peter had examined the contents of a letter and not disclosed them to Thomas, and he was tempted to torment Peter in the same way.

Now he re-read the letter more closely, ignoring the exaggerated coughs behind him. It was a short letter, only one sentence, and after reading it a few times, Thomas felt confident that he'd memorised it. The signature was Archbishop Eyre's. He was sure of that. He vaguely recognised it from the letters that Peter had deigned to show him and it was different from the writing on the envelope.

'He wants to see me,' Thomas said, looking up.

'When?'

'This morning. Eleven o'clock.'

'Today?' Peter said, standing up with a frown. 'Whatever can it be about?'

Thomas shrugged. Peter was probably wondering if his assistant was about to get a promotion but Thomas was less sure. Such news was normally announced by letter or a visit from one of the Archbishop's minions, but he was being summoned to the Cathedral. The prospect filled him with an instinctive sense of dread, though he would happily suppress it until it came time for the meeting, not least because it meant he could enjoy Peter tormenting himself as he imagined what rewards awaited the younger man. Thomas tried to smile but he was sure it looked more like a smirk. He had less than three hours until the meeting.

# 5

## PENNIES FROM HEAVEN

Mick Costello had a problem. How was he to find a man with 'a voice like the devil himself' in a city like Glasgow when it was full to the brim with wretched and damned souls round every corner, up every tenement close or propping up every bar between the Gallowgate and the Broomielaw? He would have liked time to quiz a few more people, perhaps uncover an eyewitness able to offer more than a terrified and exaggerated description of the man's voice, but he didn't want to stick around in case the police showed up. Someone was bound to have sent for them or word would have travelled fast to the London Road station, with a couple of officers perhaps already dispatched to investigate.

The last thing Mick needed was any contact with the police. It might be all the man in black was waiting for and he'd find himself heading back to Ireland quicker than you could say a prayer to St Michael the Archangel, asking for his help to defeat Satan.

Reluctantly, but with an urgency born out of necessity, Mick gathered up what few belongings were his and clambered over the broken door, heading quickly back down the three flights of stairs. Whoever had demolished the door was strong as an ox. It was a solid wooden structure that Kate had locked as well but it had been battered to the ground without ceremony, an impressive if intimidating feat of strength that gave Mick cause for real concern for probably the first time since he'd arrived in Glasgow.

His brother had sent a warning the previous night and when that had been ignored, he delivered another one in person, but it was only with Kate's abduction that Mick realised the danger he was in. What would have happened if he'd not been out with Thomas, if he'd still been lying in bed on top of Kate's naked, sweating, warm body? Would he still be alive now to think of such a marvel?

The man in black had obviously brought reinforcements with him, or acquired them on his arrival in Glasgow. He remembered the thin, spindly body who'd produced pathetic tears at the sight of his own blood on his hands, and he knew his pursuer had neither the physical nor mental strength to knock down the door.

Mick was suddenly aware of the cold as he stepped out from the mouth of the close, looking up and down the street to see if anyone – the police – was approaching. He shivered and remembered his mother's words from when he was much younger. 'That's someone walking over your grave, son,' she would say with a nod of the head and the sign of the cross. He would always follow suit even though he never knew what she meant. He'd always been too afraid to ask but he knew now.

He kept picturing Kate, the way her mouth wore a lop-sided grin as he lowered himself on top of her like it was his first time and she was going to give him the benefit of her vast experience; the sweet taste of her nipples, still lingering on his lips which he licked automatically. His fingertips tingled as they remembered running up and down her spine as she arched her back with every one of his hungry thrusts, the smooth texture interrupted by the callous scar she wore without complaint; gentle caressing of her wound only served to heighten her eagerness and her nails dug deep into his own flesh, urging him on.

He wanted to go back to just one hour ago, when he had stood vigil over her, smoking, while she enjoyed a peaceful sleep. Or he could go further back to the pub and the warning his brother had sent him, which he would now have heeded. It might have deprived him of his night with Kate, but it would have saved her from a fate he did not even want to begin to imagine.

Mick was momentarily paralysed, not knowing where to move, or even how to. The dawn wind, silent but deadly, snapped at his flesh, and he lit a cigarette with trembling fingers in the futile hope that some stray ripples of heat would wash over him. There was still a cluster of people on the pavement and one or two of the women eyed him suspiciously. He held their gaze until they looked away.

'Did any of you see anything?' he asked, blowing smoke in their direction.

No one answered. One man began to edge closer to the entrance of the building and the rest seemed to be drawn along in his undertow.

'I'll make it worth your while if you did.'

One of the women snorted, immediately taken aback at a noise she had hoped would have remained silent.

'What's that supposed to mean?' Mick said.

The woman shook her head, refusing to speak even after Mick's demands had become more insistent.

'Talk is cheap, mister,' the man nearest to the close said. 'There's only one thing loosens the tongue other than the drink round here and I haven't seen any sparkling in your hand.'

Mick's free hand fumbled in his pockets but he knew he had nothing that would impress them enough to speak, even though he had no idea whether anything he paid for would be at all useful in helping him start his search for Kate.

'You'd have my thanks,' he said. 'And many would be glad to have Mick Costello's gratitude to call on.'

Now the man snorted and scratched his grey beard with scrawny, black fingers.

'That'll not put bread on the table,' he said. 'You'll excuse me now for I've had enough of your blethering.' And with that, he disappeared into the close. Mick finished his cigarette angrily, fighting the temptation to pursue the man and knock the insolence out of him.

He was uncharacteristically restrained but at least it snapped him out of his inertia. Flicking the dying embers of his cigarette into the gutter, he turned and strode away from the group still standing in front of him. He had almost reached the end of the building when he heard urgent footsteps approaching. Balling his fists, he turned the corner and, once out of sight, spun round and planted himself firmly in the middle of the pavement, ready to punch whoever was in pursuit. And he was in the mood for a fight.

When the young woman appeared round the side of the building, Mick was glad he wasn't already swinging his arm because he would probably have killed her had he connected. She was no more than fourteen years old, probably the same age as his sister, Bridget. A dirty shawl was wrapped round her head but it couldn't hide the ghostly pallor of her skin, stretched taut across her face. Dark eyes were sunk deep in their sockets, blinking furiously like they were adjusting to the daylight. Her cracked lips were covered with weeping sores and they moved slowly as she spoke, as if every word was a painful effort.

'I saw him, mister,' she mumbled.

Mick had to lean in close to hear and she recoiled slightly.

'Sorry,' he said, taking a step back.

'He was big, so he was,' she said, stretching her right arm up as high as it could go.

'As tall as me?'

'Bigger. He had to bend to go through the door.'

'You saw him go into the room?'

The girl nodded, glancing over either shoulder to check that the man wasn't lurking nearby.

'So where were you?' said Mick.

'On the landing above. He didn't see me. I was on my way to work when I heard him stomping up the stairs so I stopped and waited.'

The girl started coughing, the effort of so many words obviously a shock to a throat not used to so much exertion at the one time. Mick hesitated, not sure whether he should offer any help and ignorant as to what that help would be should she say yes. More likely, if he moved towards her again, she'd take fright and run away, so he waited until the coughing subsided.

There were so many questions floating around his mind he didn't know which one to blurt out first, but while he was still wrestling with his words, the girl started speaking again.

'He pushed the door down like it was made of straw,' she said with an awestruck shake of the head. 'You should have heard the noise when it crashed onto the floor. Then the girl started screaming.'

'What did he do?'

'I don't know. I couldn't see inside the room and I was too scared to go any closer in case he saw me. But I heard him, mister . . .' she shivered and blessed herself.

'What did he say?'

The girl blessed herself again. 'All he said was, "You can run but you can't hide." '

'What does that mean?'

'I don't know, mister, but it was the way he said it. Honest to God, I nearly fainted when I heard that voice. I'll never forget it,' and she made another sign of the cross.

Mick was no longer concentrating on the girl, his frown now focused on the words the man had said to Kate. He had no idea what it meant, if anything at all, but he knew that Kate was in danger, and it was all his fault. He didn't even want to think about how much worse it might already be for her if they'd figured out how little she knew about him. Her potential useful-ness was probably her only chance of survival, and he hoped without too much optimism that she realised this.

The girl coughed again, a short, sharp burst to get his attention.

'I better be getting back, mister. I'll probably be late for work now.'

'Oh, right. Thanks,' Mick said, taking two penny coins from his pocket, the only money he had left in the world. He held them out to the girl who snatched them from his hand with the deftness of a fairground magician, the coins disappearing somewhere into the depths of her frugal clothing. She began to scurry away.

'What colour was his hair?' Mick shouted after her, desperate for one final piece of information.

The girl stopped and looked back at him, shaking her head. 'He didn't have any.'

'What do you mean?'

'His head was bald and shiny like a freshly laid egg,' she said, almost managing to push out a smile at the thought. She turned and disappeared round the corner, leaving Mick puzzled and penniless.

He was too late to find work. He knew that even as he headed to familiar haunts, only to be greeted by locked gates, empty offices and the occasional apologetic shrug from foremen who were normally helpful. He needed money, that much was for sure, though having the day might help in the search for Kate, if only he knew where to begin. And being able to cross a few palms with even a penny or two might well provide the vital fragment of information that would lead him to her.

Standing in the mouth of a random tenement, Mick lit another cigarette. He briefly considered asking his brother for help, but it was something he was reluctant to do. He knew that he'd get another lecture for free along with whatever money Thomas might be able to muster up for him and he'd had his fill of lectures, for one day at least.

Still, thinking of his brother had given him an idea and he strode off in the direction of the Calton, briskly sprinting across the road ahead of an oncoming carriage, the driver's abusive shouts as he reined in his horse only serving to make Mick smile.

On another day there would have been cross words, flying fists, bloody noses; on another day he might have been flat on his back while a panting beast, the sweat steaming off its glistening coat, looked down at its handiwork with a disinterested air, just another dead body to be scooped up off Glasgow's streets and deposited in a pauper's grave without a single mourning tear to feed the mound of soil piled up on top of the cheap, wooden coffin.

But Mick was now a man with a plan and the sooner he could hear his pockets jingle, the sooner he could begin asking questions.

The door of St Mary's Church was already slightly ajar when he pushed on it, the oak barrier creaking with the effort of swinging open. He shut it behind him and stood perfectly still, waiting to see whether the door had announced his presence to anyone already in the church. After a couple of minutes, when the only sound that could be heard was his own breathing, Mick ventured further into the building, walking gingerly and gently, eyes and ears alert for any sign of another presence.

He'd snatched off his cap as he stepped into the church, dipping his finger in the holy water font and blessing himself as he passed it, like he was shuffling in to attend a long overdue Sunday morning Mass. But it was Thursday, the church was empty and he wasn't here to say his prayers or listen to the incoherent, incomprehensible Latin mutterings of the priest.

His boots seemed to land heavily on the wooden floor, each step sending a noise out ahead of him, bouncing off the walls and high roof like an endless echo, heralding his imminent arrival. He began walking on his toes, which succeeded in dulling the noise slightly, but he remained on edge, ready to drop to one knee at any moment like he was only here for quiet contemplation should he encounter anyone.

A black box rested in the back row, the letters 'SVDP' scrawled across the front of it in white paint. Mick's eyes quickly scanned round the rest of the church before he picked up the box and shook it. Silence. He cursed under his breath and put the box back down. Standing still, arms folded, he tried to work out where the money would be kept, even as a thought nagged away at the back of the mind that the priests wouldn't be stupid enough to leave such temptation lying around for any weak soul to succumb to. Certainly, they would know better than to hope in the good nature of man, not when there were so many hungry mouths and empty stomachs to fill, never mind thirsts to be quenched.

A cursory check in the sacristy at the side of the altar confirmed Mick's fears and trudging back through the church, his mind raced with thoughts as to where else he might get some money. It looked as though he would have to go, cap in hand, to his brother after all.

The door of the church suddenly creaked and Mick automatically searched for somewhere to hide, slipping into the priest's side of the confessional box that nestled unobtrusively down the left-hand aisle of the church. His door clicked gently as he closed it over and he sat down slowly, eager not to make any noise that would alert whoever was coming into the church.

It might be one of the priests, in which case he'd look pretty foolish if they found him in here. At the very least he'd have to conjure up some sort of credible explanation for whoever stumbled upon him; if he was really unlucky, the police might be called and he'd already resolved to stay well away from their prying questions. Why hadn't he just slipped into one of the rows, knelt down, bowed his head and moved his lips in silent prayer? He shook his head at his own stupidity, his blind panic.

Yet, if it wasn't a priest, it could be a kindred spirit, someone else with the same eye for money and the same diabolical inspiration as to how he could get some, in which case hiding in the confessional box didn't seem like such a daft idea. The creature, no doubt desperate in his own way, the same as Mick had his personal reasons for wanting some money, would quickly discover that the St Vincent de Paul box only offered a false hope and he'd also head for the sacristy in the forlorn hope that the priests had deposited the previous Sunday's collections casually in a cupboard, trusting in God and the goodness of humanity. Mick almost laughed out loud at his own naivety – and desperation – that had seen him search the room not five minutes before.

Should he surprise the intruder, feigning mock outrage at the sacrilege being committed in this house of God and hoping that his actions might generate a reward from a grateful clergy later on? That was an even more ridiculous thought than the one he had about there being a bounty of cash in the church in the first place. So he continued sitting perfectly still, the footsteps getting closer until he was aware that he'd stopped breathing to avoid potential detection.

Then the door clicked and someone stepped into the other side of the confessional box, closing the door and shuffling noisily over to the grill which separated priest and sinner, a black veil draped across the wrought-iron giving a thin protection of identity for the person about to unburden their soul. Mick always believed the priest recognised his voice anyway, so he always felt he'd have been as well pulling back the veil, shaking the priest's hand and saying, 'Bless me, Father, it's Mick Costello here. It's been five weeks since my last confession and I've done a couple of dodgy things that I'd like you to forgive me for.'

A man began speaking in nervous tone that was so quiet Mick had to press his ear close to the veil to hear.

'Bless me, Father, for I have sinned. It is one week since my last confession.'

One week, thought Mick. How bad could you be in just one week? He thought at once of the sins he'd stacked up in the last twenty-four hours and grinned sheepishly. The man coughed. Mick stared through the veil. He could only make out the shadowy outline kneeling across from him and he knew he was just as concealed, yet he sensed the man was waiting for a response. He wracked his brain, trying to remember what the priest said to him when he had begun his own confession in a similar vein, but nothing came into his head. It had been a long, long time since his last confession. He grunted, slightly panicky, but the noise seemed to be enough for the man who began speaking again, quicker now and in a more agitated manner, like he was desperate to get everything out before he changed his mind or the offer of forgiveness was withdrawn.

He was a Derry man, of that Mick was absolutely sure. He pictured a small figure, nervous, bullied by his wife, laughed at by his workmates, scorned by his children. There was an agitated need for forgiveness in his voice which seeped through towards Mick, who had to resist the urge to tell the man to pull himself together or stretch a hand through the cloth and slap his face; if he'd done that the man was liable to figure out he wasn't really a priest.

And what of the sin? The whiney voice explained that he'd found a shilling at the factory where he worked, just inside the doorway of the canteen area where they all gathered every day for lunch. He knew who had lost it.

'I saw it drop out of Jack Gallagher's trousers,' he told Mick. 'There must have been a hole in his pocket or something. But he didn't notice – no one did except me. And I should have shouted him, but instead I stopped and put my boot on top of it. Just stood there and let a few people past before I bent down and pretended to tie my laces. And then the shilling was in my pocket. It still is, but I know what I did was wrong, Father. I know it's stealing.'

Mick grunted in agreement, only half listening. He'd been hoping for something a bit juicier, sexier. Maybe the man was riding his wife's sister, or at least had been thinking about it. But this? Bloody hell, he'd have done the same thing in a second and he wouldn't have ended up in the confessional box agonising about it.

'So I don't know what to do, Father. If I just go and give Jack the money, he'll know I'm a thief . . . and we could really do with the money ourselves.'

'Have you any more sins to confess, my son?' Mick asked impatiently.

'No, Father, that's it.'

'Well, you'll have to make a good act of contrition.'

'Yes, Father,' the man said, murmuring the words of the prayer as Mick stifled a yawn.

'And for your penance say two hundred Our Fathers, four hundred Hail Marys, a Glory Be to the Father and twenty decades of the Rosary.'

There was silence from the other side of the grill and Mick had to hold his nose to stop any laughter escaping.

'Sorry, Father. Can you say that again?' a trembling voice eventually said.

'Two hundred Our Fathers . . .'

'Two hundred?'

'Four hundred Hail Marys . . .'

'But that'll take forever.'

'A Glory Be to the Father and twenty decades of the Rosary.'

'I'm due back at work in fifteen minutes.'

'Your penance is your penance.'

'But four hundred Hail Marys? It's never been more than twenty before.'

'That's the new limits, my son. The Holy Father himself set them . . . for all the worst sins.'

'But I only stole a shilling.'

'Only?'

'I know what I did was wrong, Father, but that's a lot of prayers.'

There was a pause as Mick began coughing and giggling at the same time. As he tried to compose himself, an idea came into his head.

'There is another method of repentance,' Mick said, stumbling over the sentence as he struggled to remember the appropriate words.

'What is it, Father?'

'A shilling.'

'Pardon?'

'The shilling you stole will buy you forgiveness for all your sins without having to do a penance.'

'I've to pay for forgiveness?'

'It is the will of the Holy Father. The penance should fit the sin. Would you question that?'

'No, Father, but . . .'

'Well, it's either that or the two hundred Our Fathers, four hundred Hail Marys, Glory Be to the Father and . . .'

A silver coin appeared in front of Mick, grudgingly pushed through the grill. A thick finger still pressed down it, layers of grime coating the skin, many days' worth of earth nestling under the nail. Eventually it released its grip and retreated back across the divide.

'God bless you, my son,' Mick said.

The door clicked open after a few seconds but slammed shut and Mick braced himself for a confrontation with the unknown man. Instead, he heard angry footsteps stomping towards the front door and he sat back with a smile. A few more sinners and he'd have enough money to start looking for Kate.

# 6

## NEEDLE IN A HAYSTACK

He walked into Haggerty's, almost pushing his way through the clouds of tobacco smoke lingering in the air, much of it having refused to leave at closing time the night before. He'd already ordered a pint and a whiskey, lighting up his own cigarette and contributing to the hazy gloom, before he thought to glance round the pub. It had been an automatic reaction to get a drink and he had to remind himself why he was here.

It had seemed like the obvious place to begin his search, the pub where he had met her just a few hours before. He shook his head as he remembered. It was hard to believe that it had only been such a short time since she'd challenged the truth of his tale. He knew, even as he pushed the door open, that she wasn't going to be sitting there with a drink in one hand, a cigarette in the other and a smile on her face that said, 'Where the hell have you been all this time?'

His eyes scoured the room nevertheless, nodding at those who did so to him and studying those who didn't. There was no sign of Kate. There were no women at all in the pub. There was no sign of a giant bald man either and Mick turned back to the drinks that had now appeared before him. Handing over a couple of confessional coins, he realised this wasn't such a good idea. By the time he'd visited the half dozen pubs within a stone's throw of Haggerty's, he'd have run out of money and would be right back where he started and he'd had enough of Glasgow sinners for one day without having to hear any more confessions.

The money was meant to buy information and he'd have to use it wisely. Gulping down the whiskey, which gilded his throat with a warm, comforting feeling, he nodded to the barman.

'There was a girl in here last night,' he said. 'Donegal lass. Long black hair, eyes as brown as a nut.'

'That sounds like half the women in Glasgow,' the barman said.

'You're a Donegal man yourself?' Mick said.

'Indeed I am.'

'A fine county.'

'God's very own.'

'And here's me thinking it was my beloved Galway.'

The barman smiled. 'God shines on us all.'

'Never a truer word said . . . Her name was Kate. That's as much as I can tell you.'

'I can't help you and that's the God's honest truth. But if I were looking for a young lady who might frequent such a place as this, then I might be trying down nearer the docks.'

The barman winked knowingly and Mick glared at him.

'I'm not saying that's where you'll find her,' the barman said quickly, holding his hands up. 'It was just a thought.'

Mick nodded and attacked his pint with impatience, eager now to escape from the pub. The barman had annoyed him, even though he was only saying what most other people would as well, and Mick didn't want to give out any more details, certainly not about the man in black, not when there were six guineas waiting to be claimed by whoever delivered Mick into captivity. At any rate, it was a plan, of sorts at least, and a better idea than shuffling in and out of every pub he came to with only the vaguest set of questions to ask anyone. He knew little enough about Kate and he already knew her more than most around here, so it was unlikely he'd find any answers amongst the drunkards and degenerates he was currently rubbing shoulders with.

Draining the final drops of liquid from his mug, he slammed it down on the counter and without a word or sign of acknowledgement to the barman he strode out of Haggerty's and into the watery light of the December day. It would be about twelve o'clock now, he thought. Half the day already gone and he was no further forward in his search. He strode along the Gallowgate towards Glasgow Cross, listening out for the hungry cries of sea-gulls that would tell him when to turn and head towards the waterfront.

Mick reached his destination with an uncharacteristic burst of determination but the sights and sounds that greeted him forced a halt to his progress. The noise of the birds which had drawn him to the river could no longer be heard above the roar from the mass of bodies which thronged along the water's edge, even though hundreds of the creatures hovered in the sky, darting this way and that, occasionally swooping low whenever there was even a glimpse of food on the ground; they'd more often than not be beaten to the prize by a hungry hand on the dockside.

He could do no more than light a cigarette. Taking deep draws on it, he blew puffs of smoke out in front of him, temporarily blurring the sight before him before drifting away, leaving him yet again with the stark scene before his eyes.

It seemed like people were moving in every direction but not getting anywhere. Some shuffled away from the water, others scurried towards it, while bodies darted in and out of the throng. Their purpose was unclear, but Mick had several ideas and none of them were particularly pleasant. Part of him wanted to shout out a warning to those poor souls who had just arrived in this strange land. He could easily pick them out in the crowd. Whether on their own or in frail family groups, they shuffled aimlessly along the dockside, shoulders hunched, threadbare clothes pulled tight around skeletal frames, bony hands gripping battered luggage which held all their worldly possessions. Everything else had been left behind and lost forever in Ireland.

Eyes were wide, vacant and brimming with hopelessness, still trying to recover from what they'd witnessed on the journey over the water. Yet pupils still darted frantically, searching desperately for a welcoming face or at least a helpful one that could offer advice or guidance on where to find food or shelter. It was enough to make Mick shake his head in despair. He knew there was little chance of these people finding what they were looking for. Instead, their luggage would be snatched, what little money they possessed would be taken by fair means or foul and they'd find themselves even worse off than when they'd first set foot on dry land, something they'd never thought possible.

Relatives and friends may well have led the way just a few years before, the Great Hunger driving millions out of Ireland, many of whom landed in this city and on these docks, and memories of the famine still rumbled on in the stomach of every Irish man, woman and child who repeated the journey. The crossing from Ireland should have been bad enough. It was, as Mick knew himself, but everyone who crammed onto boats, jostling for an inch of space with the hundreds of other bodies who'd paid their pennies for passage across the Irish Sea, clung to the hope of a better life when they finally disembarked. How wrong could they be?

Two girls were heading towards him though he wasn't sure they realised they were on a collision course. They were both hunched over, probably with the cold, but it looked from a distance like they were carrying the weight of the world on their shoulders. All they did have were identical brown cases, no bigger than a folded newspaper. The cases clattered off their scrawny legs that, even though they were hidden from view by heavy, ankle-length skirts, Mick still knew existed. It was like the Holy Ghost, he thought with a smile and wondered whether something religious had rubbed off on him during his short spell in the confessional box.

As the girls got closer, he could see they were sisters. They had the same red hair, its natural fieriness dampened down by the severity of their crossing to Glasgow but more than that, when they glanced up at him in perfect timing, like a puppet master was working them from above, they had the same look of despair painted on their pale faces. Four blue eyes held his gaze only briefly before both heads bowed down again and they shuffled on past him. His eyes followed them until they disappeared round the corner into the dark shadows, which he feared would soon devour them.

It made him think of Kate again and he realised it would do no good to his search or his soul if he continued to stand witness to this pitiful scene that never seemed to change, no matter how many times he set eyes on it. He headed in the same direction as the red-haired sisters but when he rounded the corner, they were already gone and he knew better than to spend any time wondering as to their fate.

He was grateful that he could make a retreat from the sea of bodies and not plunge headfirst into its murky waters. The women he needed to speak to were nearby, in the lanes just off the waterfront, but it seemed like another world as he slipped away, leaving behind the unfortunate people either arriving or leaving Glasgow; he could never make up his mind which was worse. He could still hear the noise of a thousand human voices, all mixed in together, though it was more of a lingering murmur than the deafening roar it had been just moments before.

Within a couple of streets, it seemed like God had shut the trap door on the sunlight, pitiful though it generally was at this time of the year. Mick knew it was the tall, grimy buildings, jostling for space and stooping over oppressively which created the noontime gloom, but it set him on edge. This was a place where bad things could and did happen under the convenient cover of darkness. He wished for a moment that he was armed, but he had to be content with clenching his fists, which remained hidden inside jacket pockets.

He was past the opening of the tenement when a cough stopped him in his tracks and drew him back. A body sat in the corner, almost out of sight. At a glance it could have been a bag of rags but it moved as he came into view and coughed again. A bony hand that looked as if it had slipped up through the ground from a grave appeared from within a black shawl and pointed towards the door.

'Here. It's all here.'

It was a woman's voice, probably, but it was impossible to figure out how old she was.

'I know what you're looking for,' she said.

Mick strained his ears but couldn't figure out the accent. Years of drinking, smoking and God knows what else had robbed it of its identity and it was just a croak that escaped from the depths of her throat.

'We've got young ones here for you.'

Mick didn't reply but continued staring at the woman, though he threw occasional glances over either shoulder just to make sure he wasn't being set up for an attack. That was the sort of trick a newcomer would fall for, but he knew better.

'Straight off the boat, so they are. Worth every penny. Fresh.' Her voice held onto the last sound like the sizzling of meat in a frying pan and Mick glared at her.

She shrugged. 'Maybe you like the old ones,' she said, snatching the shawl from her head. Her cackle echoed out onto the street as she saw his reaction, his body recoiling at the sight; she was soon gripped by a coughing fit that Mick feared would take her for good. She was bald, except from a few tufts of hair that had stubbornly refused to fall out or were optimistically trying to grow back in. Her face was a mass of red lines, like someone had drawn all over her and her mouth, when it opened to fire its chilling laughter in his direction, was just a black hole. The toothless trap shut tightly again after a few seconds and the shawl resumed its vital task of hiding her from the world.

'I'm looking for a girl,' Mick mumbled. 'Her name's Kate.'

The bag of rags nodded like it was being shaken by an invisible hand.

'Is she your favourite?'

'Long black hair. She's from Donegal and her eyes are – '

The hand reappeared and pushed weakly on the door, which opened a fraction and then shut back over again.

'You'll find what you're looking for in there.'

'She's here?' he asked, moving quickly towards the door. Five skeletal fingers halted his progress and then stretched out flat in front of him, hovering at his chest. He stared at the woman's hand for a few seconds before he realised what he was meant to do and he scrambled in his pocket for a coin, finding the smallest one he could and dropping the ha'penny on her palm, which immediately disappeared back under the shawl. He could hear disappointed mutterings but she didn't stop him when he stepped past her and pushed through the door.

It was as black as a coal mine and he stood with his back pressed against the door. He could feel his eyes nervously checking out the surroundings though he knew that nothing would become any clearer no matter how long he stood here. It had been gloomy enough outside, but once he'd crossed over the doorway, he had entered a world of total darkness.

Swallowing hard and resisting a sudden urge to pull open the door and flee, he quietly stepped forward. His body was tense, alert, ready to repel any sudden attack, as he inched along the passageway, each tiny footstep taking him further away from the exit which he didn't dare turn round and look at; he wouldn't be able to distinguish it at any rate. Shouting out 'Kate' would probably make more sense. At least it would announce his presence and probably hasten the end of his search, one way or another, but the element of surprise was all he had to his advantage and it wouldn't do to give it up just yet.

His journey in the darkness ended abruptly when he met another door in front of him. He staggered back slightly, but quickly regained his balance, knowing that someone was bound to have heard the collision. He waited.

A key was turning and he heard a click as the door unlocked. He'd expected to hear footsteps but it was as if whoever was on the other side had been standing there all the time just waiting for somebody to collide with the barrier. Slowly the door began to open and as it did, a streak of candlelight scurried out from the gap and streaked up the floor.

When the door was half-open, it stopped moving. Mick waited for someone to appear, a voice to question him or at least a hand to beckon him forward. He thought of rushing the door but he didn't know what he was plunging into.

'I'm looking for a girl,' he said in a nervous voice. It was like he'd uttered the secret password because the door flew open and a girl stood before him. Her hair hung loose over her bare shoulders which she made no attempt to cover with the flimsy white house-coat she wore. She nodded towards the room behind her and he stepped through into the light. The door slammed shut and locked behind him and he spun round.

'Don't be scared, darling,' she laughed. 'We'll let you out again when you're finished.'

Her accent was pure Belfast, hard and straight to the point. She glided past him and dropped down onto one of four wooden chairs crowded round a table in the middle of the room. She immediately snatched up a half-smoked cigarette from the table, putting it between her lips and holding it close to the flame of a candle. Puffs of smoke bellowed out of her mouth and Mick reached for his cigarettes, though he was glad he still had some matches to light his own.

The girl sat back and studied him while a man sitting next to her took a deep gulp from a bottle of whiskey before wiping his mouth with a dirty sleeve. Grey stubble was dotted all over his face while his hair of the same colour was wild and unkempt.

'Will you take a drink?' he asked with a grunt.

Mick shook his head.

'Suit yourself,' the man said, taking another gulp.

'I'm looking for a girl,' Mick said, his apprehension suddenly replaced with impatience.

'So you said,' the Belfast voice said, blowing a cloud of smoke in his direction. 'What are you wanting then?'

'I told you, I'm looking for a girl.'

'Listen, darling, they're all looking for girls when they come in here. So tell me what you're after and I'll find the girl for you.'

'Her name's Kate.'

'We don't have any girls called – ' the old man began to speak but a slap on his grisly face silenced him abruptly.

'Kate, you say?' said the girl. 'Just give me a minute.'

She disappeared through another door and Mick lit a cigarette as the old man leered at him with a crooked smile, black stubs sticking out of bloodied gums. The whiskey would help dull the pain in that decaying mouth, Mick thought.

A sudden scream roared up from beneath them and startled the two men. They both stared at the floor as it seemed to howl in pain.

'What the hell was that?' Mick asked, his eyes continuing to focus on the wooden floorboards as if somehow he'd eventually be able to see through them and witness whoever, or whatever had made that noise, because he wasn't sure if it was human or not. It had scared him, no doubt about that, and he had to fight the urge to bless himself. He looked back up at the old man who was shaking his head.

'Is there somebody down there?' Mick said.

'Save your breath, mister,' the old man said. 'No good ever came from asking questions here. I'll tell you that for nothing.'

Mick began to speak again but the door opened and the Belfast girl reappeared.

'That's her ready,' she said, nodding over her shoulder.

'Kate's here?' Mick said, the hellish scream immediately forgotten as he strode towards the other room. The girl stood, arms folded, in the doorway. Mick knew right away what she wanted and he didn't even mind handing over the shilling. It would be money well spent, he thought, if it meant getting Kate away from here.

As soon as he stepped past the girl the door closed behind him though he was relieved to hear that it hadn't been locked. It was a small room, dimly lit by a tiny stub of a candle that sat on the window-ledge. The window itself was black with grime, ensuring that no natural light was ever going to break in. Mick shivered, though he wasn't sure if it was the cold or a delayed reaction to the scream.

She sat on the bed with her naked back to him. The black hair that snaked down her spine was the same colour but he knew right away it wasn't Kate. There were scars on the girl's back but none as fresh and painful as the one he'd seen the night before.

'Turn round,' he said.

The girl glanced nervously over her right shoulder. Her face was painted – the Belfast girl must have hastily applied some make-up – but Mick could tell she was still a child. Her eyes blinked furiously and a tear managed to escape, immediately turning black as it rolled down her cheek.

'What's your name?'

The girl hesitated as she tried to remember what she'd been told.

'It's okay. I know it's not Kate.'

Panic rushed across the girl's face, like she'd done something wrong even without speaking.

'It's okay,' Mick said. 'It's not you I want.'

He turned towards the door and then stopped, pulling out a penny and walking back over to the girl. He pressed the coin into her trembling palm with a wink and then walked out the room.

'Jesus, you're quick,' the old man spluttered as Mick closed the door behind him.

'That's not Kate,' he said, looking round the room. 'Where's the girl?' he asked.

The old man shrugged.

'I need to speak to her.'

'Maybe she's got nothing to say to you.'

He punched the old man who toppled backwards, chair and body landing heavily on the floorboards. Mick was upon him before the man, who'd still managed to keep a safe hold of the whiskey bottle, could pull himself up. Grabbing him by the throat, he pressed the rough flesh and the man began to splutter.

'If you know where she is, you've got about one minute to tell me.'

The old man's eyes were brimming with terror but he didn't have the strength beyond a couple of frantic punches, which landed harmlessly on Mick's shoulders, to fight back. Mick squeezed tighter as a sharp edge suddenly pressed in on his own neck. He tensed.

'We don't want any trouble, darling.' The Belfast voice was trembling but the hand that held what he presumed was a knife seemed steady enough.

'Now let Benny here go.'

Mick held his grip for a few more seconds as Benny struggled for breath before releasing the old man, who rolled on to his stomach, coughing and spluttering and holding his throat. The knife was still pressed on his own flesh.

'Now it's your turn,' he said.

'How do I know you won't turn on me if I do?'

'You don't.'

'I don't want any trouble here.'

'I'll be on my way as soon as your knife lets me. There's nothing here for me.'

He knew the girl had only two choices – to let him go or kill him – and she'd have to be strong if she wanted to do the latter. She chose wisely and stepped back from him and he stood up, rubbing his skin where the knife had been.

'Her name's Kate,' he said, 'from Donegal. She's got – '

'Sorry, I can't help you,' the girl said. 'I don't know anything.'

Mick shrugged and nodded at the locked door, which the girl hastily opened for him. He plunged back into the darkness as he heard the lock clicking behind him and he walked, arms outstretched, down the corridor, until his fingertips hit the wood of the outside door.

He stepped over the bag of rags still sitting on the stairs and walked away, annoyed at his own stupidity. It had all seemed easy, apparently finding Kate in the first house he looked, but she could be anywhere in the city. It was unlikely that the man in black would bring her here. She could be on her way back to Ireland at this very moment for all he knew. She could be lying at the bottom of the river. He was no further forward in his search to find her and he knew that the longer he took, the worse things would be for her.

There was still money jangling in his pocket and this time he strode with a purpose – to find the first pub he could. He was never very good at thinking with a clear head. Maybe a few drinks would help him figure out his next move.

# 7

## HEART OF DARKNESS

The lights had been turned out on her world and Kate lay perfectly still in a darkness so thick and oppressive you could cut it with a knife. Mind you, the fact that she could only open one of her eyes didn't help, and even that one found it difficult to adjust to the surroundings. There was nothing to focus on, not even the shadowy outline of a chair or a table, and Kate preferred to keep her good eye closed and pretend she was sleeping.

A sliver of wind crept into the room, slipping under a tiny gap at the bottom of the door and gliding across the floorboards to where she lay. It caressed her left eyelid, which fluttered irritably though it would not open, and Kate could not roll over and turn her back on the invisible draft. When she had tried moving, a pain seared through her chest like a ragged knife cruelly twisted in her flesh and she struggled to breathe as if her head was being held under water. That was where his boot had landed, how many times she could not say. She'd been unconscious for most of the attack.

The wind would sometimes subside, or increase in velocity and Kate wondered if it was actually his cold breath, just inches from her face, toying with her. It was a petty cruelty that was perfectly in keeping with his character and she stretched out her right arm, grasping blindly though she only gathered handfuls of black nothingness. She was alone in the room and the thought was strangely comforting.

If only sleep would come to her, then her dreams might offer some respite, but she'd been slipping in and out of consciousness long enough to leave her frustratingly alert and aware of her circumstances. And could she be sure that sleep would bring dreams and not nightmares? She shuddered as her mind flooded with memories, whether real or imagined, and in them all he was standing over her, silently inflicting retribution for her perceived sins. The only sounds he wanted to hear were her painful cries for mercy, he had told her, yet the louder she begged, the more ferocious he had become until there was nothing else she could say. In her mind she had known her words were wasted, but her jaw also ached from where his fist had landed.

Kate ran her tongue round her swollen lips, the drips of saliva offering a soothing balm to her tender flesh, though when she tried the same thing in her mouth, she realised a couple of her teeth were now clinging precariously yet defiantly to her gums.

A stray tear escaped from the corner of her good eye and rolled across her face. Kate stuck her tongue out and caught it, immediately licking her lips, though its salty tang only served to heighten her thirst. More tears were now pouring out of both eyes, though they stung her left one which she again tried to open without success. She tried to picture how she must look right now, like she'd been run over and crushed by a speeding horse and cart, and it only made her cry even more, though as her shoulders began to shake with the sobbing, waves of pain rippled through her body and she tried to halt the grief for her former self which was gripping her very soul.

She knew it wouldn't do any good to feel sorry for herself and anyway, hadn't she known the consequences of getting caught after running away? She'd seen it happen before, to other girls, and she'd never said anything at the time. But she thought she was smart enough to escape. If there was any anger left in her battered body, and she was scared to feel too much of anything in her current state, then it would be mainly aimed in her own direction. If only she hadn't gone home with the storyteller, then she might still be free. She knew, even as she thought it, that it didn't make any sense. No matter where she'd ended up, he would still have found her and she was only glad that Mick wasn't in the room when he had. She'd heard his tale of escape from Ireland, complete with a few dead bodies, and even if he was telling the truth – she still suspected a few characteristic Irish embellishments – he would not have stood a chance of protecting her.

She'd recognised the heavy footsteps as they approached the door though she tried to fool herself into thinking it was just Mick returning, and she'd glanced quickly around the room, hopelessly trying to find somewhere to hide and escape. The door flew into the room, landing with a loud crash on the floor, which almost drowned out her scream. His fist was already sailing through the air and just inches from her face when he'd said: 'You can run but you can't hide.'

She remembered those words now, even though it felt like his punch had almost wrenched her head clear off her body, and she knew she'd been an idiot. Better that she'd thrown herself off Jamaica Street Bridge and allowed the cold, comforting waters of the Clyde to hide her forever than to think she could stay alive and free of his clutches in this city. Once he had claimed her, not long after she'd first arrived in Glasgow, then her life was no longer her own and she'd have been better accepting this grim reality than pretending there was something better out there.

Yet . . . she let that word hang in the blackness and allowed the tiniest of smiles to break out from the outer edges of her wounded mouth. Hadn't she found something better last night? For a few hours at least she had been able to pretend that everything was normal, that she was just Kate Riordan, a Donegal girl who'd found her Galway love; in her mind there might even have been a trace of hope that if Mick's story was true, then he would have been tough enough to rescue her should the need arise. He would have slain her captor and then she would have been free – to be with him or to live in this city that she'd once hoped would be her refuge. She might even have been able to go back home.

Instead she was here, in this black prison, and Mick would have forgotten her already, her name a fading memory and her face soon to be replaced by another. Her face. The thought made her cry again. He would never recognise her, even if he were to stumble into the darkness at this very moment.

Something touched her cheek. She wasn't alone. She could feel it at her face, examining her, searching for any sign of life, sniffing to decide what she was. It was a rat. She shuddered as the beast continued its examination of her flesh.

'Jesus, Mary and Joseph,' she mouthed silently, not really sure where to direct her prayers. If she screamed she wasn't sure if that would scare it away or provoke it into launching an attack. It smelt of a backcourt toilet, and she could feel herself gagging. It was nose-to-nose with her now and she could feel its breath against her terrified skin.

She'd heard of rats eating babies before, a mother's wailing upon discovery enough to waken the dead of Glasgow, but never an adult, not a live one at any rate, but would the creature be smart enough to realise that, especially in this darkness? And if it was hungry enough, would it matter if the flesh was fresh or not?

Kate squeezed her eyes tightly shut but still a few tears managed to escape. A tiny tongue on her face began mopping them up. The rat was licking her cheeks, not hungrily but almost soothingly, like it sensed her pain. She certainly hoped it wasn't her fear. Then it was gone, as silently as it had appeared, and Kate allowed a heavy sigh of relief to escape like she'd been holding her breath for an eternity.

She thought of home. She didn't hold out much hope of ever seeing it again and she tried to fill her mind with memories of her childhood. Her family were always there, but in the background. She could see them but they didn't seem to notice her as she stood on top of Mullaghderg Hill, staring out at the choppy waters of the Atlantic Ocean, which looked so unwelcoming yet offered a way of escape. She glanced up towards the horizon, knowing that America was just beyond it. The strong sea breeze tossed her black hair and nipped at her rosy cheeks, but she didn't shiver, her head full of dreams about the new country and the life she could make for herself there.

But with only a few pennies in her purse, heading west was never a viable option. Instead, she shuffled on to the cattle boat along with hundreds of others for the short journey across the Irish Sea to Scotland, sailing up the Clyde, past Greenock and Lyle Hill, where those who had gone before her sat and watched, offering a silent greeting to this new land, when a word of warning might have come in handier.

Kate wanted to shout a warning now to that young girl back in Donegal, watching the waves and creating grand dreams for the future, but even if that was possible, her voice would have been lost in the roar of the wind, blown out to sea and destined never to be heard or heeded.

Footsteps were approaching, getting louder with each stride down the stairs and she tensed her aching body. They stopped outside the door and Kate imagined she could hear his breathing, steady and menacing, as he rummaged in his pocket for the key that was then thrust into the lock. It opened with a click and the door creaked open. The footsteps didn't move and Kate lay still as a corpse. A gust of wind that had been hovering outside now burst into the room, swirling about with the enthusiasm of a child at play, occasionally slapping her face as it skirted over her body. Kate concentrated on her breathing, trying to keep it under control and as quiet as possible.

A gritty cough. Then he spat out the contents of his throat. They landed near enough to Kate's face that she heard the dull thud on the wooden floor. His feet seemed to slam down as he moved forward, shutting the door behind him. Kate tensed in anticipation of the first blow. She tried to fill her mind with happier thoughts; her mammy bathing her and her sisters in front of the fire, the smell of the peat on her daddy's clothes after he'd been out in the fields cutting all day. Her first kiss, to a shy boy called Fergal, whose face turned as red as his hair once their lips parted, barely seconds after they first met. She was only twelve then. Or maybe thirteen? And then she thought of the Galway storyteller who had lain on top of her just the night before.

The footsteps were at her face now. Maybe a boot would come crashing down on her skull and it would all be over in an instant, the pain quickly followed by relief. Instead he bent down, his knees creaking with the effort and his arms slid under her body. As he pulled her up she cried out with pain but it didn't stop him. He dragged her across the floor and propped her against a wall. She started to topple over but he pushed her in the other direction until her shoulder crashed into another wall and she guessed she was in a corner of the room.

'Kate,' he said. 'Look at me.'

It was difficult for her to breathe, never mind lift her head. Something was pushing on her lungs, squeezing the very life out of them, and she slowly slid down the wall until the pressure eased slightly. Then she lifted her head, knowing that he never liked to ask anything more than once. Her right eye opened and she could make out the bulky outline of his body. He was sitting on something, a chair most likely but it could just as easily be a crate.

There was a flash of light and a dancing flame appeared before her face. As he moved the candle away from her, the orange glow revealed his own face. He stared impassively at her and she tried to hold his gaze, though she quickly blinked and looked away. It wasn't just that he had a numerical advantage in terms of his eyes. She felt like she was staring back into her own death and it was simply a matter of when rather than if.

'Why did you do it, Kate?' he asked in a voice that would reduce most people to quivering wrecks. It had the cold chill of hell laced into every syllable and though she was more used to it than most, it still had the ability to scare her on occasion. Now, however, she was almost in too much pain to care.

'I don't know,' she croaked.

'You're my girl, Kate,' he said, reaching out and flicking a strand of hair away from her left eye, which remained closed. 'You can't leave me. You know that.'

She flinched at his touch and he laughed grimly. At any moment, a fist would replace the fingertips and her head would jerk back like it was going to crash through the wall. She wanted to tell him to hurry up and get it over with. The waiting was the worst part, trying to second-guess the new ways he would invent for inflicting pain upon her body. But at the same time, she knew better than to provoke him.

'What am I going to do with you?' he said with a sigh. The candle moved closer to her face until the tip of the flame caressed her cheek. He moved it closer still until it was pressing in on her flesh and she let out a tiny squeak of pain. He held the flame there for a few more seconds before he moved the candle away.

'Maybe you'd like to meet up with Deirdre?'

Kate looked up quickly and her left eye opened a fraction, though the pain that shot through her eyeball was like the heat from a furnace. His mouth broke into either a grin or a sneer. It was hard to tell which was which, but there was a definite grim satisfaction as he remembered Deirdre.

She remembered too. How could anyone forget? He'd forced all the girls into the room and made them form a circle round Deirdre, who was slumped on a chair. The only reason she hadn't fallen off was because he'd bound her to it with a rope, now horribly bloodstained. Her head was bowed and her chin rested on her breastplate. It was difficult to tell whether she was still alive because there seemed to be little sign of her chest rising and falling, though when he grabbed her hair and jerked her head back, a low groan escaped from her mouth. It was a pathetic sound but Kate knew it was liable to be one of the last ones Deirdre was ever going to make.

It was as well she was wearing a dress familiar to them all because her face was purple and bloated beyond all recognition, like she had been dragged out of the depths of the river.

She could only have been thirteen or fourteen. Kate didn't know and had never bothered to ask. It wasn't an important question in their world, but she knew the girl was young enough to be valuable. 'Men pay more for fresh meat.' That's what she always heard him say, and it meant that Deirdre was his favourite. Some of the other girls resented the fact, but Kate liked her. She reminded her of one of her sisters, Nuala, and the thought of her own sister being caught up in this wretched existence was enough to break her heart.

So she had looked out for Deirdre, offering a kind word here, a warm smile there, even a shoulder to cry on if the young girl had returned from any violent encounters, which wasn't uncommon. She came from Mayo, that much she had revealed, and had arrived in Glasgow with the promise of scullery work – hadn't many of them been given the same false promise – so that she could send money back home. But a girl who was barely out of childhood herself stood no chance in this cesspool of a city where men lurked on the dockside, watching, waiting, ready to pounce.

For nearly a year she'd worked, day in, day out, making him money and keeping him happy. Then she disappeared. For four days it had been hellish for all of them, anyone within reach usually felled with a distracted punch, before he found her. Now Deirdre was back, sitting here amongst them.

'I want this to be a lesson to you all,' he said. 'No one runs away from me, whether you're my favourite or not. You're all Jack's girls and don't ever forget it.'

He rubbed his bald head with his free hand, before he slipped it into his back pocket. There was a glint of light on the steel of a blade before he ran it smoothly across Deirdre's throat, letting go of her head which fell forward even before the blood began spurting out. There were a couple of stifled gasps, but otherwise everyone stayed silent. Some of the girls tried to look discreetly away, glancing down at their feet but Kate watched the twitching body in its death throes. She said a silent prayer for the young girl and resolved to escape the first chance she could.

So he was going to cut her throat and there wouldn't even be an audience to bear witness to her final moments on earth. Kate's shoulders sagged with a tired acceptance of her fate and she began mouthing the words of the Hail Mary, which surprised her because she'd long since given up on a religion that she believed had abandoned her to this wretched existence.

'God help you, right enough, Kate,' Jack said with a laugh. He produced a knife from his pocket and held it out before her opened eye. 'Remember this?' he said. 'There might even still be a trace of Deirdre here.'

He began turning the blade in the flame of the candle as Kate took an involuntary gulp, not wanting to think about what was going to happen to her but unable to get the image of Deirdre out of her mind. She wondered if the young girl had felt anything as the blade glided across her flesh, slicing it silently open. She had already been beaten to an inch of her life by that point anyway, so it was unlikely, but Kate knew she would feel it, and as he continued heating the blade, she knew it would be burning metal rather than cold steel which would draw an end to her life.

'Maybe God is looking after you, Kate?' he said. 'Because today is your lucky day . . . Surprised?' he asked as she looked up. 'Lucky for you no one knows what you did, or I would have had to kill you. But you're my girl and good girls are hard to find. I still need to punish you, though. You know that. Just so that you don't do it again.'

Kate relaxed, relieved, but only for a second before he lurched forward on to his knees, grabbed hold of her arm and pressed it down on the floor. In almost the same movement, his free hand produced a small axe from inside his jacket and, kneeling on her arm to keep it steady, he brought the weapon swiftly down, slicing off her pinkie and ring finger of her left hand. It was over in the blink of an eye, so quick Kate didn't even have time to cry out, though she did when he pressed the hot knife on her open wound to stop the flow of blood. She screamed until she had exhausted every human sound left in her body and all she could do was whimper like a dog.

# 8

## GOD WORKS IN MYSTERIOUS WAYS

Thomas Costello patted his heart. The letter from Archbishop Eyre was still in his jacket pocket. He was outside the sacristy door, having knocked it gently, and he tried to control his breathing as he waited for an answer. Saint Andrew's Cathedral was busy. People were filling up the rows of wooden benches, waiting to confess their sins and most had given him no more than a fleeting glance as he walked quietly up the side aisle, stopping to genuflect in the direction of the altar when he reached the front.

A tray of lit candles flickered weakly beneath a statue of the Blessed Virgin, resplendent in her pale blue gown, hands joined together in prayer, her head bowed slightly to the side, full of concern for her flock. Thomas stopped in front of the statue and pushed a shilling into the collection box before lighting his own candle. He slipped into the front row and knelt down, blessing himself and praying for his own mother. He knew she was safe, and his sisters and brother too, and he hoped that would remain the case.

John McDonagh was a good man, and had helped the family before, particularly after their father had died, making sure that the rent was paid until they had worked out how to bring in their own money and who would have to do the necessary work to make that happen. Mick used to joke that John McDonagh was making an investment for a future wife – he'd never married himself – but Thomas knew there were no ulterior motives. And hadn't he helped pay for Thomas' studies, especially after he was sent to Rome? Thanking God for his old neighbour's kindness, Thomas stood up and headed for his appointment.

The sacristy door slowly opened and a priest emerged into the doorway.

'Father Costello,' the priest said with a slight bow of the head.

'Father McNeill,' Thomas said, returning the greeting.

A quick flicker of a smile stole across Father McNeill's face, or it could have been a distasteful sneer, Thomas thought, as he studied his fellow priest. There was a silent standoff for the best part of a minute as the two men held each other's gaze.

Father Angus McNeill was the Archbishop's right-hand man. His official title was Chancellor of the Diocese, but many of his fellow priests had less complimentary names for him. No one got to the Archbishop except through the Chancellor and that access was jealously guarded. It didn't help that Father McNeill was Scottish, a native of South Uist who had forged a beneficial relationship with the Archbishop while he'd been in charge of the Church in the Western Isles.

When he moved to Glasgow, the Archbishop brought Father McNeill with him who, in turn, brought an inbuilt distrust and dislike of all things Irish. Given that just about all of Glasgow's priests were from Ireland and the overwhelming majority of their flock were of the same nationality, it made for a frosty and sometimes fraught relationship.

Now he stood before Thomas, content to be the physical barrier between him and the Archbishop, happy to let the visitor be the one to break the silence. Thomas, however, had resolved not to be the first to speak. Father McNeill patted down a patch of black hair that was already plastered to his skull as if he'd just come in out of the rain. His nose kept twitching involuntarily, a habit which had always amused Thomas but one that Father McNeill was either unaware of or had long since got used to it.

The Scottish priest's head suddenly spun round at the sound of a cough from within the sacristy and he stepped aside, gesturing with another nod of the head for Thomas to enter. Not waiting for a second invitation, Thomas stepped past his fellow priest and into the room. The door shut quickly behind him but he didn't turn round, although he knew that Father McNeill stood there, now barring his exit.

It didn't take Thomas long to realise there was no one else in the room and he wondered if the whole thing had just been an elaborate hoax, though he couldn't think of any reason why that would be the case. He was on the verge of turning round to ask Father McNeill when a voice spoke up from beyond the deep purple curtain in the far corner of the room.

'Come through, Thomas.'

He recognised the voice right away. It was Archbishop Eyre. He stepped forward nervously, resisting the urge to look back towards the door for reassurance from Father McNeill. Reaching the purple barrier, he gently nudged it open and stepped into another room. This one was smaller than the sacristy and sparse except for the desk which sat facing him against one of the walls, on which was a simple wooden crucifix with a silver figure of Our Lord. Behind the desk sat the Archbishop, though he didn't look up. He was reading a black leather Bible, the pages illuminated by a single candle, which cut a lonely figure on the right-hand edge of the desk.

Having let the curtain fall shut behind him, Thomas stood waiting, hardly daring to breathe and conscious of not wanting to make any sound that would announce his presence. The Archbishop continued reading, his balding head bowed as he studied the book intently. He brought his thumb and forefinger to his mouth before using his dampened fingers to turn the page, all the while maintaining the same level of concentration as before. Wiry, gold-rimmed spectacles perched precariously on the edge of a stubby nose; Thomas had an irrational desire to stretch over and push them up.

'There is much to be learned from the letters of Saint Paul, don't you think?' the Archbishop eventually said without looking up at Thomas.

'Yes, Your Grace.'

' "You may be quite sure that in the last days there are going to be some difficult times. People will be self-centred and grasping, boastful, arrogant and rude; disobedient to their parents, ungrateful, irreligious; heartless and unappeasable; they will be slanderers, profligates, savages and enemies of everything that is good; they will be treacherous and reckless and demented by pride; preferring their own pleasure to God. They will keep up the outward appearance of religion but will have rejected the inner power of it. Have nothing to do with people like that." '

There was a pause as the Archbishop sat back, removing his glasses and placing them on the Bible, which remained open at the page he'd just read from. Thomas kept his eyes focused on the holy book rather than risk catching the other man's eye, hands clasped behind his back. He prayed that he wouldn't have to endure such a long silence this time.

'Saint Paul's second letter to Timothy, chapter three.'

Thomas nodded.

'Such profound words of wisdom that still resonate today, wouldn't you say?'

'Yes, Your Grace.'

'Yet they were written almost nineteen hundred years ago. Remarkable.'

'Yes, Your Grace.'

'Sit down, Thomas, sit down,' Archbishop Eyre said, gesturing towards the empty seat which faced him across the table. Thomas gently pulled the chair back to give himself some leg room and then sat down.

'You've caught me in the middle of a guilty pleasure. Saint Paul is such an inspiration that I always find I want to share it with everyone. Forgive me this little self-indulgence.'

Thomas smiled and shook his head dismissively, not really sure what to say in reply. He'd studied the same letters himself but they had evidently not left the same indelible mark on him as they had on the older priest.

'Some refreshments, Thomas? Tea maybe?'

'Thank you.'

The Archbishop picked up the little silver bell that sat opposite the candle and rang it in three short bursts. On the third ring, Father McNeill appeared through the purple curtain.

'Tea for our guest, Angus, if you would be so kind.'

'Of course, Your Grace,' Father McNeill said with a cold smile, bowing slightly before disappearing back through the curtain.

The Archbishop picked up his glasses and began examining them intently as he twirled them back and forth in his hand. The gold ring he wore on his right hand, the symbol of his priestly authority, occasionally seemed to glow as it captured the reflection of the candle.

'Are these the last days that Saint Paul warned about?'

'I don't know, Your Grace,' Thomas shrugged.

'I'm not sure about that myself, but I do know that they are difficult days. Our people are suffering, Thomas. I know that and so do you. Every day you see it with your own eyes, the hunger, the poverty, the spectre of death that stalks the streets day and night . . . Mourn, mourn for this great city whose lavish living has made a fortune for every owner of a sea-going ship; ruined within a single hour . . . The Book of Revelations,' the Archbishop added by way of explanation.

'And it is still not a welcoming place, Thomas. We are strangers here, you and I, and are treated as such. Our religion is despised, while our people who flee from Ireland in search of a better life are treated worse than any beast on the poorest of farms. I am English, Thomas, as you know, but in my heart I feel the pain of Ireland and all her children.'

Thomas nodded as Father McNeill appeared through the purple curtain, the clatter of china on the tray announcing his entrance. The Archbishop closed over the Bible and slid it to one side of the table, putting his glasses back down on top of the black leather cover. Father McNeill placed the tray gently on the table and took each cup and saucer off in turn, putting one in front of the Archbishop, another before Thomas and a third which Thomas presumed was his own, beside the candle.

'So we must help our flock whenever we can, wouldn't you agree, Thomas?'

'Yes, Your Grace.'

'But we must also guide them, steering them away from the work of the evil one, which is so prevalent at this time.'

The tea had now been poured and Father McNeill stood to the side, sipping from his cup and never taking his eyes away from Thomas, who'd waited for the Archbishop's invitation before taking his own cup. It wasn't a patch on Mrs Breslin's, he thought, but smiled appreciatively at his superior when he looked up.

The three priests continued drinking their tea in silence, the only sound to invade the room the dying hiss of the burning candle, though Thomas wasn't sure if the other two men even heard it. Remember you are wax and unto wax you shall return, Thomas thought and had to stop himself from smiling.

'Now to business,' the Archbishop eventually said in an urgent tone that had previously been absent.

'I need your help, Thomas,' he said, slipping his glasses back on and peering over the edge of them. Thomas couldn't understand why he needed them now but thought better than to ask. 'Will you help me?'

'Yes, Your Grace,' Thomas said nervously.

'These are difficult days, Thomas, and we have many enemies, but when there are enough good men willing to come to her aid, then Holy Mother Church will survive. More than that, she will survive and prosper.'

Father McNeill moved towards the table, nodding in agreement as he put his empty cup down. He remained standing at the table, towering over Thomas, who refused to look up at the Scottish priest.

'Our people are being led astray, Thomas, and it is up to us to steer them back onto the right path. We are the shepherds and we have to round up these stray members of our flock.'

Archbishop Eyre pushed his glasses up from the tip of his nose and smiled as he told Thomas what he'd have to do.

St Alphonsus' was to become a meeting place for the Irish Republican Brotherhood, the Archbishop explained. The group, agitating for Irish independence, had increased their presence and influence in the city and Thomas' parish was going to hold out its welcoming arms to the secretive organisation.

'And after every meeting, you will give Father McNeill a list of all those who attended,' the Archbishop said with a nod to his Chancellor, who stood wearing a sneer that Thomas was sorely tempted to wipe off his face.

'Why me?' he asked in a nervous whisper. He wasn't even sure if he actually made a sound and he was as surprised as the Archbishop evidently was that he'd said anything at all.

'Politics is not the path to salvation,' the Archbishop said after a minute of awkward silence, 'and so we must ensure that those who are misguided do not propagate these beliefs but are brought back into the fold.'

'You want me to spy on them?'

'Don't be so dramatic, Thomas. This is hardly a penny dreadful story we find ourselves in.'

Father McNeill snorted and Thomas glared at him.

'I simply want you to watch over them, as any good pastor would,' said the Archbishop.

'But what if they find out?'

'They won't.'

'But what –'

'You will offer to help them and they will trust you because you are a priest.'

Thomas could only presume that the Englishman and the Scotsman were ignorant of what the Irishman knew about the Brotherhood. Detection would mean his demise, and his dog collar would offer no deterrent to these people, not when betrayal was his crime. He was uncomfortable, too, about having to spy on his fellow countrymen, though he knew that his first loyalty – at seminary they'd insisted it should be their only loyalty – was to the Church before Ireland. It had never been something that troubled him, though he knew the distinction for some of his fellow priests was much more blurred. If he was being honest, patriotism had always played second fiddle to his prayers, even when he was a young boy. His wariness was more to do with self-preservation and that would remain his main priority.

'What about Monsignor Dolan?' he asked.

'This is a matter between us,' the Archbishop said.

'But it's his parish. He'll want to know why these men are holding meetings in his church hall.'

Archbishop Eyre smiled, taking his glasses off and placing them on top of the Bible.

'Monsignor Dolan is a faithful servant of the Church, but that faith is simple and straightforward. I fear he would not understand what we are trying to do here, Thomas, and perhaps not appreciate the need for secrecy . . . confessional secrecy. You, on the other hand, can see the bigger picture. That is why I have called on you. I know I'm asking a lot of you,' he said, sensing the apprehension from across the table. 'But the future of the Church in this city, indeed, in this country, could be at stake . . . I hope I'm not being too overdramatic?'

Thomas knew he didn't have a choice. A priest could not disobey his bishop and he sensed this was not the time to ignore that rule.

'Father McNeill will show you out,' the Archbishop said with a dismissive gesture towards the purple curtain and Thomas stood up, not caring that the chair scraped noisily along the stone floor. He was face-to-face with his fellow priest who smiled grimly like he was already picturing Thomas's funeral and Thomas shivered uneasily. It was as his mother had always said. Someone had just walked across his grave.

# 9

## ACROSS THE WATER

It was a recurring nightmare that always ended with the sound of a splash, forcing Mick's body to jolt, and he'd sit up in bed, gasping for breath like it was him who'd been thrown overboard. These were fitful sleeps and frantic dreams but the sound that rang in his ears long after he had wakened was real enough. It made him shiver whenever he remembered and he'd quickly bless himself, sometimes trying to piece together a few words from prayers that he now only half-remembered. It was enough to bring a tear to a statue, as his mother used to say, and he was always glad no one ever saw him in this state.

He wished he could dream of something else, even the fact that he still hadn't found Kate despite three days of looking for her. At least that would have made him angry, if more than a little frustrated, but sleep would bring him no such comforts. All his mind could remember was the boat trip when he escaped from Ireland . . .

The boat was already full by the time he managed to shuffle up the gang-plank. At times it felt like the movement of the other passengers, all crammed together shoulder to shoulder, was pushing him towards the boat rather than anything he might be doing himself, like putting one foot in front of the other, and he was glad for his height and weight, which prevented him from completely disappearing under the desperate surge.

At the time he thought he'd been lucky to get on the vessel at all. He had managed to acquire the fare – two pennies that he'd robbed from a drunk who'd been foolish enough to venture up a dark lane to relieve his bladder. Mick had felt guilty even as he'd smashed the man's head off the brick wall, knocking him clean out so that rummaging quickly through his damp pockets had been an easy task, but he told himself it was the lesser of two evils; he told God that, if truth be told, and hoped forgiveness would come his way at some point in the future. For now, he needed to leave Ireland and he couldn't do that without money. His unconscious victim only possessed a few coins, but it would be enough to get across the water.

Even when he finally managed to get on board, he kept moving in the hope that some space might suddenly appear, even just enough so that he could stretch his limbs, still aching from the exertions of his escape. He'd been afraid to stop, even for five minutes, and he'd punished his body while running the beast into the ground. When he'd left it some twenty miles from Belfast, its weak legs barely able to hold the weight of its panting body, Mick knew that it would be dead soon, either collapsing under its own exhaustion or hastened to its end by whichever hungry soul stumbled upon what he was sure they would think was a gift from God.

The horse came back into his mind as he finally came to a stop halfway up the side of the boat. The smell of animals seeped up from below him and when he strained to hear above the tired drone of his fellow passengers, he could make out the restless cries of nervous beasts in the hold. It was most likely cattle that had been herded on board and he was almost envious of them as the first drops began falling onto his head. It took no more than ten minutes of thick, angry rain before everyone on deck was completely drenched

'That's Our Lady's tears for Ireland,' a woman was telling her son, who stood ignoring her as he stared through the sheets of rain towards the dock, where people were still queuing up to get on the boat. No one else seemed to hear her and Mick wiped those heavenly tears off his face, a pointless exercise since more immediately replaced them, and so he stood with everyone else, silently accepting the fate that the dark clouds overhead had decreed for them all.

It was another half hour at least before the boat finally pulled away from the dock. Mick wondered how many passengers were on board, not to mention the animals down below, the vessel groaning under the pressure of its cargo as it inched away from land. He resisted the urge to look back – he didn't want to risk it being his last ever glimpse of Ireland – instead focusing his gaze on the choppy waters ahead which waited menacingly for them.

Ten minutes out of Belfast the rain stopped, the wind having blown itself into exhaustion, the water calm as a bath tub. That's when the shivering started. Every item of Mick's clothing was soaked and the wet garments clung to his skin as if they were trying to suck the heat out of him in order to dry themselves. He couldn't stop the tremors shaking his body and he felt colder with every passing second. It was then that he heard it . . . the cough of the dying.

The little girl could not have been more than two years old. Her mother was crouched down as comfortably as the limited space would allow and the little girl sat on her lap, her head buried into her mother's chest, blonde hair hiding her face. At first glance it looked like the child was asleep but every few minutes a cough would grip the tiny body, shaking it callously so that the mother would wrap her arms even tighter round the child's frame.

Mick didn't want to catch the woman's attention, not least because he was afraid that she would read, in his own eyes, the grim inevitability of the situation. If she asked him, he wouldn't lie. He couldn't tell the truth either, but false hope was the cruellest gift to give anyone in these circumstances. So the child kept coughing, each one sounding weaker and more deadly than the one before. The Scottish coastline was just about visible when there was just silence. He looked down as discreetly as he could, desperate now to avoid contact with the woman, but she was staring at her daughter, her lips pressed to the blonde hair and muttering silent prayers in between gentle kisses. Mick swallowed deeply and wished it would start raining again so that his own tears could mingle with Our Lady's.

One or two shouts alerted everyone else to the approaching land and it seemed to restore people's ability to speak, a steady murmur beginning to rise up from the boat like steam from an exhausted animal. Mick knew better than to tell anyone that they were still hours away from Glasgow and the chance to put two feet firmly back on dry land. Still, the sudden wave of optimism was contagious and he couldn't help but grin himself.

He stopped as the woman stood up shakily, still holding her daughter. He reached out a hand and gripped her elbow to steady her until she was facing him. He wanted to hold her gaze – he didn't know why because he knew it wouldn't bring her comfort – but he had to look away after a few seconds. She shuffled forward and there was a parting of bodies, as much as was possible in the cramped circumstances. It was as if everyone knew that she needed some space.

She took a few steps and didn't stop when she got to the side of the boat. Mick could never figure out how it happened so quickly but one minute she was there in front of him and the next she had disappeared overboard with her daughter, vanishing beneath the frothy water being churned up in the boat's wake, the only sound ringing in Mick's ears that of the splash when the bodies hit the waves, even as gasps and shouts from other passengers raised the alarm.

Even after he'd got dressed and headed out, Mick still couldn't shake that haunting sound from his mind. There was nothing anyone could have done on the boat to save the child – her life had been in God's hands alone. Still, he couldn't help but admire her mother's courage, for what life awaited her in Glasgow without her daughter? It was hardly likely she had enough money to bury the girl and an existence full of pain and poverty was the only guarantee. She chose instead to be with the little girl and Mick was sure God would understand that too.

He strode along the street with a determined purpose, pushing the boat trip to the back of his mind, at least until he closed his eyes that night and drifted off to sleep to discover himself back on board. He had a job to find and he knew better than to be late. The word in the pub was that Lorimer's factory was offering a few days' work, and he knew that many of those who'd supped alongside him last night would be heading in the same direction at this very moment, unless they were still sleeping off their over-indulgence. It would only be a morning's work today but that suited Mick well enough. He was of a mind to head back to the streets near the docks one last time. He knew it was a hopeless search – hadn't the man in black struggled to find him so far and that was with the benefit of six guineas to loosen tongues – so what chance did he have of finding Kate? With each passing hour his guilt was fading away, however, and he knew his search was drawing to a close.

There were already plenty of bodies gathered outside the factory gates when he arrived but it didn't stop him from pushing his way towards the front, ignoring the angry shouts from those he elbowed out the way. He wanted to make sure he was within easy eye contact of the foreman, though he didn't have to worry. He knew the man – they'd drank together on more than one occasion, but more importantly, he was also from Galway and he looked after his own. Mick nodded as he passed through the gates.

'Thanks, Mr O'Rourke,' he said with a smile and O'Rourke winked, so quick that no one else was likely to notice and complain, but Mick noted it gratefully.

It was a labouring job; mind-numbing, back-breaking and relentless, but it was a job all the same. An old store-house at the back of the factory needed demolishing so Mick and his fellow workers, with sledge-hammers in hand, attacked the frail old building without mercy. They were all covered in dust and debris within seconds but there were no complaints to be heard above the grunts of bodies that would be tired soon enough. Mick was glad of the early finish, with it being Saturday, and he continued the assault on the walls, dreaming of the one o'clock whistle that would set him free.

Mr O'Rourke appeared around ten, giving them the nod that they could stop for five minutes to have a smoke. He'd brought a bucket of water with him, which he put down at his feet, a few splashes escaping onto his boots. He held up a ladle and the men shuffled forward, grateful for the chance to refresh parched mouths. There was no way to avoid inhaling the dust which covered them with silent menace and as the cold liquid touched his lips, Mick was almost moved to offer a prayer of thanks to God.

O'Rourke now stood away from the queue of men, drawing heavily on a cigarette. He nodded to Mick as he handed the ladle to the next man in line and he headed over to the foreman. Lighting his own cigarette, Mick began spluttering. The tobacco bonded with the dust as it glided down his throat and he had to dredge up whatever he could from his mouth and spit it out.

'Dirty work,' said O'Rourke.

'Aye,' said Mick with another cough.

'There's a week's worth here if you want it.'

'Thanks.'

'Be here just before seven every morning.'

'I'm grateful to you, Mr O'Rourke.'

'If a Galway man can't help one of his own, what sort of world is that?'

'That's true and not a word of a lie.'

Both men continued smoking in silence. Mick watched the men devouring the water and he knew he'd have to be quick if he wanted another drink before starting back at work. O'Rourke had almost finished his cigarette and that would signal the end of the break.

'So are you a fan of the football then?'

Mick looked at O'Rourke, not sure the question had been directed at him, but there was no one else within earshot. Mick shrugged.

'A few of the boys are going to see the Celtic this afternoon.'

'The Celtic?'

'We'll be at Flaherty's in Cornfield Street if you're of a mind yourself. The game starts at two.'

'Thanks for the invite,' Mick said, drawing on his dying cigarette one last time before he flicked it away. O'Rourke nodded as he stepped forward towards the bucket, calling time on the short break. Within minutes, clouds of dust once again swirled in the air above them and the relentless crash of steel on brick echoed out against the chill Glasgow morning.

Mick swore he'd never heard a sweeter sound in all his life than the whistle that called time on their exertions. The final strains hadn't even faded away before he'd thrown the sledge-hammer down on the pile of rubble resting at his feet which, just a few short hours before, had been a solid wall. Everyone else had done the same, though their eagerness in discarding tools was not matched in their departure. Mainly they shuffled painfully towards the exit, backs that were bent slowly beginning to unravel and it seemed like some of the workers gained feet in height as they managed to stretch to their full length again.

Those battered bodies would enjoy the benefit of a day of rest, tomorrow being the Lord's Day after all, before they'd be back on Monday morning to continue where they'd left off. The thought was a daunting one, Mick realised, but he had no choice. None of them did, and he was in no mood to feel sorry for himself, even if every bone in his body felt like it had been trampled underfoot by a thousand cattle.

He stopped when he walked out the factory gate, still of a mind to resume his search for Kate, but knowing he'd have to clean up first, when a hand touched his shoulder. He glanced round as O'Rourke walked by, muttering, 'Flaherty's,' with another wink. Mick licked his lips as all thoughts of Kate disappeared, already imagining the taste of whiskey on his tongue.

They walked towards the football ground, six of them. He'd only known O'Rourke, but after a few drinks the rest of the men had started to seem like his oldest and dearest friends. If truth be told, Mick would rather have stayed in the pub but he was in a minority of one. Still, the plan was to head back to Flaherty's after the game.

Two more of the group were Galway men – Gallacher and Big Dan – though Mick hadn't recognised either of them, while there was also Gerry from Derry, who was the most anxious to leave the pub.

'Lateness is a sin, as my old mother used to say, God rest her soul,' he kept piping up every few minutes until O'Rourke vowed to kick his 'bony Derry arse all the way back to that bloody wall of yours' if he didn't shut up.

The last of the group was also the quietest. Cahal was a Cork man with the strongest handshake Mick had ever had the misfortune to experience. He had to stop himself from frowning as the grip began to crush his own hand. Cahal grunted a greeting and that was the only sound Mick heard him utter in the pub. He stood with a pint of Guinness permanently poised at his lips, listening to the conversation that continued around him, though he contributed nothing to it. After a while, Mick forgot he was there.

They walked through the graveyard – a short-cut Gallacher suggested but which unnerved Mick – and clambered over a wall, dropping down onto the ground and finding themselves in the middle of a crowd of men queuing noisily to get in through the one gate that seemed to be open.

'We'll miss the start of the match at this rate,' Gerry said as he bobbed anxiously in and out of the line, looking to see if there was a gap he could scurry through.

'Calm yourself down, man,' Big Dan said. 'When does anything happen at the start of the game anyway?'

'That's not the point,' said Gerry. 'What if they score and it's the only goal of the game?'

'If that happens I'll eat my hat,' Big Dan said.

'You've got yourself a deal,' Gerry said, spitting on his palm and holding his hand out.

'And if it doesn't, then you have to eat yours,' Big Dan said with a laugh that was quickly drowned out by the rest of the audience who'd been listening. Gerry hastily pulled his hand away and began bobbing in and out again, this time in silence.

The queue was moving fairly quickly, however, and after paying his penny entrance fee to a man who snatched the coin out of his hand without a word of thanks, throwing it into a dark green biscuit tin along with the many others, Mick found himself inside the ground. He followed his companions, though he felt his body drawn towards the noise of the crowd, which he soon saw was several hundred strong. He quickly realised that the volume of the roars seemed to rise and fall in time to the action on the field that was a patchwork quilt of mud, hay and just a glimmer of green from the tiny sections of grass that hadn't succumbed to winter's assault.

The game might have excited the bulk of the crowd – even Cahal could be heard shouting 'Give it to Madden!' – but Mick had to admit it made no sense to him. He didn't know who Madden was; he didn't know who any of them were and it just seemed like a bunch of men wearing strange outfits, the likes of which he'd never seen before, charging round a field after a leather ball. O'Rourke stood at his left shoulder, occasionally whispering words of explanation, but while Mick nodded gratefully it didn't make things any clearer.

'Give it to Madden,' Cahal cried out again and Mick looked round.

'Does he ever shout anything else?' he asked O'Rourke discreetly out the side of his mouth.

'He says Madden's a Cork man,' O'Rourke offered by way of explanation. 'Mind you, he was born in Dumbarton so I don't know how he figures that one out.'

Cahal glared at O'Rourke but said nothing.

'I think he maybe lay with a Cork girl one time,' said Big Dan, 'but I don't know if that counts.'

The other men laughed but Cahal's glare switched back to the field.

Then the ball went through one of the sets of the white sticks that were planted at either end of the field and everyone around

Mick cheered. Hats flew into the air and several hands heartily slapped his back.

'That's a goal for the Celtic,' O'Rourke said. 'Good old Peter Dowds.'

Mick smiled and hoped the game would finish soon. He was keen to quench his thirst and was already imagining his first pint back in Flaherty's when a brown paper bag was thrust into his hand.

'This'll keep you warm,' Gallacher said.

Mick put the bag to his mouth and took a gulp from the bottle inside, almost spitting it straight back out and coughing and spluttering, much to the amusement of his companions.

'Not used to the old poteen then?' Gallacher said with a shake of the head. 'You're letting the county down.'

Mick handed the drink back to Gallacher, the liquid still burning the lining of his throat and he continued coughing for a few minutes more. He wanted a smoke but was afraid his mouth would go up in flames if he stuck a lit cigarette into it. He watched as Gallacher took a healthy gulp with barely any reaction at all and he stretched out a hand.

'You want more then?' Gallacher laughed as Mick nodded. 'Are you sure you can handle it?'

As he snatched the brown bag from his companion's hand, a flash caught his eye and he looked round. It wasn't light, however, which had stopped his second battle with Gallacher's lethal liquid. Standing not more than twenty feet away, arms folded and leaning on one of the iron railings dotted around the ground, was a man who towered above everyone around him. He stood nodding at what he was watching on the field.

A sudden wave of nausea gripped the pit of Mick's stomach and it had nothing to do with the poteen. It was the sight of the man running his hand across a head that was as bald and shiny as a freshly laid egg.

# 10

# THE FALLING MAN

Celtic had scored another goal. There was more cheering and
backslapping and caps flying everywhere, with most people happy
enough to wear whatever landed nearest to them regardless of
who the previous owner had been. Someone further back in the
crowd started singing *The Bold Fenian Men* and soon many voices
were joining in.

Mick nudged O'Rourke, gently at first but soon with an
urgency that was already gripping every bone in his body.

'Who's that?' he asked.

'Which one?' O'Rourke said, his eyes scanning the field as the
players resumed their competitive pursuit of the ball.

'Him,' Mick said, nodding towards the tall, bald man.

O'Rourke looked round and then spun his head back to face
Mick.

'You don't want to know,' he said nervously. 'And stop staring
at him, you eejit.'

Mick looked away, his gaze stopping restlessly once more on the
game, though he still tried to watch the bald man out the corner of
his eye. He was smoking now, though it seemed to Mick that he'd
only taken a couple of draws before he'd completely destroyed the
cigarette, flicking what remained callously into the crowd in front
of him, yet no one turned round to complain. An arm stretched up
from one of the men who stood around him and he snatched a lit
cigarette from the hand, quickly devouring it as well.

'Who is he?' Mick said, nudging O'Rourke, who frowned at him.

'Keep it down will you? Do you want to land us all in trouble?'

Mick shook his head, but looked past O'Rourke towards the bald man again.

'Alright, alright,' O'Rourke said, glancing over either shoulder. 'That's Jack Duffy,' he whispered so quietly that Mick had to lean in to hear. 'That's about as much as you want to know about him and even that is too much.'

'So what does he do?'

'Did your mother not dig the tatties out of those big Galway ears? I told you, you don't want to know.'

'But I need to. He's taken something – someone . . .'

'Well, don't tell me,' O'Rourke said, holding up his hand to stop Mick talking. 'And if you've even got the sense you were born with, you'll forget whatever it was, or whoever it was.'

'I can look after myself.'

O'Rourke shook his head with a sigh.

'There are bad men and there are evil men,' he whispered. 'And then there is Jack Duffy. The devil would be shaking in his boots if he had to face him. Mind you, some people say he is the devil himself, and it wouldn't surprise me, not one little bit.'

Mick already knew that Duffy had a voice like the devil – at least that's what two terrified women had told him – but now O'Rourke seemed to be quaking in his boots as well and Mick was of a mind to tell the foreman to pull himself together and start acting like a Galway man. He needed more information, however, so he stopped himself from saying anything.

'Jack Duffy runs District 14,' O'Rourke said without prompting. 'You name it, he's involved in it. Anyone who tries to stop him or challenge him . . . Well, none of them live to tell the tale. So take this warning, Costello, from one Galway man to another: if you want to live to see eighteen ninety-two, then you'll turn away right now, start watching the game and say nothing more to a living soul about Jack Duffy.'

The game had stopped. Mick thought it was finished – he hoped it was – but Big Dan pointed out that it was only half-time, following that up with an explanation when he saw a puzzled expression break out across Mick's face. The players disappeared slowly into the pavilion, which stood in splendid isolation across from where they were. Enthusiastic applause followed them as they trotted off the field, while the stop in play seemed to herald a frenetic burst of smoking, white clouds bursting out from the crowd all round the ground. Mick joined in too, though he declined another gulp of Gallacher's special brew, preferring instead the soothing caress of the tobacco on his throat.

The rest of the group were discussing the game, though Cahal once again stood on the edge of the conversation, listening intently but making no contribution and Mick wondered whether, in fact, his shout for Madden was all that the Cork man was capable of uttering. He, of course, could contribute almost nothing himself since he still didn't really understand what he had just witnessed. As far as he was concerned it would never catch on but he thought better than to voice these doubts in the middle of such enthusiasm.

So he nodded and laughed and groaned at the appropriate moments, taking his lead from O'Rourke, and all the while keeping a discreet vigil over Duffy. Not that there was any chance of losing him in this crowd. He must have been about seven feet tall, thought Mick, because he was near six feet himself and he knew that if they stood toe to toe he'd be straining his neck to look up at the bald man.

After ten minutes or so, the players began to drift back onto the field, the Celtic team in their green and white striped shirts appearing first, which sparked sporadic cheers around the ground. They were followed quickly by their opponents, Kilmarnock Athletic, whose blue shirts were greeted with casual indifference and a few half-hearted jeers.

'Give it to Madden,' Cahal shouted as soon as the game started again and Mick couldn't help but grin.

The game was only a few minutes old when Duffy stood up to his full height – he really was a giant, thought Mick – and began bound-ing through the crowd, which parted fearfully before him. He was heading towards the gate, followed by three or four men who scur-ried in his wake, struggling to keep up with his massive strides.

Mick tapped O'Rourke on the shoulder. 'I'll be away now.'

The foreman looked round as Duffy disappeared out the gate and shook his head.

'I'll see you on Monday,' Mick said.

'I hope so, you big eejit. I hope so.'

If it had just been Duffy's cronies he was following, then Mick would have had no problem tracking them, but they were losing ground with every passing stride and Mick realised he'd soon be upon them if he continued at the pace he'd set off on from the football park. He sprinted across the road until he was on the other side from the group of four, all of whom had slowed down simultaneously to light cigarettes, and he quickly passed them by without any of them noticing him. Now he could focus on the bald head which remained well in front of him.

Duffy was heading back towards the centre of Glasgow, and given what O'Rourke had told him, Mick's guess was that he was bound for District 14. It was a name that would send a shiver down any spine. It was home to beggars and thieves, prostitutes and pickpockets; men who would steal the shirt off your back and others who would cut you open for the price of a pint. God had long since abandoned District 14 to its hellish fate and the poor, forsaken souls who couldn't escape their terrible existence endured it all in the dirtiest, dampest and most foul buildings that ever claimed to be called houses.

Mick knew that many of those who stumbled off the boats after dragging themselves across the Irish Sea found themselves, through no fault of their own, in District 14 and once there, there was very little chance of a happy ending or even the hint of a better life which they had fled their homeland to find. And with someone like Duffy in charge of such a place, the only guarantee was a life of terror.

Duffy had arrived at the crossroads, but he turned left when he should have headed straight on towards his home territory and Mick stepped up his own pace, occasionally breaking into a jog so that he didn't lost sight of his quarry. By the time he reached the corner and got round it himself, the bald man was disappearing into a doorway at the far end of the street and Mick slowed down as he headed towards the last building in the row.

He was almost out of breath, due mainly to the exertions of trailing Duffy, though he was nervous too now that he had a moment to think about what he was going to do. The truth was, he had no idea, other than go in the building. Whether he'd come back out alive was the big question and it wasn't one that Mick was able to answer. He'd long since left Duffy's companions behind, though he presumed they'd know where their boss was going and he expected them to arrive eventually. It meant that he would have to be quick and also hope that he'd catch the other man by surprise. Even allowing for that, however, there was no guarantee of success.

For one final time he hesitated outside the entrance to the close which had swallowed Duffy. This was his last chance to escape, even if it meant abandoning all hope of finding Kate again, but a blast of guilt surged through his body. Hadn't he been to blame for her abduction in the first place? And when they'd finished with Kate, they'd be back looking for him again.

He leant on the empty cart that lay abandoned on the road and took a deep breath before almost stumbling up the stairs. He pushed open the door and stepped into a gloomy close, though a broken window at the far end of the passage cast enough light to guide the way for him. There were two doors, one on either side but he heard the groan of floorboards above him and he decided instinctively to head up the stairs, creeping as quietly as he could, all the while trying to calm his breathing and stifle the thunderous beating of his heart which he feared would announce his approach.

Stopping at the first door he came to, he gripped the handle with his sweaty palm. It turned easily and he pushed the door open. It creaked as it swung back, destroying any chance of surprise he may have enjoyed. The room was surprisingly light and Mick, whose eyes had adjusted to the gloom of the passageway, now had to cope with natural sunlight and he blinked furiously.

A bed sat in the middle of the room, the cover crumpled untidily on it. Standing at the window was a black-haired girl. Her head was pressed against the grainy glass as she stared out into the street below and he could see the window misting over as her breath caressed the pane. She wore a flimsy yellow dress which hung lazily off her left shoulder, revealing some fresh wounds on her back.

'I'll be right with you,' she mumbled, not looking round and Mick let the door gently fall shut.

'Kate,' he said in a trembling voice. She looked round. 'Jesus,' Mick gasped. 'What happened to you?'

He moved slowly towards her while she remained rooted to the spot, watching his approach through the one eye she could fully open. He noticed her left hand was heavily bandaged and when she saw him staring at it, she swiftly hid it behind her back. They stood face to face and suddenly Mick had no idea what to say. He had imagined rescuing her but he'd never got as far as trying to figure out any conversation they might have, and with Kate unwilling to speak, Mick felt it was up to him to break the silence.

Words which usually fell out of his mouth like raindrops on a cloudy day had suddenly dried up and instead he leant closer to her and lightly kissed her closed eye.

'That was beautiful.'

Mick spun round, his body gripped with an overwhelming fear that he hadn't anticipated. Duffy's voice had breathed an icy chill all over the room and Mick sensed Kate's body tensing as well. He wanted to clutch her good hand and squeeze it tightly, to let her know that everything would be okay and that he would look after her, making sure that no more harm would come to her, but he couldn't move his own hand. He couldn't move any part of his body, if truth be told, and even if he could have, his assurances to Kate would have been meaningless.

Duffy stood at the doorway with his arms folded, not blinking as he kept the two of them in his gaze. Mick had to look away before glancing back at the bald man but only for a few seconds. He was aware of Kate brushing past him but he still couldn't stop her.

'Jack, just let him go,' she said quietly.

She was getting closer to Duffy, repeating her mantra of 'please' while he continued to hold Mick in his gaze. Standing directly in front of him, she came up to his chest and she stared up at him.

'Please, Jack,' she said. 'For me . . .'

Duffy began nodding, looking down at Kate and for a split second Mick thought he might actually be allowed to leave. Then Duffy gripped Kate's arms and moved her aside, letting her go and striding towards Mick in the same movement. In two steps he was in front of Mick. His right arm stretched out and a massive hand gripped Mick's throat. He couldn't breathe and his own hands grasped frantically at Duffy's arm as fingers tightened and red spots appeared before his eyes.

Mick could feel his feet being lifted off the ground. Any strength he had seeped out of his body and he stopped clawing at the grip that was crushing him. With barely any effort, Duffy pushed Mick's body away, releasing his hold and firing him through the window. Mick was flying and for a few seconds he actually managed to smile though he didn't know why. The grin was soon wiped off his face as he dropped like a stone to the ground. He wanted to think of Kate, or of his mother. Even an image of Galway would have comforted him but all he could picture was the football match he'd just left and he wanted to curse O'Rourke for having taken him in the first place.

He closed his eyes and began to pray, though he'd barely managed to mouth the words 'Hail Mary . . .' before he hit solid ground. He lay perfectly still on his back, eyes closed, and held his breath for a few seconds, not sure whether this was how it felt to be dead. Then he groaned, opened his eyes and saw the grimy building he'd just been thrown out of. He glanced to his side and realised that he'd crashed through the empty cart that had sat outside the house. It was enough to break his fall and even as he lay on the road, his body still aching from the impact, he knew he was still alive and he thanked Our Lady.

It was a premature prayer of thanks, however, as Duffy burst out of the close-mouth, bounding over and kicking him hard in the ribs. It felt like he'd been shot and Mick struggled to find even a tiny breath. He braced himself for another blow, knowing Duffy was standing over him, but nothing came.

Slowly, Mick rolled onto his side, letting out a scream as his body weight rested on his left arm, which he guessed was broken. Still, he managed to push himself onto his knees and crouched in the street on all fours like a dog. He barely had time to draw breath before Duffy's boot crashed into his body, sending Mick sprawling across the road. He heard a crack and was sure that a few ribs had just been broken.

He was on his front now and lay still, reluctant to move again. He guessed that Duffy was waiting to pounce again and he wanted to delay the inevitable. Screaming suddenly filled the air, building up to a crescendo as Kate rushed down the stairs and out into the street.

'Don't kill him, Jack,' she shouted.

Mick glanced up at the same time as Duffy looked round and he saw the bald man point at Kate. It was enough to halt her in her tracks. She was brave enough to plead for his life but not stupid enough to risk her own. Duffy still stared at Kate and Mick tried to grab the window of opportunity, slowly crawling towards the pavement on the other side of the road.

His fingertips had just about managed to touch the kerb when he felt his ankles being gripped and he was dragged back across the cobbles, the rough stones attacking his face as it scraped along their surface. His body shuddered to a halt and Duffy pressed a boot down on his broken arm until he began to scream like a starving child. When the pressure was lifted, Mick's screams evaporated into groans while Kate sobbed helplessly. Then it started again and it felt like his arm was going to fall off. Duffy seemed to know exactly how long to apply the pain and after it happened a fourth time, Mick was praying that it would all be over soon. He wanted to die.

Voices began hovering above him but he was drifting into unconsciousness and couldn't really make out anything that was being said. He was grateful enough for their arrival, however, if only because it had distracted Duffy's torture, for a few moments at least.

His left arm was useless. He'd have been worried the damage was permanent if he thought that he'd have use of it in the future, but since that future looked set to last for only a few more minutes, it was not a great concern. He stuck his right hand into his trouser pocket, as much to try and conceal it from Duffy so that he wouldn't alternate between either arm.

He heard a voice say, 'Not out here, Jack,' and suddenly he was floating as several pairs of hands grasped his limbs and hoisted him off the ground. He relaxed and let them carry him back into the building, past Kate, who stretched out an arm and briefly touched his cheek, before she was pushed away. He knew they were taking him inside to kill him and he suddenly realised too that it had nothing to do with the man in black. This wasn't his style, or if he had been intent on exacting such a brutal revenge, then he would have emerged from the shadows himself, even if it was only to fulfil the role of gleeful spectator.

He was dropped callously onto a wooden floor and he lay perfectly still, breathing heavily even though every time he inhaled, a pain shot through his body from his broken ribs.

Duffy crouched down and pushed his face close to Mick's so that he could feel the warm breath of his tormentor on his cheek. A stale odour of tobacco and whiskey washed over him and he noticed Duffy's teeth were a combination of yellow and black. A crooked grin broke out across his face and Mick knew that it was time. Duffy had tired of him and was now going to put an end to this torture. The sharp point of a blade pressed into his cheek and Duffy pressed hard until Mick sensed his skin being punctured.

'Now, should this be quick or slow?' Duffy said. 'What do you think? Should I slit your throat or cut out your eyes and tongue first?'

Mick automatically clenched his fists but he knew it was a pointless exercise. He'd barely have enough time to swing a solitary punch before Duffy would dispatch him with his knife. Or worse, it would convince him that mutilation was better than murder. He relaxed his hands, feeling in his pockets as Duffy stood up. The bald man grabbed Mick's jacket and hauled his broken body to its feet. If he let go Mick knew that, in all likelihood, he'd topple over.

'I'll make it quick for you,' Duffy said with a grim smile.

Mick closed his eyes just as the sound of urgent banging on the door invaded the room.

'What is it?' Duffy growled.

A muffled, nervous voice shouted something from the other side of the door though Mick couldn't make it out.

'I'll be right there,' said Duffy, turning back to face Mick who threw a handful of pepper into the bald giant's face. He let go of Mick and began clawing at his face with his hands, groaning furiously. Mick fell to the floor at the same time as the knife that Duffy had dropped and he immediately grasped it, thrusting his arm out and lodging the blade in Duffy's thigh. It provoked a scream to scare the devil himself, but Mick was already at the window which bore the signs of his previous exit, clambering over the ledge and dropping out without a moment's hesitation. He knew he never would have made it to the door and, even if he had, Duffy's men were on the other side.

That argument still seemed to make sense to him as he tumbled once more to the ground, knowing that there was no cart to break his fall this time and accepting that he was going to die. He was glad that he had deprived Duffy of that particular pleasure, however, and as the bald man continued howling in the room above, Mick closed his eyes and smiled. The footballers he'd seen before had disappeared. Now there was only Kate, who stood waving from outside a cottage, like she was welcoming him home after a hard day's work in the fields. It would be a comforting image to take to his grave.

## II

## HEAVEN CAN WAIT

It was a strange feeling to be dead. It wasn't how Mick imagined it would be, though it still made him smile. Thomas stood at his side, rosary beads entwined between his fingers, lips moving in silent prayer. He wanted to ask his brother what he was doing here, but when he tried to speak no sound escaped from his mouth and he had a sense that he wouldn't be able to hear Thomas either if he said anything. He guessed it was just another comforting image, like Kate waiting for him in Galway, and that if he closed his eyes for a few seconds Thomas would be gone when he opened them again.

He didn't want to lose sight of his brother; perhaps he was offering up last-minute prayers to let Mick into heaven? He would need more than that to persuade Saint Peter to open those gates, and even then Mick still didn't fancy his chances.

He could feel his eyelids growing heavy, like someone had placed a couple of pennies on them. He remembered they had done that to his daddy as he lay in bed, dressed in his Sunday best. If it wasn't for the coins resting in his eye sockets, it would have been easy to think his daddy was only sleeping. His hands were joined together in prayer though it had been a long, long time since that had happened when he was alive and Mick knew that if his daddy was at that moment praying for his own salvation, he'd be slurring over the opening words to the Our Father.

His mammy sat on a chair at the side of the bed, her head bowed. She wore a black lace veil that concealed a face that had shed barely a tear for her dead husband. Not that Mick blamed her. She'd suffered enough when he was alive. Maybe God had finally answered her prayers after all this time.

Mick hoped someone would be crying at his bedside but he couldn't think who that might be. His mammy would, if she knew what had happened, but those tears would be spilt on Galway soil when she heard the news. He barely dared to hope that Kate would take on the role of chief mourner, and why would she? She no more knew his last name than he hers, so she would be crying for a stranger, their only connection one night of messy passion, the details of which were already beginning to fray at the edges.

Mick couldn't fight the pressure any more and his eyes snapped shut. He hoped his brother was still conducting a prayerful vigil over his body. He would miss him, of that he was absolutely certain. There was ten years between them and Thomas had been absent from the family home for as long, given up to Holy Mother Church like any good Irish family would do. Yet there was a bond that had never been broken and Mick wished that they could have spent more time in each other's company. Now it was too late.

His brother stood over his body and would no doubt stand over his coffin when it came time for the funeral. Mick wondered whether Thomas would be able to perform the ceremony in his usual cool, detached manner or would he shed a tear or two for his dead brother? Thomas Costello was a Galway man, Mick thought, so there would be no tears, at least not in public.

Would they be spilt on the letter he'd have to write home, probably to John McDonagh, who would be the man to break the news to his mammy? McDonagh would like that, Mick realised with a grin. The old man had been hovering round their mammy from the moment their daddy's coffin had been dropped into the ground, or at least that's what Mick had always believed, so he would relish the opportunity to provide a shoulder to cry on for a grieving mother. The rest of his family would mourn too, he realised, but they were younger and in time memories of him would fade. The thought that he would one day be forgotten made him sad.

He managed to open his eyes again and Thomas was gone. Mick smiled and tried nodding his head as if to say, 'I told you so,' though he found it impossible to move it at all. Kate glided into view. Her eyes were glistening – well, the one that could open was – while she kept wiping her nose on the dirty bandage covering her left hand. Mick tried to speak but he didn't know if his lips even moved. Certainly he realised that no sounds escaped from his mouth, but as he tried again to say something, even if it was only an incoherent grunt, Kate smiled, a relieved grin breaking out across her bruised face, and Mick knew at that very moment that she had been the most beautiful girl in the world. The realisation that he wouldn't see her ever again brought tears to his own eyes.

Kate leant over and began kissing his wet cheeks, which only made him cry harder, and as she moved closer to him, her leg pressed against his arm, sending a pain shooting through his body and he screamed, loud enough to be heard in Galway. Kate staggered back and suddenly the room seemed to be filled with a thousand noises, as if someone had unblocked Mick's ears. Maybe they had pulled the tatties out of them? He could now hear his brother's voice.

'Thank goodness for that,' Thomas said. 'I thought we were going to lose you.'

Mick strained for another sight of his brother but it was sore moving his eyes, never mind trying to manoeuvre his head. His arm, meanwhile, continued to throb but he had a growing sense things were not as he'd imagined them.

'Is this heaven?' he whispered.

'No, it's Glasgow,' said his brother and Mick smiled.

# 12

# LOVE ME TENDER

Mick had drifted back into unconsciousness almost as soon as he spoke and nothing Kate or Thomas could do or say would drag him out of it. Still, a sense of relief washed over her like a warm bath and she smiled, though almost immediately she began crying. Heavy sobs shook her body violently and although Thomas guided her gently towards a chair, she could sense the awkwardness in his touch. Slumped on the seat, tears continued to run silently down her face, yet she refused to look away from the now hazy image of the body on the bed.

Thomas remained standing, the low murmur of his prayers the only sound in the room. Kate found it strangely comforting and her gaze would occasionally drift to the priest, whom she studied with curiosity. There was no obvious resemblance between the two men that would suggest they were brothers, yet it was clear that Thomas' vigil was more than that of a concerned pastor. He was praying for his brother, as a brother, and she was glad that someone was.

She tried doing so as well, though the words just seemed to stay jumbled up in her head and she eventually resorted to mouthing, 'Thank you, God,' silently a few times as she watched the unconscious Mick. It felt like all her dreams and nightmares had rolled into one long and exhausting fantasy and she still couldn't quite believe what she'd seen when she thought about it again.

He had dropped out of the sky, landing on top of one of Duffy's men who'd been standing outside the building, making sure she couldn't get back inside to try and save him. Mick cracked his head off the ground, the sound like a gunshot making Kate flinch, and he lay perfectly still. She feared he was gone but she wasn't sure she had the strength to try and thump his body back to life and she only had the use of one good hand.

She looked at Duffy's man and knew for sure that he was dead, a sliver of blood flowing out his ear as he lay, crushed and broken. Duffy's terrifying scream had subsided and he leant out the window as Kate glanced up. He said nothing but she knew that look on his reddened face. There was murder on his mind.

She looked round helplessly, knowing he'd catch her if she tried to flee; she wasn't leaving Mick behind either, not after he'd finally found her. It was better that both of them met the same fate, though from the state of the Galway man, he'd feel the wrath of Duffy a lot less than she would. The clatter of urgent hooves grew louder and she glanced up as a horse and cart drew to a stop beside her. Two men jumped out of the back and roughly grabbed Mick's arms and legs, bundling him into the cart. Kate started to protest but the driver climbed down and took a firm grip of her arm.

'Come with us now, miss.'

She tried to shake off his hand, which remained clamped to her limb.

'You'll be safe.'

Still, Kate resisted as the man tried dragging her towards the cart. He stopped with a sigh.

'You can choose the easy way or the hard way. It makes no odds to me, but you're getting on that cart.'

The man had a quiet determination in his manner and Kate was reluctant to see what the hard way was. She started to move when Duffy staggered out into the street, holding his bloody leg and breathing heavily.

'Kate,' he snapped and both she and the cart driver stopped. He stepped forward, edging Kate behind him. Duffy limped towards him.

'Not today, Jack,' the man said in a firm voice, thrusting his hand in his jacket and producing a gun. Duffy stopped and stretched himself to his full height, grimacing with the pain of putting weight on his wounded leg.

'Is that a wise thing to do?' Duffy said.

Both the driver and Kate inched towards the cart, and she quickly climbed on board, stumbling over the step as she moved across the seat. The gun was still pointed at Duffy, who was edging forward as well.

'Don't be daft, Jack. Stay where you are or this'll stop you.'

Duffy stopped, a grin breaking out across his face.

'Another time, then.'

'I wouldn't count on it,' the driver said, now sitting up beside Kate. He grabbed the reins and snapped them, the horse immediately sprinting away, leaving Duffy standing on the pavement, oblivious to the dead man who lay at his feet.

'You can run but you can't hide, Kate,' he shouted after her and she put her head in her hands, not looking up until the cart drew to a final stop. Her sight was blurry at first when she looked up but her eyes quickly focused as Thomas stepped forward from the front of the church.

'Good man, O'Connor,' he muttered, shaking the cart driver's hand. 'Bring him into the house,' he said to the two men in the back, and they immediately jumped to attention, nudging Mick to the edge of the cart before they grasped his limbs again and began manoeuvring him towards the front door of the house which sat directly next to the church.

'And it's good to see you again, Miss – '

'Kate.'

'Miss Kate,' the priest said, holding out a hand, which she took and let him guide her down from the cart. He stood aside and gestured for her to head into the house and he followed behind her as she moved unsteadily into the building.

Mick was in a small room on the ground floor at the back of the chapel house. The men had put him down on the bed and when Kate and Thomas walked in, O'Connor was slicing his shirt open with a small knife. Thomas closed the curtains and lit the two candles on the table opposite the bed. An oppressive gloominess enveloped the room despite the feverish efforts of the candles to shed some light on proceedings.

With an impressive delicacy and steady hand, O'Connor had cut Mick's clothes away and was now pulling them off until the unconscious man was lying on the bed wearing only his underwear. There was blood and bruises and lumps where there shouldn't have been and one of the men who'd carried Mick into the house draped a thin cover over him.

When O'Connor and his two assistants left the room, Thomas followed them and Kate could hear the deep voices talking outside. After a few minutes, the priest reappeared and walked over to his brother. He stood studying the unconscious man for a few minutes before leaning over and gently pushing a stray strand of Mick's brown hair off his forehead. It took all of Kate's best efforts not to cry when she saw the gesture.

Thomas asked her what had happened and she told him as best as she could, apologising for the gaps in her tale and aware of trying to speak properly to the priest. Slowly, and not without confusion, she managed to get him to understand that Mick hadn't rescued her from his own pursuers, but from her demonic nightmare. When she explained about Mick's miraculous survival after tumbling out of the window, she began laughing nervously.

'It's just as well I had O'Connor following him,' Thomas said. 'I knew that brother of mine wouldn't be able to stay out of trouble, even after I warned him. We should thank God that both of you managed to escape. It's that bloody guardian angel of his,' Thomas said, and she'd looked up, startled.

'Sorry,' he muttered almost immediately, red flashes of embarrassment creeping out across his cheeks, and he looked away towards his brother. She followed his gaze and couldn't help but think that the priest was telling the truth. Either that or he was just the luckiest man in the world. Whatever the reason, Mick was alive when he should have been dead.

He was still sleeping, though she knew it was not a peaceful rest. He would groan suddenly and without warning but to Kate it sounded like the most beautiful song of a nightingale because it meant that he was breathing. His body would be aching, and it was as if tremors of pain were shaking it every few minutes. She wanted to do something – anything – to help, but didn't know what that could be. A sense of helplessness was beginning to replace her relief and she stood up, groaning as a pain shot up her left arm.

'I've sent for a doctor,' Thomas said as Kate sat back down. 'And we'll get him to look at you as well.'

She smiled gratefully, a smile that Thomas returned briefly before glancing back to his brother.

'What happened to your hand?' he asked without looking at her. She stared at the dirty bandage and shuddered as she imagined what might be underneath it. Duffy had stemmed the flow of blood and had actually left the bandage with her, though she'd had to wrap it herself. It still throbbed, often without provocation, and it only served to remind her of the disfigurement.

He'd left the fingers with her as well – 'Just so you don't forget,' he'd told her, though how was she ever going to be able to do that? Still, she had kicked the bloody digits out of sight anyway, while remaining aware that they still lurked in the blackness surrounding her. They would soon enough become an unexpected feast for the rats.

There was a knock on the door and they both looked round. Thomas moved towards the door, opening it and speaking to the person on the other side – it was a woman's voice – before closing it shut and returning to the room with a bowl of water in his hand.

'The doctor will be here soon,' he said, placing the bowl on the floor at the side of the bed. 'We'll need to clean him up first.'

Thomas looked down on his brother and Kate followed his gaze. After a few moments she was aware that he was watching her. She could tell from his face what he wanted her to do, though he seemed nervous about asking her. She nodded knowingly and relief spread across his face. The priest waited for a few minutes, still watching Mick though he had stopped praying, and an awkward silence filled the room.

'I'll go and wait for the doctor,' he said eventually as he stepped towards the door and she waited until he had closed it behind him before she turned her attention towards the bed.

She slowly pulled back the cover, her fingers shaking nervously in her anxiousness to avoid hurting him. It was bloodstained and the outline of his battered body was clearly visible on the white material. Her eyes scanned his torso, trying to figure out where to start, but she was reluctant to begin. She'd never done anything like this before and she was scared; she wanted to help him, to soothe his pain, but she was worried it would hurt him more than help him. Mick groaned again, his face wearing a mask of pain, and it dragged her out of her dithering.

She took the cloth and immersed it in the bowl of warm water. Squeezing it, she wiped his face, so delicately at first that it made no difference, but as she applied more force, the dried blood began to disappear and with each sighting of his cleansed flesh, she would leave a soft kiss – on his forehead, his cheeks, his chin and, finally his lips. She let her own lips rest on his and sighed with a trace of contentment she barely thought possible. Mick groaned again. It could have been her ears deceiving her but Kate was convinced there was less pain in that noise and she pressed her lips more heavily down on his.

Once his face was clean, she began on his arms, performing the same ritual as before, first on his right arm until she was sure she'd kissed every inch of it, and then onto his left arm, though he flinched as soon as the cloth touched flesh, and she remembered what had happened when she'd leant on it. Looking at the limb, she should have realised because it was bent and broken out of shape from where Duffy had repeatedly crushed it and she wondered whether there would be much the doctor could do to heal it.

After two or three attempts at cleaning it, she gave up, realising that it was only going to cause him more pain, and her attention turned to the rest of his body. Her cloth freshly rinsed, she began under his chin before her tongue caressed his Adam's apple. It moved across his throat, tracing a faint line across his skin, before it reached his ear. As she nibbled the lobe, his head moved slightly and the briefest glimmer of a smile broke out from the edges of his mouth. Her tongue retraced its route across to the other ear, where she repeated the same action, provoking the same response.

Now she began to wipe his chest, aware again of where Duffy had landed his heaviest blows. It rose and fell weakly as her fingers playfully toyed with his chest hairs before her lips caressed each of his nipples in turn. She wanted to rest her head on his torso but she was afraid the weight would only add to his agony, so she continued wiping the blood off his body.

She could feel the jagged edges of his ribs and knew that was where he'd been kicked. She hoped that the doctor would be gentle when he carried out his own examination.

When she reached his waist, she wiped round the edges of his underwear, before transferring her attention to his legs, beginning with his feet and working her way up until she met the material again. As the cloth ran up and down each leg in turn, she began humming a tune her mammy had sang to her when she was just a girl. It seemed like a lifetime ago but the words soon came flooding back to her much easier than the prayers she'd struggled to recall.

*'The pale moon was rising above the green mountains, the sun was declining beneath the blue sea; When I strayed with my love by the pure crystal fountain, that stands in the beautiful Vale of Tralee . . .'*

Her mammy had always seemed to be singing, no matter what she was doing, whether it was cooking or cleaning or sitting for five minutes in front of the stove in what was a rare break from the endless chores that piled up on top of her.

Kate's favourite time was just before bed, when she would wait in line behind her sisters, all of them freshly scrubbed and ready for bed. Each of them would sit on their mammy's knee in turn, and she'd sing to them in a voice that sounded like an angel's as she brushed their hair until it was smooth and shiny.

'She was lovely and fair as the rose of the summer, yet 'twas not her beauty alone that won me; Oh no, 'twas the truth in her eyes ever dawning, that made me love Mary, the Rose of Tralee.'

That was her mammy's name and that was her song. She was beautiful, even after the years of hardship, the nine children she'd borne, of whom only six had survived beyond infancy.

'You're your mother's daughter,' people used to tell Kate and she'd blush, though secretly pleased with the compliment, which she treasured, while willing each day to pass quicker than the last so that she could grow older and more like her mammy.

She ran her tongue along her swollen mouth, suddenly reminded of her own injuries, thankful there was no mirror to cast that image back at her. It certainly wouldn't remind her of her mammy and she was glad that she had her memories of happier times.

Satisfied that Mick's body was clean, or at least as clean as it could be without causing him untold pain, Kate dropped the cloth into the basin and pulled the bloodstained cover over his body. She leant over and kissed him once more and then inched the cover back again. She moved his right arm, giving herself a tiny space on the edge of the bed and she slowly squeezed herself onto it, draping her right arm softly across his chest and letting her head rest on his arm which now acted as a pillow for her. She pressed closer to his body until she could feel its heat beginning to seep into hers and she smiled as she closed her eyes, kissed his chest one last time and let the exhaustion wash over her until she began to drift into the first contented sleep she'd enjoyed since the last time she'd lain with her Galway boy.

# 13

## SECRETS AND LIES

She stood before him as he sat on the edge of the bed. His hands were shaking and his heart was booming. She smiled as his nervous eyes watched her and she nodded as if to calm him. Her hands slowly stretched up and peeled the straps of her negligee off her shoulders. He stared at the bare flesh which slowly revealed itself as the garment slid silently down her body. She was as naked before him as he was to her. Her fingers ran through her black hair as she stretched and his eyes tried to memorise every inch of her. Stepping forward, she sat across his lap; his own flesh tingled as it touched hers and her body was so close to his that, as he breathed in deeply and anxiously, he could smell her aroma, like freshly picked apples. He looked up as she moved her face towards his and their lips met . . .

Thomas woke with a start and glanced around him, though he knew he was alone in the church. He held out his trembling hand and he could feel his heart pounding. He breathed deeply, two or three times, trying to calm down, and then pushed himself off the kneeler and sat up.

One minute he had been praying the Sorrowful Mysteries – the Crowning of Thorns – and the next he was dreaming of her. It wasn't the first time it had happened and he worried that it wouldn't be the last. At least before he'd been in bed and had woken suddenly, momentarily unaware of his surroundings, before his eyes adjusted to the dark and he realised that it wasn't real; she wasn't there with him, beside him, under him. Thomas shook his head and frowned. These were not the thoughts of a good priest and this was certainly not the place to be having them.

The church was empty. This was normally Thomas' favourite time, when it felt like his personal chapel, and he would kneel in silent prayer, sometimes for an hour or two. He prayed for his family, especially his mother and his brother and sisters back in Galway, though, in truth, the main focus of his prayers was actually Mick. It had been that way before his brother got into trouble and it was even more so now. Mick was still in the chapel house, a guest that Monsignor Dolan knew about but chose not to enquire of too deeply. His lack of curiosity surprised Thomas, but he was grateful for it nevertheless.

'I will ask no questions, which means you will tell me no lies,' Monsignor Dolan said.

'Thank you, Peter,' Thomas said. 'It will only be for a few days.'

'Discretion, Thomas. That is all I ask for,' he said with a final nod before retiring to his own room.

The girl also remained and the Monsignor asked even less about her, if only because he didn't know of her presence. Thomas could think of no plausible or acceptable explanation that would appease the parish priest so, with the help of Mrs Breslin, he'd managed to keep her hidden from prying eyes.

Kate. How many times each day did he say that name, out loud or in his head, the sound of which made his spirits soar? And when he saw her, his heart wanted to explode into a million tiny, painful pieces. He watched her when she tended his brother's wounds, gently washing and drying and cleaning them and sometimes adding a gentle, soothing kiss. He smiled cautiously whenever she did so at him, pocketing each one to recall and savour later. He'd memorised every conversation they'd had, whether brief or not, replaying them in his mind over and over again. And when he slept he dreamt of her, picturing her naked body pressed close to his. The feeling of desire would almost suffocate him, at which point he would wake up, the desire instantly replaced by guilt and then confusion. He wasn't supposed to feel like this. He

115

wasn't allowed. Yet, he couldn't help it and he didn't want it to stop.

Dozing off in the church was taking it too far, however, and he knelt down and resumed his prayers, his own forgiveness now at the forefront of his thoughts, though he kept his eyes opened and focused on the crucified Christ on the wall behind the altar. He didn't want to run the risk of falling asleep again. There were other things that he should have been concentrating on, though even as he tried to remember them, thoughts of Kate wouldn't disappear.

At this moment she was lying in bed with his brother, the two of them probably still sleeping. They had been when he'd gently pushed the door open and saw them, wrapped together, oblivious to his silent vigil. Mick was bruised and battered and she wasn't much better. Her injured hand, freshly tended to and dressed properly by Doctor Hannah, lay across Mick's bare chest.

Thomas had stood outside the room when the doctor treated her, though her cries of pain seeped through the wooden door and pierced his heart, and he had to resist the urge to go in and hold her in a comforting embrace. That feeling had crept up on him and left him surprised and disorientated, but it had merely been a foretaste of what was to come.

When the doctor emerged from the room, he wore a grave expression that Thomas recognised from when he was about to announce a death in a sombre, dispassionate tone, and he was instantly worried.

'That is a bloody mess, if you'll pardon the language, Father,' the doctor said with a shake of the head.

'Will she be okay?' Thomas asked, desperately trying to disguise the concern in his voice.

'She'll be fine, no doubt about that, but she'll never play the piano again,' the doctor said with a grim chuckle, though any trace of a self-appreciative grin instantly disappeared when he saw the expression on Thomas' face.

'God forgive me, Father,' he said.

Thomas nodded disdainfully, gesturing with his head in

the same movement towards the way out and the doctor quickly scurried away.

The priest pressed his ear to the door. He could hear sniffles, the remnants of tears that had flown more freely not five minutes before, but it was not enough to justify his sudden entrance. He wanted to console her, but feared that if he stepped over the threshold at that moment, it would only lead to an awkward and embarrassing scene. After a couple of minutes, he slipped away, but she was never far from his thoughts.

Now, having finished his prayers, he made the sign of the cross, stood up and walked to the front of the aisle, genuflecting and then heading through a door at the side of the altar that led into the chapel house. He was tempted to check on the sleeping couple but headed instead for the dining room where Mrs Breslin would soon be serving dinner. He was eating alone tonight. Monsignor Dolan was visiting St Mary's. It was a fortuitous visit, thought Thomas as he sat down at the table, breathing in deeply as he detected the odours of his food drifting through from the kitchen. There was another meeting in the hall tonight and the less the Monsignor knew about it, the better. He had decided against asking about Mick, but Thomas wasn't so sure the same lack of curiosity would apply to the group of Irishmen who would soon be gathering in the parish.

It had been Padraig Clarke who first approached him one Sunday after Mass. He hadn't actually attended the service himself but he appeared as everyone poured out of the church, pushing against the tide of bodies as he made his way inside. Thomas was hanging up his surplice when there was a knock on the sacristy door and he turned to see Padraig, cap in hand, waiting at the doorway for an invitation to enter.

The request to use the hall was brazen. Padraig had never, even for a moment, hesitated about revealing the name of the Irish Republican Brotherhood. It didn't surprise or startle him, but Thomas still felt uneasy and he looked at Padraig, wondering for a brief moment if this was the last face he would stare at should his own intentions ever be discovered. The Brotherhood was a name he remembered from his childhood, whispered warily in public or boasted of loudly in private. They were fighting for 'the cause', and every shot fired in anger at a barracks or any pane of glass smashed at a police station was down to them. Even broken wheels on army carts or carriages were apparently the work of the Brotherhood. This is what he remembered from his daddy's drunken lectures, that and the heavy slaps on the back of the head whenever he didn't supply the right answer to questions that were often barely coherent.

His daddy would stumble into the cottage, imbibed with an alcohol-drenched patriotism that he wanted to impart to his oldest son. It didn't matter that Thomas had to be dragged, half sleeping, out of bed, and made to listen to tall tales of fallen heroes and lavish boasts of heroes yet to come.

'The Brotherhood will free Ireland,' his daddy would slur, leaning into Thomas' face so that the whiskey fumes washed over his face and stung his own throat, and he'd swallow hard to stop himself from throwing up.

Sometimes the lectures would last for hours or they might end abruptly when his daddy's head, weighed down by drink and tiredness, crashed onto the table. Thomas would wait a few minutes until the snoring began before creeping back into his own bed. It would take him longer to fall asleep again. He was cold and felt sick every time he breathed in and smelt traces of alcohol that clung to him like a damp cloud on a winter's morning.

He wondered who they were, these mysterious men who were part of the Brotherhood. He knew his daddy wouldn't be involved – drink was the only thing he thought worth fighting for – but he imagined these men to be big and strong and heroic and sober, interested only in Ireland's freedom.

Now, Thomas knew that they were all of these things and none of these things. They were just men, no more or less, and one of them now stood before him in the sacristy. He frowned as Padraig repeated the name of the Brotherhood, though he quickly replaced it with a pained smile. He didn't want to appear unhelpful, but Padraig didn't seem to notice.

Just as he knew Thomas would agree to the request, Padraig must also have been sure that the priest wouldn't betray the Brotherhood's confidence, though that may well have just been the assurance of talking as one Irishman to another. It was enough to make Thomas shake his head when he thought about it later. If there was any lesson to be learned from the history of their troubled land, it was that an Irishman's worst enemy was one of his own. Still, he had no intention of proclaiming loudly the purpose of the meetings, content instead to report back to the Archbishop as he'd been instructed.

There were seven of them in total who had attended the three meetings. As well as Padraig, the group consisted of Daniel Lafferty, Sean Dempsey, Sean Doherty, Denis Lyons, Harry O'Donnell and Martin Higgins. Those were the names that Thomas had scribbled down in his diary after the first meeting. He'd been in the hall to welcome them, ushering them towards one of the smaller rooms that branched off from the main part of the building.

They all sat round the table he'd put in especially for them, though none of the men spoke. Some of them had greeted him on their arrival with a nod or a deft touch of the cap but once they were together, silence descended on the gathering. They were all waiting for him to leave.

'Do you want me to say a prayer before you get started?' he'd asked dutifully, but Padraig shook his head. Thomas quickly scanned the room, hoping to locate at least one pair of eager eyes but most of the men wouldn't return his gaze. They were obviously desperate to begin their meeting and he could sense that he had overstayed his welcome, even though this was home to him. He closed the door, briefly thinking of standing outside and trying to listen, though he knew that if he was caught, the repercussions would not be pleasant.

He was sitting at the table in the meeting room after dinner when Padraig walked in, accompanied by another man that Thomas had never seen before.

'Father,' Padraig said with a brief nod, sitting down opposite the priest and gesturing for his companion to take the seat beside him. As the man sat down, Thomas studied him discreetly, committing to memory the colour of his hair, the shape of his crooked nose, the clothes he was wearing, though this information was surplus to requirements. All that the Archbishop wanted was names.

'Father Costello,' he said, stretching a hand out across the table.

The stranger grasped it with his, revealing a firm grip and course palms.

'Nice to meet you, Father,' he said with a nod.

Padraig coughed and Thomas knew he was being asked to leave. He remained sitting at the table, smiling at Padraig.

'That's a heavy fall of snow we've had tonight,' he said.

'We'll need to watch we're not snowed in,' the stranger said in an accent that Thomas couldn't quite place. If he had to guess, he'd have said Cork, but he did not have his brother's gift.

The other men began to drift into the room, one or two also remarking on the weather. They all dropped onto the nearest empty seat and, as before, a cloak of silence seemed to drop over them and Thomas decided it was time to go. As he stood up, Sean Dempsey walked in.

'Dan Foley,' he said with a sudden burst of enthusiasm, striding over to the stranger who stood up, grinning. Both men hugged, patting the other's back enthusiastically but Thomas noticed Padraig's stern face and reckoned Dempsey was minutes away from a reprimand. Excusing himself, he closed the door behind him and walked across the church hall to the entrance. Glancing back cautiously, he took out his diary from his jacket pocket and quickly scribbled the name in his book. At least it meant something new to report to Father McNeill when they met tomorrow.

Thomas edged the hall door open and caught a blast of cold air, which took advantage of the gap and flooded into the building. Handfuls of snow that had been piling up against the door spilled onto the floor inside and as he pushed it open a little further, he could see the white powder lying inches deep on the ground outside. It was still snowing, though not as heavy as before and he shivered as he pulled the door shut again.

He walked halfway across the hall, heading towards the door that led back through to the church. A sudden burst of laughter from the room stopped him in his tracks for a moment. Curiosity that had lurked in the background since the first meeting now began to grip him and he couldn't resume his journey out of the hall. It was because of the stranger's presence, he realised, and he found himself quietly creeping back towards the room.

A low murmur slipped out from under the door but it was indistinguishable even as Thomas stood, holding his breath and pressing his ear to the wooden barrier. Occasional loud words were recognisable but nothing that made any sense. He was about to turn away again when there was a click. He knew right away what it was and the realisation momentarily paralysed him. When he took a step back he was aware that he was still holding his breath and he slowly and silently began to exhale.

There was another click and this time he knew for sure. There was a gun in the room, perhaps even more than one. He knew that sound, even though it had been many years since he'd heard it, when he was a boy back in Galway and he'd gone hunting with his daddy, looking for dinner, but the noise still made him nervous even now.

He took another step back and pressed down on a loose floorboard, which creaked loudly for a second. Thomas decided against waiting to see whether the men in the room had heard it, and strode quickly out of the hall and into the church. His mind was racing, though it was struggling to keep up with his heart, which beat with a nervousness that only Kate had previously managed to provoke.

All he'd been asked to do was provide a list of names. Hadn't that been what the Archbishop said? He'd spoken about apocalyptic dangers the Church faced, though in such cryptic terms that Thomas couldn't understand why his task had any relevance.

He now had a new name, but more than that, he had other information.

Certainly, it was unsettling to know that there was a weapon on Church property. He could think of no good reason for the gun's presence, but he could imagine a few bad ones; these men were not planning a hunting trip, at least not one where the only target was a rabbit, and he wished he had not agreed to Padraig's request. The reality, however, was that it was the Archbishop who had asked and he was not in a position to say no, even though he couldn't imagine his superior would be pleased to hear about the gun. If only he could speak to Monsignor Dolan about it, then he might feel better, but the Archbishop had demanded 'confessional secrecy' and for now Thomas felt compelled to maintain that.

He slipped into one of the pews and knelt down, closing his eyes and asking God for some help. His lips moved as he began muttering familiar prayers, the Hail Mary and Our Father, ones that he'd learned on his mammy's knee and which remained a source of spiritual comfort to him even now. He smiled as he remembered the small boy who'd declared when he was only nine years old that he wanted to be a priest. His mammy had burst into tears while his daddy shook his head and muttered, 'That's all Ireland needs. Another bloody priest.'

He'd been chased out of the cottage for his blasphemy, complaining loudly but heading gratefully for the pub, while Thomas knelt at the side of his bed beside his mammy and said prayers – 'For your father's black soul,' she'd hissed bitterly.

Thomas fumbled in his pockets, bringing out a set of rosary beads that gave structure to his prayers.

'Do you think he hears you, Father?' a voice whispered in his ear.

Thomas looked up and came face-to-face with Padraig, who was leaning over from the row behind him. He was startled and almost tumbled sideways. Padraig leant forward again.

'I'm not convinced that he does, to tell you the truth. I think maybe that's what has held us back all these years. All these superstitions and rituals, promising a better time in the next life so that we accept the misery we've got in this one.'

'We're all entitled to our beliefs,' Thomas said nervously.

'If only that were true, Father.'

Thomas sat back in the pew and looked round at Padraig. He was not a familiar face at Sunday Mass, even though he stayed no more than a stone's throw from the church. He would appear only at funerals, standing morosely at the back, slipping in at the last moment and leaving just as discreetly before the coffin was even carried out. If he was a notable absentee, then his wife was the opposite. Mary Clarke sat in the second row, right-hand side every Sunday morning at half-past-nine Mass, her head covered by a veil and bowed in prayer, no doubt for her non-believing husband.

'Is that the meeting finished already?' Thomas asked.

Padraig shook his head. 'I just decided to take a breather. It gets a bit stuffy in there with all those sweaty Irishmen.' He laughed gruffly, the noise echoing out across the empty church and drifting high up to the domed roof above the altar. Thomas forced his mouth into a smile.

'We appreciate your help, Father. It's a handy wee room.'

'You're very welcome.'

'A bit of privacy's hard to find. I mean, you just never know who might be listening outside the door. You can never be too careful, can you, Father?'

Thomas shook his head.

'That's the way we like to keep it, Father. Silence is golden, as they say. So every noise makes us jumpy, a gust of wind, a banging door, a loose floorboard. I'm sure you understand.'

'Absolutely.'

'So it might be better if you left the key with us,' Padraig said.

'The key?'

'For the room. It would save you having to disrupt your busy schedule just to see us in and out.'

'It's no bother,' Thomas said.

'I think it would be better, Father. You've done enough for us already, so I don't want to put you out any more.'

Padraig stood up, suddenly towering over Thomas, who thought of voicing more objections but knew what the end result would still be. All the time the click of the gun was ricocheting through his mind. He rummaged in his pocket and brought out a bundle of keys, taking a few seconds to prise the meeting room key off the thick silver ring that held them all. He handed it to Padraig, who immediately slipped it into his pocket, nodded and walked back to the hall, his footsteps falling heavily on the stone floor as he disappeared through the door. Thomas remained sitting for a few minutes after he'd gone. The urge to pray had left him though his mind still raced with thoughts of what was going on in that room. He would have to be more careful from now on, or perhaps just a little less curious. Avoiding any loose floorboards might help as well.

# 14

# DEAR DIARY

He could tell that Father McNeill was anxious to leave and that just made Thomas go all the slower. He opened one drawer and rummaged about inside, shaking his head and frowning before closing it and opening the one below it.

'I'm sure I put it in here last night,' he said as Father McNeill stood in the middle of the room, arms folded and fingers drumming impatiently on his sleeve. Even just glancing round at his fellow priest, Thomas could see the coating of dandruff which covered the shoulders of the black jacket and he had a sudden urge to get up and brush them clean. It would certainly have startled his guest and he suppressed a smile as he thought of the reaction it would provoke.

'Are you just going to tell me the same names as before?' Father McNeill said with a heavy sigh.

'No, there's more. Somebody new . . . Where did I leave that diary?'

He finished searching the third drawer and then stood up with a shrug.

'If it's only one name, can you not remember it?'

Thomas shook his head. 'Probably, but I want to make sure. I don't want the Archbishop getting inaccurate information.'

Father McNeill walked over to one of the armchairs in the far corner of the room and dropped down onto it, dislodging some of the dandruff, which floated in the air like tiny flecks of snow. He produced a pocket watch that he opened and studied, snorting angrily before snapping it shut and plunging it back into his pocket.

'My carriage is waiting outside,' he said curtly.

'I know, and I'm sorry. I've got a terrible memory.'

The diary was close to Thomas' heart, literally. It sat in the inside pocket of his jacket, ready to be produced at any moment, but he was enjoying the other man's irritation. He'd been surprised that Father McNeill came to see him. He'd presumed it would have been the other way around, or that they would have agreed a designated meeting place where neither man would be recognised, but the Archbishop had insisted. St Alphonsus' would just become another port of call on his Chancellor's tour of the city's parishes, not arousing any suspicions amongst the parishioners or parish priest.

The arrangement suited Thomas. It was certainly more convenient, and he enjoyed witnessing the discomfort that Father McNeill evidently felt whenever he ventured out from the cosseted comforts of the Cathedral. It was bringing him into close proximity with ordinary people – ordinary Irish people – and the Highlander's distaste was barely concealed.

Thomas also remained curious as to what was going on. He didn't want to ask bluntly. For one thing, he knew that he wouldn't get a straight answer, if any answer at all, but to have raised any questions might have been seen as a sign of dissent towards the Archbishop and that was not recommended.

'It just seems like a talking shop,' he said at last as he stood, hands on hips, facing Father McNeill.

'What do they talk about?'

'I don't know. I'm not allowed in when the meeting's started.'

'Well, at least we know who's doing the talking. Are you going to find this diary or not, because I have a busy schedule.'

Thomas patted his pockets absent-mindedly, affecting a startled expression as he touched the diary.

'Would you believe it was in here all the time?' he said with a laugh, mentally complimenting his own acting skills as Father

McNeill stood up. He flicked through the book until he came to the last list he'd scribbled down two nights ago.

'Are you not curious to know what the Archbishop wants with this information?' he said, holding the page open.

'Have you got the names there?'

'I mean, he's got you charging round the Archdiocese collecting names of men who sit in a church hall chatting about the old country, and without you even knowing what for.'

'Who says I don't know?'

'Maybe you do. It was just the impression that I got. It seems pretty secret to me, so I didn't think His Grace was for telling anyone, not even his Chancellor.'

Father McNeill smiled grimly as he copied down all the names from Thomas' diary, scribbling each one down in an untidy script, though he printed the name 'DAN FOLEY' in heavy capital letters.

'We are an old Church and a young Church in this country,' Father McNeill said as he wrote. 'And our resurgence has been a blessing for those of us who kept the faith alive during the dark days.'

'And rightly so,' said Thomas.

'Even if we have had to rely on the help of others to build ourselves back up.'

Thomas knew what he meant by others, but resisted offering any defence of his fellow countrymen and women. Others had done so in the past and found, to their cost, that the Chancellor could be very unforgiving with those who dared to disagree with him, and Thomas had no great desire to find himself dispatched to some far-flung corner of the diocese.

'Our enemies remain strong too,' Father McNeill continued. 'We cannot give them an excuse to kill the sapling before it has taken root, if you know what I mean?'

Thomas nodded.

'So a few men sitting in a room talking about the old country, as you describe it – talking and planning and plotting – puts the whole future of the Church in this country at risk. And when that risk is spelt out to the Archbishop then he must act to prevent any such disaster from happening. We've worked and prayed too long and too hard to let a few Irishmen jeopardise that.'

He almost spat out the word 'Irishmen' as if a fly had lodged itself in his throat and he was trying to get it out. Shutting his own diary and pocketing it, he nodded briefly and headed for the door.

'Same time next week,' he said, disappearing out of the room without waiting for any reply. Thomas was glad that he'd mentioned nothing of the gun to the other priest. He hadn't intended to keep it a secret but there was something in the Chancellor's words that had stopped him. Or was it simply the smug expression that always seemed to rile Thomas? He stared at the list of names on the page in front of him, gripped once more with a curiosity to find out what plans were brewing inside that room, though he realised he couldn't risk standing outside the door again.

# 15

## ONE SMALL STEP

A pain shot through his side like a knife being thrust in and out as she held up his right arm, sliding it into a freshly washed white shirt which he didn't recognise. Mick frowned but managed to suppress the urge to cry out. He knew she was being as gentle as she could, and it would be worse when she tried his other arm. He looked down at it, lying listlessly at his side. The doctor had pressed a splint on it, which he'd strapped tightly, though he'd been honest enough to explain that it might make no difference.

'The bone will heal,' he'd said as he finished, 'but it was a bit of a mess. We'll just have to wait and see.'

'And pray,' Kate had piped in from the corner of the bedroom. The doctor smiled, but Mick could tell he was a man of medicine rather than faith, and Mick wasn't convinced that prayers would make much of a difference either. Still, it wouldn't do any harm and it felt good to think that somebody had him in their thoughts.

Kate didn't even attempt to push his left arm into the shirt, instead wrapping the garment across his body and buttoning it up so that it hid his injured limb. He watched as she managed to push each button through the hole with her one good hand and he could feel tears beginning to well up in his eyes though he quickly blinked them away. It wouldn't do for her to see him like this – it was just as well that she was concentrating on the task – but he wanted to thank her; the words refused to take shape in his mouth, however. He waited until she'd finished, struggling to push the last button through the tiny opening in the material which she eventually did with a triumphant grin. As she stood up, he leant forward and kissed her, a tender caress that he hoped would let her know how he felt.

They were venturing out for the first time since the attack. The doctor had recommended fresh air and Mick was grateful for the chance to escape the confines of the chapel house. It had proved to be a safe haven and he'd thanked his brother for saving his life. He'd wanted to thank O'Connor as well but Thomas had said he would pass on the message. There was an air of mystery surrounding the man who did his brother's bidding and Mick didn't have the strength to press for more information. He was still in a lot of pain and only sleep brought him any relief. Even that was not guaranteed, though the smell and the sound and the touch of Kate alongside him proved more soothing than any balm.

'Ten minutes a day to start with,' the doctor had said, 'just to build up your strength. Try walking to the end of the street and back and see how you get on.'

It had seemed like nothing at all when the doctor said it, but now that he'd taken a few steps outside, slowly putting one foot in front of the other, Mick glanced up the street and thought the end of it seemed as far away as the horizon. He shivered in the winter chill, though Kate had slipped on a heavy winter coat over his shirt. It was one of his brother's, as was the shirt, and didn't quite fit; the sleeve that he'd managed to use stopped just short of his wrist but it was warm enough.

There was still a heavy covering of snow on the ground, though it had been packed down by the heavy tread of countless pairs of feet, and it only made Mick step forward with even more caution. He leant gratefully on Kate, who clutched his right arm and guided him up the street, occasionally squeezing his hand affectionately. Rain was falling lightly and Mick noticed the snow at the side of the ground was turning brown like a mysterious disease was slowly and silently devouring the pure white flakes.

Every half-dozen steps or so, he would stop, almost breathless.

'Are you okay?' Kate asked each time.

'I'm fine,' he said with a nod, taking short breaths in quick succession until he felt capable of going on. Deeper breaths only made the pain in his tightly-strapped ribs even sorer than it was during every other waking moment.

'We can turn back if you want,' Kate said.

'No, the doctor said the end of the street and back and that's what we'll do.'

Another squeeze of his hand, a smile that would melt the coldest heart and a kiss to set his heart racing.

He looked into Kate's eyes – she was now able to open both of them, though the bruising, purple and yellow and sickly, remained – and he was reminded to thank God for his good luck.

'Why me?' he'd asked her as they lay in bed last night. She leant up on her elbow and even though it was dark, he felt he could see her face in perfect clarity. Maybe it was just because it seemed like the only thing he'd looked at in all the time he'd been in the bedroom, but he'd committed it to memory and it was the last thing he thought of before he drifted off to sleep and it was the first thing he thought of when he woke up.

'What do you mean?' she asked.

'Why are you here with me? What makes me different from . . .'

'You mean, from all the other men that I've been with?'

'No, I didn't mean that. What I was trying to say was . . .'

'It's okay, I know what I am.'

'What you were,' he said, touching her arm gently with his fingertips.

'I could ask you the same thing,' she said. 'Why did you look for me? It would have been easier just to let me disappear and forget about me.'

'Guilty conscience, I suppose.'

She laughed, leaning over and kissing him quickly.

'So why me?' he asked again.

'Because you wanted me.'

'I know, but – '

'You wanted me just for me. Not because you had the money or anything like that. It just felt normal and I hadn't felt like that for so long . . .'

Tears glistened on her cheeks and she pressed her face into his chest. He could feel more tears dropping onto his flesh like thin rain and he felt happier at that moment than he had done in many a long day.

When they reached the end of the street – it took a lot longer than the ten minutes the doctor had recommended – they stopped. Mick leant against the tenement wall and glanced back at the route they'd just travelled. It was no more than a hundred yards, but it felt like they'd been walking for miles. He was breathless and sore and exhilarated at the same time. Kate lit two cigarettes and passed one to him, which he began smoking gratefully, filling his lungs up with tobacco and breathing out with a contented sigh.

'It'll be dark by the time we manage to walk back,' he said and she laughed.

The rain was getting heavier and he sheltered his cigarette in the cup of his hand, feeling its heat tingle his skin.

'Let's go,' he said, taking a final draw before flicking the cigarette away. 'We'll get soaked if we stay out here for much longer.'

She took his arm again and they began the slow trek back to the chapel house. Mick knew it was all in his mind but he suddenly felt as if there was a spring in his step that hadn't been there when they'd first set out.

The following day they repeated the journey and already it didn't seem quite such a daunting prospect. Kate remained his crutch and each foot forward was a slow and measured action, but he was heading in the right direction and it felt good. Thomas had been pleased when they'd told him the previous night, though Mick knew that his recovery would soon herald his departure from the chapel house. He'd always known that it was a temporary arrangement, but he would miss it when he had to go; he liked living in the same house as his brother, even if it was secretive.

He'd also been amazed that Kate had been allowed to stay with him without so much as a word of chastisement, if not downright condemnation, and he was grateful for his brother's understanding. The scandal of the arrangement, if it ever got out, was one Thomas was unlikely to survive.

Neither Mick nor Kate had given much thought to what would happen next, though he presumed it would involve the two of them together, regardless of any practical difficulties that would involve. For one thing, his labouring days were over for a while, at least until he could see whether his left arm had any future use or not.

'You need to get out of Glasgow,' Thomas had urged.

'That's what I keep telling him,' Kate said as Mick shrugged. 'It's too dangerous here now.'

'Everywhere's dangerous,' Mick said.

'But Duffy'll kill you next time for sure,' she said.

'I'll be ready for him.'

'Don't mistake bravery for stupidity, Mick Costello,' Thomas said with a frown. 'And it's not just Duffy who's after you, in case you'd forgotten.'

Mick knew his brother was right. Glasgow was the worst place for him to be right now, and maybe it always would be from now on. It was now just a case of choosing where he could go – where they could go, because he was determined that he wasn't going anywhere without Kate. He had a few more days at least before he would be well enough to leave St Alphonsus', so he would be able to bide his time before making any final decision. They'd already been told they could stay until beyond Christmas Day, which was less than a week away, and Mick reluctantly accepted in his mind that he would leave Glasgow, for all that he wanted this city to remain his home.

Each day now followed a similar pattern and he looked forward to their walk. He could pretend that they were just a courting couple – married, perhaps – as they strolled along the pavement. No one seemed to pay much attention to them, despite the fact that they were walking wounded, two stray casualties from some unknown battlefield, but he liked the fact that they could enjoy the anonymity of their ordinariness, though he knew Kate was still on edge, throwing nervous glances all around her whenever they were out.

'He'll be looking for us,' she said every time he tried to reassure her.

'We're safe here,' Mick said, hoping that the conviction he tried to inject into his voice made up for the lack of it in his heart.

' "You can run but you can't hide." That's what he said.'

'They're just words.'

'But he found me last time.'

He would squeeze her hand tightly, and whisper what he hoped were words of reassurance. The truth was, he expected Duffy to reappear at any moment, though he hoped it would be long enough to let him get his strength back, otherwise they were both in trouble. He knew well enough the power that the other man possessed, and even if he fully recovered, there was no guarantee it would make any difference.

On the fourth day, he decided it was time to try walking without any help.

'It's the only way I'm going to get better,' he insisted when Kate protested.

'But what if you fall?'

'I'll be fine.'

It was a strange sensation to have someone care for him and it was slightly unsettling. He felt the same way about her in return, even if he wasn't ever able to articulate those feelings; he hoped that his actions did speak louder than words.

Thomas had yet to see him walk – he'd always been too busy with work in the parish. Mick thought about surprising him at Sunday Mass, walking up the aisle to receive Holy Communion; he'd love to see his brother's face at that moment, but the thought of having to actually sit through the service was so unappealing that he contented himself with imagining Thomas' reaction.

They were going to go to Mass on Christmas Day, however.

Both of them. He had insisted, even though Kate protested that she'd vowed never to set foot inside a church again. He'd started to laugh when she told him but quickly realised from her glare that it wasn't a joke.

'But Christmas Day is special,' he said.

'So let's spend it together in here.'

'I want to go, and I want you to be with me.'

'But why?'

'Just to say thanks.'

'To Thomas?'

'No, to God.'

'What for?'

'. . . For you.'

He could almost feel the heat of her blushing cheeks and he grinned at her discomfort.

'I could dig you in the ribs right this very second, Mick Costello, and then where would that smile be?'

He held up his hands in mock surrender but he could tell she wasn't annoyed at all.

'Well, maybe I better go and thank him as well then,' she said, cuddling into him and wrapping her arm across his bandaged chest.

'What for, then?'

'Don't you go fishing for compliments,' she said, nipping the skin of his arm. 'I don't want you getting all big-headed now.'

When they stood outside, Kate seemed reluctant to let go of his sleeve and he had to prise her fingers off his jacket.

'I'll be fine,' he said, kissing the tip of her nose as she frowned. He started laughing, even after she playfully punched his arm.

Each step seemed like a shuffle to Mick and anyone would have been hard pushed to get a cigarette paper under his feet when they moved. He did try lifting them off the ground but it felt like his boots were made of concrete and the effort of trying to walk was draining his energy. Still, he was determined to get to the end of the road on his own, even if he had to wait for Kate to come and help him back to the house.

He could hear her shouts of encouragement as he got closer to the end of the street. He still found it strange to accept that this was the limit of his physical exertions, though he kept telling himself it wouldn't always be this bad. He remembered his flight from Ireland, and the pursuit through misty fields, thinking it had been so long ago, when the fact that it remained fresh in his mind reminded him that it had happened less than three months ago.

There were only about another ten steps to go, and he thought of the cigarette he would have as a reward when he stopped. It was enough of an incentive to boost his shuffling and he managed to get to the end of the building within a couple of minutes, grateful for its solid presence to lean against as he kept breathing in and out quickly until there was a regular pattern to it once more.

He stood up and waved back at Kate who remained outside the front of the church house, jumping up and down and waving both her arms. He could hear her joyful shouts and pictured the smile on her face, which always made him smile as well. He gestured for her to come to him and she started running up the street. He hoped she wouldn't jump straight into his arms. For one thing, he didn't have the strength and he knew his ribs couldn't cope with the impact.

Rummaging in the coat pocket, Mick brought out his cigarettes and stuck one in his mouth, searching in the other pocket for matches. One was struck against the tenement wall and he looked up quickly.

'Fancy a light then, Mick?' said a voice that Mick vaguely recognised, and a hand held out a flame that flickered briefly in the winter chill before it was extinguished. Mick's cigarette hung limply from his lips as the match was flicked away. A tall, burly man stepped out of the shadows and grabbed the lapels of his jacket, lifting him off his feet and carrying him to the cart which sat out of sight, just yards from the tenement corner.

Mick was once again flying, though only for a brief second as he was thrown onto the back of the cart. He landed roughly and it felt like someone had stamped on his ribs all over again. He groaned as the man jumped up behind him, dragging a heavy cover over him and then sitting down on top of him. The weight was squeezing the air out of his lungs at an alarming rate and Mick slammed his good arm on the floor until the man stood up.

The cover was dragged back until his head was visible as the cart started moving briskly. Then another face was close to his.

'It's good to see you again,' a voice whispered. 'I've been waiting a long time for this moment.'

Mick tried to look away but a hand grabbed his chin and forced him to remain staring at a cold, grinning face.

'We've got a lot to catch up on,' he said. 'And there will be no running away this time.'

Mick stared back for a few seconds before he spat in the man's face. He let go of Mick and stood up, wiping his cheek with the back of his black leather glove. He moved forward and made to kick his prisoner, but stopped as Mick tensed, ready for the blow.

'Patience is a virtue,' the man said. 'And I've got all the time in the world.'

# 16

## VANISHING ACT

One moment he had been standing at the end of the street, waving at her as she raced towards him, the next he was gone. Her heart, which had been beating with excitement the closer she got to him now seemed to freeze and it felt like she was running on air, moving her arms and legs frantically but not getting anywhere fast. She wanted to shout out his name as a cry for help; even if it was to be the last thing he ever heard, she was determined that it would be her voice, but her mouth could only open and shut again, taking gulps of air which filled up her lungs and caused her to choke.

'NO!' she eventually managed to scream, and the sound seemed to give her a burst of energy and she ran and stumbled and fell and picked herself up and sprinted again to the end of the street. Almost crashing round the corner, she caught the briefest glimpse of a cart as it disappeared down another street and out of sight. She looked around, frantically searching for Mick but knowing that he was gone. A young mother dragging a crying toddler roughly by the hand passed by on the opposite pavement and Kate ran blindly across the road.

'Did you see what happened, missus?' she blurted out as the woman recoiled, grabbing the little boy and sheltering him within the folds of her skirt.

'There was a man, just there, on the corner,' Kate said, pointing to where Mick had been standing. 'They took him. Just this minute. You must have seen them?'

The woman shook her head quickly and started to edge past Kate, keeping her back to the tenement wall and a secure grip of her son.

'Please,' Kate pleaded. 'Help me.'

With another shake of the head, the woman quickened her pace, scurrying along the street without a glance back at Kate, who stood, bewildered, on the pavement. She gazed after the woman and child for a few seconds before looking back down the road. Then she suddenly started running towards where the cart had turned, her panicked gasps hurting her throat and a pain began to stretch across her chest like a rope had been wrapped round her and an invisible hand was tightening the bounds. She wanted to push herself faster but found herself slowing before she reached the corner.

Even as she did so she knew the cart wouldn't be there. There was one coming towards her, but the driver gave her barely a glance as he careered round the corner; the back of his cart was empty at any rate, and it was hardly likely that he would be heading back to the scene of the crime if he was the guilty party.

Kate felt that her throat was on fire and she was suddenly desperate for a cooling cup of water. Slowly she was sinking as all the strength in her legs began to seep out of her. As her knees hit the wet ground, her body began shaking and dry sobs escaped into the air every few seconds. The wind attacked her face, nipping her cheeks and flicking her watery eyes, and she buried her head in her lap, a muffled and incessant cry of pain causing passers-by to keep their distance as they continued on their way.

She must have remained there for ten minutes at least, though the final sounds had quickly drained out of her and her shoulders, which shook with every sob, gave the only clue that she was not just another bag of bones to be scooped off the street and deposited in a hastily dug hole. It was difficult for her to swallow and every time she tried coughing, her throat seemed to seize up. A hand touched her back, gently at first and then with a greater sense of urgency.

'Are you alright there?' the voice said. It was a woman. Kate didn't hear her at first though when she repeated her question, she guessed it was an old lady. When she finally managed to look up, her eyes barely able to focus, her nose running with snot that she carelessly wiped on her sleeve, she could just about distinguish a face peering at her.

Kate wiped her eyes with the same sleeve and looked again. The woman's head was wrapped in a scarf, which gave her face a round, kindly shape. A few stray hairs hung limply from her chin while a heavier concentration gathered around her top lip, which she occasionally caressed with her tongue.

'You'll catch your death lying there, darling,' the woman said. 'Come on, I'll help you up.'

She touched Kate's elbow and pushed it, encouraging her to stand up. Kate managed to put her body weight on her legs but almost stumbled over immediately. The old lady managed to keep her upright and Kate swayed back and forth like a flag in a summer's breeze.

'A wee cup of tea. That's what you need,' the woman said, beginning to steer Kate down the street, but she resisted.

'I have to tell Thomas,' she blurted out breathlessly.

'Who?'

'Thomas. Now. I've got to go.'

She broke free of the woman's loose grip and stumbled back, muttering, 'Thanks,' as she retraced her steps towards the church house.

Thomas had barely put the cup to his mouth when Kate burst into the room.

'They've taken Mick,' she shouted.

Thomas almost dropped the cup and a few drops of tea splashed onto his trousers. Kate darted over as he placed the cup on the table beside his chair and grabbed his shoulder.

'Did you hear me? Mick's gone.'

'But who – ?'

'Who do you think? Duffy! We need to go. We need to find him. Now!'

She almost dragged him up out of the armchair, ignoring the pain that flashed across her left hand. She could sense his reluctance and she glared at him, which seemed to inject a greater sense of urgency in him. Every second wasted here increased the danger for Mick. She tugged at his sleeve, almost pulling him towards the door.

'Thomas, you must introduce me.' Monsignor Dolan's voice pierced the room and Kate glanced round to where the parish priest sat, legs crossed, his hands joined together as if in prayer, and wearing a frown that reminded her of the stern priests of her childhood.

Kate froze and she could feel her jaw hanging open. She hastily shut her mouth, though her face was burning like the fires of hell and she stared at the scuffed toes of her shoes which peeked out from under the hem of her skirt.

'Monsignor, this is . . . well, she's . . . I mean . . .'

'You must be our other house guest,' the older man said, slowly standing up, the leather chair creaking painfully as he eased himself out of the seat. He held out his hand and nodded. She stretched out her own nervous hand, which Monsignor Dolan shook briefly but firmly.

'Nice to meet you,' he said. 'I'm Monsignor Dolan.'

'Kate,' Thomas blurted out. 'This is Kate Riordan.'

'So are you enjoying your stay here, Miss Riordan?' Monsignor Dolan asked.

'Yes, Father,' she whispered.

'It's Monsignor,' Thomas prompted.

'That's okay, Thomas,' the parish priest said. 'I don't think we need to stand on ceremony. Now, I believe your brother might be in trouble, if I am to understand Miss Riordan. Is that the case?'

Kate nodded.

'Well, don't let me detain you.'

'Thanks, Peter,' Thomas said as Kate smiled gratefully.

'We'll have a chat later on, Thomas. When you get back,' Monsignor Dolan said as they disappeared out of the room. Kate glanced at Thomas, whose face seemed to be as pale as hers was crimson but she thought better of saying anything. When they got outside, they made their way back up to the corner where Mick had disappeared. Thomas walked alongside her, having to check his own stride every few steps so that he didn't leave her behind. When they stopped, Kate took a few seconds to regain control of her breathing.

'What now?' Thomas said.

'This is where they took him,' Kate said.

Thomas glanced around him and then shrugged. 'So what do we do next?'

'We have to go back to Duffy's.'

He raised his eyebrows and Kate stepped forward, grabbing hold of his arm.

'We've got no choice.'

She sensed him flinch at her touch and she let go of his sleeve, muttering, 'Sorry, Father,' and blushing again.

He plunged his hands into his pocket, frowning as he began pacing back and forth in front of her. Kate watched him like the pendulum of a grandfather clock. Eventually he stopped in front of her and nodded.

'We'll go back to the house.'

'But – '

'We'll go back just now and I'll get some help. I don't really think you and I would have much chance of success on our own, do you?'

Kate shook her head reluctantly, though she knew he was right. If they went charging into Duffy's place right now, it would just give him two more victims. She knew if he caught her again, she'd lose a lot more than a couple of fingers and Thomas' dog collar wouldn't protect him.

'But you'll need to be quick,' she said. 'Mick doesn't have much time.'

'I know, Kate,' he said.

She stared at him, as shocked as if he'd slapped her suddenly across the cheek. It was the first time he'd said her name and not sounded like he was embarrassed to be uttering it. She had to suppress a grin that threatened to burst out across her face as she saw his own face quickly regain its colour and much more besides, and she felt that she could warm her hands on his cheeks if she held them close enough.

'What is it?' he asked nervously. 'What have I said?'

'Nothing,' she said, looking away.

He brushed past her as he began walking back towards the church and she followed in his wake, not bothering trying to keep pace with him this time but also noticing that he wasn't slowing down to wait for her either.

The clock had stopped. She was sure of it. Every time she stared at the face, it seemed like the hands hadn't moved at all, even though she knew that wasn't the case. She could hear it, the machinery hidden behind the grand exterior going through its noisy motions, letting her know that it was working and time was, indeed, moving on. She sat on the chair facing it, adopting a lonely and silent vigil. Thomas would sit, stand, pace up and down the room, disappear completely and then re-emerge five minutes later, shaking his head when he saw how little time had actually elapsed.

Kate felt sick. Every second that Mick was gone left her feeling more worried and she feared that she'd never see him again. She wanted to speak, if only to break the tension hovering in the room but she couldn't think of anything to say that didn't involve pleading with Thomas to go and look for his missing brother. He'd ignored all her other pleas so she was aware that any new ones would fall on deaf ears.

He was waiting for O'Connor, the man who had rescued them before, but so far he hadn't responded to the priest's call for help. He'd sent out messages, stressing the urgency of the situation to those who he'd asked to deliver it, but it hadn't made any difference.

'I don't understand it,' he muttered, as much to the window as to Kate. 'He usually never takes this long.'

'Well, we can't just sit here like this. We've got to do something.'

There was an impatience in her voice which made Thomas frown. She knew she was stating the obvious but she stared him down until he looked away again out the window. Five more minutes, she thought, and then she was going to Duffy's, with or without Thomas. With just seconds to spare, there was an urgent knocking at the door and Kate relaxed slightly, glad that she wasn't going to have to face the danger on her own. Thomas rushed over to the door and pulled it open.

A man stood, cap in hand, head bowed, his bare scalp wearing a purple splash like someone had squashed blackberries on it.

'Where's O'Connor?' Thomas asked brusquely.

'I'm sorry, Father,' the man stuttered. 'But you'd better come with me.'

'I can't. Not now. I'm waiting for O'Connor. It's urgent.'

'So is this, Father. O'Connor's dead.'

They could see the body lying in the middle of the road as soon as they turned the corner. Thomas jumped down from the cart and broke into a run as the man who'd accompanied them shouted, 'Be careful, Father.' Kate sat beside the man who steered the cart, though there was a storm in her stomach that felt like a rough crossing on the boat from Belfast. This was Duffy's street and she feared she was heading towards her own death.

When they reached the body, Thomas was already kneeling over it, muttering prayers that Kate vaguely recognised whenever the wind caught snatches of the incantations and carried them out into the air. She presumed it was O'Connor lying on the ground, though the face was bruised and bloodied and swollen beyond recognition. His arms were outstretched across a plank of wood with his hands nailed to either end. He was naked from the waist up and a pool of blood formed on the cobbles underneath the gaping wound in his side.

Thomas had finished his prayers and shuffled over on his knees to examine O'Connor's hand. He tugged on it gently and then stopped, glancing round.

'We need to get him off the wood,' he said in a voice that seemed on the verge of cracking. The man beside Kate brushed past her and knelt down beside the priest, quickly examining the same hand and then peering underneath the wood.

'The nail's gone right through,' he muttered. 'We'll need pliers for sure unless we just pull . . .'

Kate saw Thomas shake his head furiously and the man shrugged before moving over to examine the other hand. Kate knelt down beside Thomas and took off her shawl, crunching an edge up in her palm and then wetting it in her mouth. Gently she began wiping O'Connor's face until pockets of flesh began to appear through the blood. She used different patches of the shawl until it was patterned with blotches of blood, but she continued her job quietly as Thomas' helpless sighs echoed mournfully in her ears.

'I'll need to get some tools,' the other man said after a few minutes, standing up and shaking his head as he glanced again at O'Connor. 'I'll be as quick as I can.'

He started to walk away towards the cart when there was an angry clash of metal and stone and the three of them glanced round. A claw hammer lay on the ground just a few feet from O'Connor's head. Kate was the first to look up. Duffy stood, arms folded, leaning on the wall at the mouth of the close and wearing a satisfied grin.

'That'll probably help you,' he said.

The other man snatched up the hammer and began trying to lever it under the nail head on O'Connor's left hand.

'Where's Mick?' Kate suddenly shouted, managing to suppress the fear that had gripped her body at the sight of Duffy, who just shrugged.

'Where is he?' she screamed, moving towards him and only held back by Thomas' firm grip.

'Still as fiery as ever Kate,' Duffy said. 'I'm glad you've come back to me.'

Kate pushed forward again but Thomas kept hold of her arm while continuing to stare at the giant who still leant against the tenement. A sudden creak caused them both to look round. The other man had managed to free the first nail from both the wood and O'Connor's hand, though patches of flesh clung to the thin piece of iron. He took O'Connor's arm and slowly laid it across his bare chest before transferring his attention to the other hand, which remained attached to the wood.

'I want my brother back,' Thomas said in a firm voice.

Duffy shrugged.

'Did you hear what I said?'

Duffy pushed himself off the wall and stretched to his full height.

'I don't think this is a place to be making demands, Father,' he said.

'I just want my brother.'

Duffy limped towards them, retrieving a small tin from his jacket pocket as he did so and pushing a cigarette into his mouth. Lighting it, he blew a heavy cloud of smoke towards Thomas and Kate.

'Well, you've got something of mine, Father,' he said, nodding at Kate. Thomas immediately stepped in front of her and Duffy laughed coldly.

'How very gallant of you, Father,' he said. 'I'm sure she'll reward you later. Well, if the collections have been good enough.' He laughed again as he flicked away the cigarette which had almost vanished within a couple of seconds.

'So what about a trade then, Father?'

Thomas shook his head and gently squeezed Kate's arm, which he still held.

'Oh well, God loves a trier as they say,' Duffy said with a smirk.

'I'm not leaving without my brother,' Thomas said, his voice still steady though Kate, almost pressed against him, could feel his whole body trembling and she hoped Duffy wouldn't notice.

'You're either brave or stupid, Father, but I'm wondering if you've noticed your friend there,' he said, nodding towards O'Connor, whose body was now released from the wood. 'That's what can happen to brave, stupid people around here.'

Duffy had stopped just a couple of feet from them, and he leant heavily on one leg, a brief glimpse of pain flashing across his face and Kate realised he was still feeling the effects of the wound Mick had inflicted on him. If he stretched out his long arm now he'd be able to grab her and she inched her way behind Thomas' shoulder, even though she knew the priest would be flung aside like a bale of hay if Duffy wanted to get to her.

The cart driver coughed and Kate glanced round. He stood over O'Connor, who'd now been released from his wooden cross. Both arms were laid across his chest and Kate could see the holes in the back of his hands, which still seemed to her to be weeping with blood. She knew, even as a shudder rippled through her body at the thought, that O'Connor would have been alive when the nails were hammered into his hands.

She wondered whether he was married. Someone would have to tell his wife – Thomas probably – though she was sure he'd spare the gory details. Or maybe he lived alone? She hadn't really even had a chance to thank him for saving her life before he'd vanished as quietly and quickly as when he'd arrived in front of Duffy's house with a gun in his hand and a cart to escape.

This was his reward and she felt guilty, even as her thoughts returned to Mick. If Duffy had done this to O'Connor, what did he have planned for the man who'd actually stabbed him? She bit her tongue to stop any tears escaping – she didn't want Duffy to see how scared she was, and as she pressed down on it, she could taste the blood beginning to swirl around in her mouth.

'So what do we do now?' Duffy said, lighting another cigarette.

Thomas shrugged. 'I already told you, I'm not leaving without my brother.'

'And I've told you to be careful what you say around here.'

'I don't think you want the hassle that would come with a dead priest, do you?'

'Don't tempt me, Father,' Duffy laughed. 'But here's the thing. I don't have your brother. I can see you don't believe me but there you go.'

'Why should I believe you?'

'Trust me, Father, if I meet him again, it'll mean more work for you arranging another funeral. So take this chance to leave here while I'm in a good mood and you still can. And don't worry, Kate, I'm sure we'll meet again soon . . . now that I know where to find you.'

He turned and limped back towards the building as Thomas tugged her shoulder and they shuffled over to O'Connor's body.

'So where is he?' she whispered.

'I don't know,' Thomas said, shaking his head. 'Maybe they've caught him.'

'Who are "they"?'

'It doesn't matter.'

'Thomas!'

'It's nothing,' he said quickly, avoiding eye contact. 'Come on. Let's get O'Connor out of here.'

He leant down and gripped the dead man's ankles as the cart driver took his shoulders and they lifted the body gently up and into the back of the cart as Kate climbed up onto the seats at the front. She closed her eyes and tried to imagine how she'd feel when they were doing the same thing with Mick's body and now she didn't try to stop the tears escaping.

Thomas slid in beside her and squeezed her arm again – it was the third or fourth time he'd done so – and she found his touch gently reassuring though she sensed it was better not to say anything.

'Don't worry,' he said quietly. 'We'll find him. You know what he's like. He can look after himself.'

# 17

## SUFFER IN SILENCE

Kate was sleeping. Thomas sat watching her shoulders gently rise and fall and her eyelids occasionally flicker like she was going to waken up. She'd probably get a fright if she did open her eyes and discover his silent vigil, yet he didn't move. He wondered what she was dreaming about and hoped that it might involve him. They had returned to the chapel house in silence, a sense of defeat and despondency accompanying the cart on its weary journey away from Duffy's street. Thomas wouldn't look round at O'Connor but the guilt that was beginning to gnaw at his conscience made him constantly aware of the dead body.

The cart had delivered them safely home before continuing on its journey to deposit O'Connor at the morgue, though not before Thomas instructed the driver to let the authorities know where the funeral would be held. It was the least he could do, even though he didn't know whether O'Connor had any family. He didn't even know the man's Christian name. It wasn't that kind of friendship. It wasn't any kind of friendship, if truth be told, but it was a convenient relationship that had often benefited the priest but which had now cost O'Connor his life.

It had started with some work in the chapel – the window in the sacristy needed fixing to stop the rain pouring through the cracks that had developed over the years; he didn't know if O'Connor was a joiner to trade but he'd done a good job, even Monsignor Dolan was impressed – and he soon became a regular presence in the church, turning his hand to all sorts of odd jobs that suddenly seemed to spring up. But he also became Thomas' eyes and ears in the parish and beyond, in the murky world of tenements and pubs where the priest feared to venture.

He had saved Kate's life – and Mick's too – and Thomas was torn between guilt and gratitude, though as he looked at the peaceful body now sleeping in the room, he remained thankful that O'Connor had intervened.

Kate's face was buried deep in the pillow. Her eyes had closed and sleep embraced her almost as soon as her head dropped onto the bed. Thomas was envious, not least because he knew that sleep would put off his meeting with Monsignor Dolan that was looming ominously on the horizon. Yet, even when he did shut his eyes his mind remained alert, and he couldn't resist looking again just to make sure Kate was still there. Not that she was going to go anywhere else. She was safe here, at least for today, though Thomas realised that he'd have to find somewhere else for her to stay now that Duffy knew where she was.

He stood up and shuffled over to the side of the bed. He leant in and tenderly pushed a strand of hair off her face that was threatening to drift into her eye. He wanted to move even closer and brush her cheek with his lips, the urge gripping him like a fever and he imagined kissing her, slowly at first and then with an urgency born out of years of frustration. He imagined her sighs, which would only make his passion even more frantic, his eyes remaining wide open, wanting to take in every tiny sign of pleasure that he could detect on her face.

Thomas stepped back with a jolt like someone had slapped him hard on the face and he stumbled to his seat, dropping onto it almost breathlessly like he'd just run a mile. Kate remained sleeping, oblivious to the body that had been hovering above her, and to the mind that harboured such lustful thoughts.

It felt like a sickness was eating away at his insides and there was a pain in his chest like he was having a heart attack. Every time he looked at her he wanted to kiss her or touch her;

sometimes the urge to tell her how he felt was overwhelming and it was as if he was drowning. He'd gulp for air, trying to imagine what it would sound like if he actually pushed the words out of his mouth, but they seemed so ridiculous when they floated around in his head that he knew he'd never tell her.

But what if she felt the same way? The idea was enough to restore some sense of reality to his thinking and he felt like punching himself hard in the face, just to knock some sense into his mind. He was a priest and she was . . . well, she was with his brother and that really should have been the end of that.

He stood up quickly, realising that he needed to get out of the room, which was beginning to suffocate him. Yet, even as he opened the door there was a reluctance to leave. He stared at Kate for a few moments, silently mouthing, 'I love you,' part of him hoping that she'd wake up at that exact moment and catch him, but part of him terrified at such a prospect. He closed the door and walked slowly down the hallway, though the image of Kate sleeping in the bed followed him all the way into the church, where he sat praying for help – and forgiveness – until the dying embers of daylight had seeped away and he was just a shadowy figure in the darkened building.

He had almost finished the Glorious Mysteries – the Crowning of Our Blessed Lady as Queen of Heaven – when he heard a noise. At first he ignored it, presuming it was the building painfully contracting in the winter chill, but after a minute of silence, he heard another noise. It was coming from the hall. Thomas got up slowly, his natural instinct to avoid confrontation battling with his conscience, but he knew the latter would win out, since he had a duty to investigate what was going on. He walked towards the hall, sometimes on tiptoe, and then telling himself not to be so scared. He was a priest of this parish. This was his home and he had every right to be here.

He knew, even before he reached the hall and saw the faint light creeping out shyly from under the door, that it was Padraig's room. That's what he called it now, ridiculous though it sounded even to him. Thomas hesitated a few steps from the door, knowing that the easier option would be to turn and slip back into the church, or scurry up to his bedroom. He already felt nervous about spying on these people and was even more reluctant to find out what they were doing.

The click of the gun suddenly rang in his ears again and he shuddered. That made his mind up for him and he turned to head back the church. There was another click and he realised it wasn't memories he was hearing. There were guns in the room again. The noise momentarily paralysed him and it was in those fleeting few seconds that the door opened, casting a wider trail of light across the hall which rushed towards him, capturing his frame in its glare.

'Father, what are you doing here?' It was Padraig's voice, though Thomas didn't immediately look up. When he did, he saw the man standing in the doorway, looking surprised and guilty like a child caught stealing from its mammy's pockets. He was holding a wooden crate and Thomas spotted a few stray strands of straw sticking out the side of the lid. Padraig's discomfort lasted just seconds, however, before he stepped forward.

'This is a surprise,' he said.

'I heard a noise,' said Thomas. 'I didn't know anyone was using the hall tonight.'

'We'll not be long, Father. We've just got a few things we need to move.'

'Well, I'll leave you to it then,' Thomas said nervously.

'Your help would be much appreciated, Father,' said Padraig, thrusting the crate into Thomas' arms, and he struggled at first to hold the heavy object. 'More hands make idle work,' Padraig said with a wink. 'I'll show you where it goes.'

He led the way to the main door of the hall, which he opened. Thomas didn't know how he could have done that since there was only one key that was still part of the main bundle, but he thought better than to ask. A cart was parked outside the hall, with a couple of crates already loaded on the back. Denis Lyons, one of the men from the meetings, stood patting the horse and he looked startled when he saw Thomas appear through the door.

'Don't worry, Denis,' said Padraig. 'Father Costello has kindly agreed to give us a hand.'

Thomas smiled grimly at Denis, who nodded as the priest lowered the box gently onto the back of the cart and slid it alongside the other two.

'Just a few more, Father, and then we'll be off,' said Padraig, opening the hall door and gesturing for Thomas to come back inside.

They walked in silence to the room, Padraig leading the way. There were at least a dozen crates stacked on the table and Dan Foley stood beside one opened crate, a hammer in one hand and a pistol in the other. He nearly dropped both of them when he saw Thomas. Padraig scurried over to his comrade, whispering a few words in his ear that Thomas couldn't hear. Dan nodded reluctantly but Thomas could tell he wasn't happy.

He frowned at the priest as he tucked the gun into the crate, stuffing it under some straw to conceal it. Then he placed a lid on top, quickly knocking a succession of nails into it until the crate was sealed.

'It's just a few Christmas presents for the boys back home,' Padraig said as Thomas stared at the crates. 'But we don't want to spoil the surprise now, do we?'

'Of course not,' Thomas said as Dan grunted, and he knew the other man would have preferred to use one of the guns, or even the hammer, to guarantee Thomas' silence.

'We'll keep this to ourselves, Father,' Padraig said as he handed another crate to Thomas, who was more prepared for the weight this time. 'Careless talk and all that . . .'

Thomas nodded.

'After all, I'm sure the authorities would be interested in finding out everyone who's involved, even those who are just lending a helping hand.'

The two men stared at each other before Thomas turned and shuffled slowly back through the hall towards the cart, burdened by his load as well as the guilt which was now weighing even heavier on his shoulders.

★ ★ ★

Monsignor Dolan wanted to see him. Thomas nervously trudged towards the sitting room where he knew the parish priest would be, no doubt having commandeered the armchair nearest the fire. It was a meeting he'd been expecting, and dreading, ever since Kate had burst into the room to demand his help in rescuing Mick. His anxiety had increased after what had happened with the crates and he could only pray that the other priest was so focused on what was happening in his house that he hadn't noticed what was going on in the hall.

Whether the Monsignor had known about Kate's presence or not – and it appeared that he had – now that she had emerged out of the shadows, he was left with no choice but to act, and Thomas knew Kate would have to leave. They still hadn't found Mick either, and he sensed Duffy had been telling the truth when he denied knowing anything about it.

Thomas knocked gently on the door and waited for a grunt from within before pushing the door open and walking in.

Monsignor Dolan was standing in front of the fire, hands clasped behind his back, which was being caressed by the heat of the fire shimmering out into the room.

'No need to be so formal, Thomas,' the older man said with a smile. 'This is your house as well. Sit down.'

As Thomas dropped slowly onto the chair furthest from the fire, Monsignor Dolan took a small bell from the mantelpiece and rang it. He'd barely put it back above the fire when Mrs Breslin appeared at the door.

'A cup of tea would be lovely, Mrs Breslin' the Monsignor said.

'What about a wee sandwich as well?' she asked.

'Nothing for me . . . but maybe Thomas is hungry?'

'No, I'm fine, Mrs Breslin. Tea's fine for me.'

The housekeeper closed the door and Thomas stared out the window, anxious to avoid any eye contact with his fellow priest. He feared that the older man might read his thoughts and then he'd be in a whole lot more trouble than he was already; there was no chance of him confessing any of it either, regardless of the sanctity of the confessional box.

Monsignor Dolan sighed and sat down on the chair nearest the fire – his chair by virtue of superiority – and clasped his hands together. Thomas noticed for the first time that he played with his thumbs when he did this, both of them circling anxiously around each other. After a few minutes of unbearable silence for Thomas, the older man slapped his palms on his thighs.

'Where do we start, Thomas? Where do we start?'

'I don't know.'

'Your brother?'

'I've no idea where he is,' Thomas said, shaking his head. 'I don't even know who took him.' He couldn't bring himself to explain about the man who'd pursued Mick from Ireland. It was just another secret to keep from Monsignor Dolan.

'That is not good news,' the parish priest said, joining his hands together and pressing them to his lips. 'So what are you going to do now?'

'I don't know. Ask about and see if anyone's heard anything, I suppose.'

'Your man is dead, I hear.'

Thomas nodded as O'Connor's crucified body suddenly appeared before his eyes. He clenched his fists, his fingertips running up and down his palms and trying to imagine the pain of them being pierced by a nail.

'And the girl?'

'She's asleep now.'

'She will have to go.'

'I know.'

'We can't have anything that would embarrass the Church. That would never do. What would the Archbishop say?'

'I know, Peter, and I'm very sorry. I wasn't thinking . . . She'll be gone by tomorrow morning.'

Monsignor Dolan coughed briefly as the door opened and Mrs Breslin appeared, a rattling tray of cups and saucers announcing her presence. She began laying everything out beside either chair, not looking up as the two men watched her, waiting until she'd gone back to the kitchen for the pot of tea before speaking again.

'Mrs Breslin has a sister,' the Monsignor said. 'She's on her own with two children since her husband died, God rest his soul.'

'I didn't know,' Thomas said.

'She has space in her house. The girl can stay there for just now, and she'll be able to help with the children as well. Mrs Breslin will take her there tonight, after she's finished here.'

'I don't know what to say, Peter. Thank you.'

Monsignor Dolan shook his head dismissively, stretching across to the table beside his chair and lifting up the cup and saucer, holding it ready for Mrs Breslin who re-emerged with the tea. She filled the cup slowly, conscious of not spilling any of the hot liquid onto the priest's legs, only stopping when he nodded to indicate so. She repeated the task with Thomas' cup and he muttered, 'Thank you,' as she took the pot away. Tiny spirals of steam floated up from the tea and Thomas blew at them, causing them to break up and disappear.

'Thank you, Mrs Breslin,' Monsignor Dolan said as the house-keeper left the room once more. 'There's nothing quite like a cup of tea, Thomas, is there?'

'No.'

The parish priest sipped his tea in silent appreciation as Thomas watched him, grateful for his continued and uncharacteristic understanding, though he was beginning to think that he might have misjudged the older man. Thomas had tried to be discreet, secretive, even devious, hiding them downstairs in the guest room at the back of the house while Monsignor Dolan occupied the main bedroom upstairs, but the parish priest seemed to know everything, almost as soon as it happened. What if he could read minds, Thomas wondered, instantly dismissing the idea with an imperceptible shudder as he remembered the thoughts that were constantly running through his own head. Whatever the Monsignor's secret was, and he suspected the infor-mation was probably served up to him along with his tea, he wasn't going to ask, though it did make him wonder whether Padraig's activities in the hall were as secret as Thomas believed. He was relieved, more than anything else, however, that Kate would have somewhere safe to stay because it was quite clear that Duffy was not going to let her get away. Hadn't he told her that she could run but not hide? Well, hopefully, she would now be able to hide.

'Right, now that's sorted,' Monsignor Dolan said as he put down his cup, his voice dragging Thomas back from his thoughts, 'let's see if we can't find your brother. Now who do you think would snatch him off the street just like that?'

# 18

## SINK OR SWIM

Mick closed his eyes and heard the water splash against the side of the ship, which rocked gently in the calm sea. It was a comforting sound and the movement of the vessel soothed him, like he was a baby being cradled in his mammy's arms again. He could feel himself drifting off to sleep, though at the very moment he began to relax and move to make himself more comfortable, the chains which bound him to a damp, wooden pillar jolted his body back into position and he had to start all over again.

It would begin with an image of Kate running towards him, arms outstretched, her face lit up with joy, and he'd breathe in deeply, trying to recapture her smell though his nose would fill up with the odours that drifted over the deck – dampness and decay, sweat and salt, blood and brine. Overpowering all of these was the stench of death, hovering in the air, so thick that Mick felt he could taste it every time he opened his mouth and he'd gag like he was going to throw up. He had already been sick a few times, the evidence of which adorned the front of his torn shirt, but though his stomach was now empty his throat still insisted on trying to produce more debris.

He had lost all feeling in his left arm. They'd chained it to the pillar anyway, ignoring his agonised screams as they twisted it behind his back. He'd got a kick in the teeth to shut him up and his chin still throbbed where the toecap had connected. He couldn't see his captors and they didn't speak so he wasn't even able to guess where they were from. He could smell them, however – it seemed like the only sense that was still working and, certainly, right now, it was the only one that was proving to have any use.

There were two of them, both big and burly. One wore the stale odour of the unwashed; Mick guessed it had been weeks, if not longer, since the man's body had last come into contact with water and soap, and every time he leant in close, Mick had to swallow hard and hold his breath for as long as he could. The other man, however, smelt like a woman. The thought was enough to make Mick grin, though he was grateful the darkness hid his amusement. He actually smelt like a prostitute, drenched in the same perfumes those women wore, not so much as an alluring feature, but more to hide any traces of the previous customer. Mick guessed the man had, at least, the self-awareness to disguise his own odious smell beneath the intoxicating fumes of a cheap bottle of scent.

Once they had bound his arms to the pillar, using heavy chains that Mick knew would be impossible to break free of, they stood back from him. It felt like they were admiring their own handiwork, though he realised he was barely identifiable in the blackness because he couldn't even make out their shadows.

Footsteps moved closer to him, lighter than the other two men, and Mick sensed they belonged to the voice that he'd just about recognised in the cart. Of course, once the face had thrust itself close to his, there was no mistaking the identity. The crooked nose, evidence of his own intervention back in Ireland, was a visible calling card, and he was sure it was the same man who now slowly circled his tired and broken body.

He waited for the inevitable blows to begin raining down on him and he tensed, hoping his body would be able to cope with whatever would be thrown at him, but instead the footsteps drew to a halt. A match was struck and a candle lit. The orange glow created an instant image of hell and Mick quickly scanned his surroundings. He already knew he was on a ship – the vessel was rocking back and forth – and he figured he was being kept out of sight and out of mind. Before he could fully check out the hold, however, the hot flame of the candle drew ever closer to his cheek and, as well as illuminating his own face, it also shed light on his captor who had crouched down and moved close to Mick.

'It's nice to meet up again,' the man in black said. 'You have no idea how eagerly I've waited for this moment.'

Mick continued staring at the man as the flame danced between them, determined not to be the first to look away.

'Ireland is waiting for you, Michael Costello. And there's a nice long rope with your name on it . . . You look surprised. Surely not? You were destined for the gallows even before you began killing soldiers. That just made me even more determined to catch you.'

Mick shrugged, and swallowed hard, already feeling the knot of the hangman's noose tightening around his neck.

'We'll be setting sail in the morning on the high tide. You're going home, Michael. What do you think about that?'

Mick shrugged again.

'Nothing to say? That's not like you. I hear you're quite the storyteller, letting anyone know who'll listen or buy you a drink how you managed to escape from Ireland. Have you not got any stories for me now, Michael? I'm very disappointed.'

The man in black stood up, still holding the candle close to his own face.

'I'll give you some time on your own to collect your thoughts,' he said, 'and then we'll have a little chat. There are a few things we need to catch up on . . . just you and me.'

He turned and strode towards the steps that led up to the deck, disappearing out of sight with the light, the two men quickly following in his wake. Mick lay back and pressed his head against the pillar, closing his eyes and realising there was going to be no great escape this time around.

He had seen a hanging or two in his time and the memories made him swallow again. It was never a pleasant sight, the body swinging back and forth like a tall stalk of corn in the breeze, legs flailing and trying desperately to find a step or anything solid to take the weight of the rest of the body. It was a hopeless fight against the inevitable and the life would drain out of the victim, sometimes quickly, if they'd accepted their fate and realised the futility of the struggle; others choked and kicked but the result remained the same. A lifeless body, rocking gently, almost hypnotically, as the crowd began to disperse, muttering prayers for the repose of the soul, the only sound left in the air the howling grief of relatives.

That was the fate that awaited him back in Ireland and he wondered whether he would be a fighter or whether he would go quietly. He pictured his mammy standing at his feet, just out of reach, kept back by armed soldiers so that she could offer no last comforting caress or even try to save him, holding him up until the strength in her own body had drained away. No, she would have to stand and weep and wait until they cut his body down before she could hold her son again. And that could be days. If they wanted to send out a message – and he feared the man in black was just the sort of person who would insist on doing so – then it would be a decaying corpse that his mammy would have to prepare for burial.

His sisters and brother would help her, of course, but they were just children and shouldn't be exposed to such horrors. Sometimes they seemed like strangers to him. He hadn't really got to know them yet, and now he would never be able to watch Patrick grow from boy to man or cast wary eyes at would-be suitors who would surely come calling as his sisters got older.

He was so tired he felt like he could sleep for a week, but even a few hours would have helped. He wanted to be alert when his captors returned but trying to rest was proving to be an impossible task. He was glad at least the sea was calm. He wasn't sure his body could cope with the turmoil of stormy waters. His chest ached and the pain which shot through his body, starting at his ribs and then spreading out until it felt like a giant hand grasping him and squeezing hard, left him breathless. He sometimes held his breath, grateful for the few moments of respite that it offered before he was forced to exhale and the vicious cycle began all over again.

161

There would be no great escape this time around because no one knew he was here. Mick had realised that despairing fact very quickly and it spared him the false hope that would otherwise have come with every strange noise or faint voice that drifted into the hold. He didn't even bother screaming for help, preferring instead to conserve what little strength he had for the interrogation that awaited him.

He heard rats scurrying back and forth across the ship, occasionally running over his legs in their haste to get to wherever they were going, rather than skirting round the human barrier. He heard them too, whispering to each other and he imagined they were talking about him, perhaps discussing how good he would taste. They were waiting for him to die. He hoped they were, otherwise he was facing the prospect of being eaten alive, and he was determined to deny them a fresh meal at least.

A mouthful of water; that's all he wanted. At this very moment, if he could be granted only one wish, then it would be for a cool, refreshing, life-affirming drink of water. Of course, that wasn't strictly true. He'd ask for freedom and the chance to lie one more night with Kate's hot flesh pressed against his own, but he'd settle for the water just now. It was also a more realistic wish. Kate was gone, though she still accompanied him in his thoughts and dreams; he was sure she'd be there, in his mind, as he breathed his last on the Galway gallows. But he'd never see her again, face to face, touching her, kissing her, holding her. He never did tell her that she was the last thing he thought of before falling asleep at night and the first thing he thought of when he woke up each morning. The poetry of his thoughts would have come out as clumsy, awkward words anyway, and he only hoped that she realised how he felt. He tried to tell her in every kiss and caress, but it was too late now to find out if he'd been successful in his physical communications.

Thomas would pray for him. His brother had helped him more than he could ever have hoped for, though he never got the chance to thank him. That would have been an awkward conversation for both of them. But actions speak louder than words –

that's what his mammy had once told him – and Thomas' actions told Mick everything he ever needed to know. Still, it bothered him that the feelings might not be reciprocated. Perhaps Thomas thought he was taking advantage of the kindness offered, and Mick cursed his own inability to say what he meant or felt.

He closed his eyes again and yawned, his mouth so dry it felt like his tongue was stuck the roof of it. A drink of water and I'll tell them anything, he thought. He tried to conjure up some saliva to swallow, though he knew that wouldn't begin to quench the thirst which was now raging in his throat, but even that simple task proved impossible, and he groaned, a long, low murmur of discontent that, to any passer-by, might have sounded like the ship itself crying out in pain.

Mick knew he hadn't been sleeping long, but he was grateful nevertheless for the few relaxing moments. His brief nap was interrupted by the sound of heavy footsteps crashing down the stairs that led to the hold and he knew the two guards were returning. The man in black followed immediately behind them, an orange glow embracing his body. The candlelight also revealed the other men. One of them carried a chair that he placed in the middle of the hold facing Mick while his colleague headed for the pillar and began the awkward process of loosening the chains.

Freed from the metal shackles, Mick toppled over onto his side. He felt light, almost weightless, and he couldn't stop himself. The side of his head cracked off the wet wooden flooring and a pain shot through his skull. A pair of hands roughly grabbed his collar and dragged him across to the chair, sitting him on it and propping him up, though after a few moments, he began to regain a sense of balance and the guard released his heavy grip.

The man in black now stood in front of Mick. He held the candle just under his chin and the flickering light made his face seem like a grotesque mask with a crooked grin painted on. There was a grating noise as something was dragged across the floor from behind him, though Mick resisted the urge to glance over his shoulder. It was to the left of him anyway, and the incessant pain which seemed to have permanently gripped that side of his body, starting at his fingertips and spreading all the way up his withered arm, made the prospect of turning round incredibly unappealing.

Eventually, the source of the noise was revealed as the two guards pushed a large barrel into view, letting it come to rest between him and the man in black, who nodded to the men. They grabbed both of Mick's arms – he screamed in pain as a heavy grip squeezed the flesh of his left arm – and dragged him off the chair and over to the barrel. They tipped him backwards and plunged him into it. Mick was under water and he immediately closed his eyes and held his breath, occasionally trying to let an air bubble escape from the side of his mouth though he could feel the water rushing up his nose. Panic quickly seized his body. It must have been twenty or thirty seconds before they pulled him up and he began coughing and spluttering, blinking furiously as the water rolled down his face and out of his nose.

'So here's the question, Michael Costello. Are you going to help me?'

Mick coughed again and spat up a mouthful of the salty water.

'Who was in charge?'

'In charge of what?'

'Who was in charge?'

'I don't know what you're talking about.'

The man in black laughed and nodded again. Mick found himself in the barrel again, this time for a minute at least. He moved his head frantically and tried to push himself out of the water but the two guards held him down firmly. Then they brought him out again and he repeated the cycle of coughing and spluttering and trying to clear his throat and nose of water which had threatened to suffocate him just moments before. He was being propped up by the two men and he let them take the strain of his body weight, unable to muster any strength to hold himself up.

'Who was in charge?'

Mick shook his head. He didn't want to say anything that

would put him back in the barrel. He deliberately bowed his head, staring intently at his feet and trying to calm his breathing as streams of water poured down his face.

'Come on, Michael. Don't be shy. We're all friends here. You can tell me. Who was in charge?'

'I don't know. I really don't. I've no idea what you're talking about.'

'Fair enough, Michael.'

The Mayo accent was still fresh in his ears as he was plunged backwards into the barrel again, for even longer this time. He struggled more and they held him tighter, pushing his body down until the water was almost at his waist. His head thrashed about, banging off the sides and still they held him down. One minute. Two. He wasn't sure what was going to explode first, his head or his chest as his lungs prepared to collapse. Three minutes. He was ready to give up; he was only fighting to stay alive long enough to swing from a rope anyway so why not accept his fate here, in this dark and damp hold? They'd keep his body until they were in the middle of the Irish Sea when it would be tossed overboard, sinking quietly to the bottom never to be found as the creatures of the water, big and small, fed on his decaying flesh.

He was out of the water, dragged up from the depths at the last moment, and his breathing was frantic, grateful, his lungs stocking up on the oxygen they had been so cruelly denied. His head throbbed, like it had been caught in a vice, the pain so severe it actually made him forget his arm. He was almost on his knees now, the two guards still holding him but beginning to feel the strain of his limp body.

'Michael, Michael. What are you doing? I just need a name. That's all. Just one name and then this will all be over and we'll leave you here in peace until we get back to Ireland. Surely you want that?'

Mick had no strength to shrug or shake his head, never mind attempt a reply. He felt like crying. His eyes were moist, salty even, but he wasn't sure if they were filled with water or tears. There were jumbled images of people he knew and places he loved, or was it the other way around, but he was unable to focus on anything in particular. He tried thinking of Kate, but even attempting to repeat her name in his head was impossible. A pain gripped his chest like a sudden and unexpected punch and he flinched.

'So I will ask you one last time. Who was in charge?'

There was no reply. Mick wanted to die. He wondered if he already was dead but the pains in his head and his chest and his lungs and his arm were all competing for attention so he guessed he was still alive. He just wanted all the pain to disappear and if he stopped breathing he knew that it would. Water dribbled out of his mouth, spilling onto his vomit-stained shirt like his body was leaking and he had neither the strength to spit it out nor seal his lips to stop it escaping. There was a rushing sound in his ears, like there was a storm brewing within them, and he wanted to clean them out with his fingers. That was impossible, of course, and he didn't think he'd be able to lift his hand to his face, even if he got the chance. The man in black sighed.

'Is that your final answer? . . . Okay, Michael. So be it.'

Mick could feel his body being lifted up again and it was like he was floating on air. After a few seconds, however, he was being tipped into the barrel and as his head touched the water he let out a noise that he hoped made sense, though he feared it just sounded like the final groan of a drowning man. But it was enough to bring him to a halt. He tried again, just in case no one had heard him first time around.

The two guards guided him back to the chair and dumped him on it, binding him once more but still keeping a firm grip on him.

'Who was in charge, Michael?'

He looked up at the man in black, his face still an orange, glowing mask. Only the grin had changed. Now it was satisfied, triumphant even as it moved towards him.

'Who was in charge?'

'Dan Foley,' Mick whispered, his head hanging low with exhaustion and shame.

166

# 19

## BROTHERS IN ARMS

Thomas leant his head against the side of the confessional box and sighed wearily, having just given absolution to another sinner. Already he'd forgotten what sins the woman had confessed but he guessed they were tame and boring and probably no more serious than taking the Lord's name in vain. Even in his current distracted state, he knew he'd have remembered if it was at all illicit or explicit. Those confessions were few and far between in this parish, however, despite everything that he knew went on in the area; people did not feel the need to unburden themselves on him, which was a pity because it would have made for a more interesting time.

His own confession would probably be more exciting than anything else he'd ever be likely to hear. He wasn't sure Monsignor Dolan could have coped with the dark revelations that were lurking in his heart, eating away at it with every passing hour. Even in here, when he was supposed to be concentrating on the sins of others, he kept thinking of his own. Kate was out of sight now, safely ensconced with Mrs Breslin's sister, but she was not out of mind. He pictured her sleeping, laughing, talking, eating; he imagined her naked – both of them together   and then he prayed to God for forgiveness which he was not convinced would be forthcoming.

The door of the confessional box opened and Thomas sat up, glad of the temporary distraction. He could hear the shuffling of a body on the other side of the box, and a nervous male cough, and he moved closer to the black veil draped across the grate that concealed the identity of the sinner.

'In nomine Patris et Filii et Spiritus Sancti. Amen,' he said in a low voice, imagining the man making the appropriate gestures in perfect synchronicity with his words. He waited for the man to speak, to begin unburdening his black soul of whatever sins had stained it, but there was only silence. Nothing was said for a minute at least. Thomas was reluctant to say anything, not wanting to make the man any more nervous than he evidently already was. After another minute had passed, Thomas cleared his throat and made to speak, but the man's voice broke through the veil to stop him before he even got the first syllable out.

'I know where your brother is,' he said.

Now it was Thomas' turn to have difficulty speaking. Did he really hear the man properly? He moved closer and pressed his ear against the black material.

'I know where your brother is,' the man repeated.

'Who are you?'

'Don't you want to know where he is?'

'Yes, of course I do,' Thomas snapped.

'He's on the *Star of the Sea*.'

'What's that?'

'What do think it is? It's a ship and it's moored down at the Broomielaw at this very minute.'

'Thank you,' Thomas said, not sure what else to say.

The man sighed and dragged his side of the veil back. Thomas reluctantly followed suit. Padraig Clarke stared at him through the grate.

'Surprised to see me?' Padraig said with a grin.

'How do you know?' Thomas asked, almost stuttering over the words.

'People tell me things, Father. It pays to know what's going on.'

Thomas nodded, though in the back of his mind he suddenly heard the click of a gun catch again and he shuddered.

'So what are you going to do now?' Padraig asked.

'I don't know,' Thomas shrugged. 'Go down and get him, I suppose.'

Padraig shook his head and frowned.

'It's a wee bit more difficult than that,' he said. 'I think the people who've got him would be reluctant to let him go, even if you are family and a priest.'

'So what would you suggest then?'

'Well, I know you don't have much time. The ship's leaving for Ireland in the morning and once it's gone, then I think that will be the last you'll ever see of your brother.'

Thomas nodded, suddenly wishing he could call on O'Connor because he would have known what to do. He made the sign of the cross for the dead man's soul.

'I don't think that's going to help him, Father,' Padraig said, shaking his head.

'Why are you doing this?'

'Doing what?'

'Helping me.'

'One good turn deserves another, Father. Isn't that what they always say?'

Thomas wanted to rush down to the ship. He wanted to rescue his brother. He wanted to tell Kate, and he realised guiltily that it was this urge that was gripping him more than any other. He knew she'd be delighted, and he longed to be the bearer of the good news, even though her joy would be solely at the prospect of seeing Mick again.

'I do have one idea, Father,' Padraig said and Thomas looked up. 'It's worth a try, though I can't promise anything.'

'Whatever you think,' Thomas said, eager to begin right away. 'So who's got him then?'

'It's probably best if you don't know, Father,' said Padraig. 'Ask no questions and all that.'

Padraig stood up and nodded towards the door and Thomas followed suit at the other side of the box, both men appearing out the door at the same time. There was still a small queue of people kneeling in the row facing him waiting for their confession to be heard and Thomas quickly muttered a few words of apology which he wasn't even sure that any of them understood before he followed Padraig towards the back of the church, knowing that they were heading for the river. He also knew, even as he stepped out of the church, that disapproving words were already being whispered in Monsignor Dolan's ear about his sudden desertion, but he'd face the consequences of that later. For now, his only thought was for his brother and he only hoped that they wouldn't be too late, though he had no idea how the other man intended to rescue Mick.

The biting night-time cold of winter harried and harassed them, searching for any traces of bare flesh to attack as they stood in the shadows, back from the waterfront and out of sight of the ship, which they could see whenever any of them took a peek round the corner of the building. It wasn't going anywhere at this time of night anyway, though Padraig had checked the departure log at the dock master's office just to confirm when it would be setting sail. Six o'clock the next morning, so there was still time.

Thomas wasn't convinced the rescue plan would work, though he kept any doubts to himself. There was no alternative, certainly not anything he could think of, so this was his, and Mick's only hope. He moved forward and glanced out at the *Star of the Sea*. The mast stood proud and erect in the gloomy darkness, and he could make it out clearly, though the rest of the ship was just a dark cloud bobbing along on the restless waters of the Clyde. He tried to imagine his brother within the ship, and he prayed that he was still alive. Padraig had assured him that he was – he seemed pretty confident about it – though he also believed that Mick would be heading for home and certain death, even if he remained suspiciously vague on the details or the reason for his belief. Thomas could only presume it was something to do with the man who had been offering money to find Mick. If only he'd been more forceful in helping his brother escape to Liverpool, then none of this would have happened.

He stepped back again and Kate gripped his arm, shivering

quietly and pressing herself against his body. He closed his eyes for a moment and tried to remind himself why it had been a good idea to bring her. He had insisted on telling her, even if Padraig had argued against it. Thomas knew he was probably right but when he saw the delight on her face and felt her crushing, grateful embrace as she impulsively wrapped her arms round his neck, then all sense seemed to drain out of his body and he offered no resistance when she invited herself along.

'What are we waiting for?' she whispered and Thomas glanced round at Padraig who shook his head angrily.

'Someone else is coming to help us,' Thomas said. 'We need to wait for him.'

She sighed impatiently but kept hold of his arm, and he was reluctant to move or say anything else lest she release her grip. Even just a couple of days with Mrs Breslin's sister had done her good. Her face was on the mend and he could see her brown eyes coming back to life. Thomas had also arranged for another visit from the doctor, if only just to change the dressing on her hand wound. She wore a fresh white bandage, though it was temporarily hidden underneath her black shawl.

A man suddenly appeared before them and Padraig stepped forward with a grunt and shook his hand. He didn't offer an introduction and Thomas wasn't concerned with any formalities. He had never seen the man before but he presumed that he was one of Padraig's comrades. It didn't matter that there wasn't a name he could scribble down later for the Archbishop. His only thought was to rescue his brother and if this man was able to help, then he could be the leader of the Brotherhood for all Thomas cared.

'Have you got them, Father?' Padraig said and Thomas nodded towards the sack behind him. Both Thomas and the nameless man quickly slipped into the dark brown robes that he'd collected from Brother Clare, a Marist who taught in the school next to the church. He was obviously a sympathiser and he'd handed over the garments to Thomas without any questions when he'd visited the school.

When they both pushed the hoods over their heads, the two men were suddenly transformed into faceless bodies and Thomas quickly pulled the hood back.

'You need to keep that up, Father,' Padraig said. 'We don't want them seeing your faces. Now, do you know what you're doing?'

The two hooded heads nodded and Padraig gave them both a nudge that propelled them out onto the road. They started to walk silently towards the ship.

'Wait,' Kate said and ran over to him, lifting back his hood and planting a quick kiss on his cheek. 'For good luck,' she said and Thomas was glad of the darkness and the hood to hide the embarrassment that had instantly crept across his face.

The two men were approaching the *Star of the Sea* and Thomas couldn't see any sign of life on it. There were no guards on the ship, as far as he could make out, though Padraig had warned that it wasn't going to be easy. Thomas had expected men with guns to be peering down at them from the vessel but he couldn't quite bring himself to believe that they were actually just going to walk up onto the ship, find Mick and then bring him back home. They were at the gangplank and his accomplice had just put one foot on it when a voice shouted a warning out from the ship.

'Let me do the talking,' the man whispered as footsteps thundered across the deck and they both looked up, peering out from their hoods. 'And if anyone asks, I'm Brother Jerome.'

A bulky shape appeared at the top of the gangplank and stood, arms folded, blocking their way onto the ship. Another figure lurked behind his left shoulder.

'What do you want?' the first man said.

Brother Jerome took another step forward.

'Stay where you are,' the man ordered, and the hooded figure stopped again.

'We're here to see the prisoner,' he said, nodding round at Thomas.

'I don't know anything about this.'

'We've to hear his confession before he heads back to Ireland tomorrow.'

'No one said anything to me.'

'Mister Walsh arranged it. He said everything would be fine. I thought he would have told you.'

The man at the top of the gangplank shook his head but Thomas could see he was suddenly hesitant at the mention of Mister Walsh's name. Thomas didn't know who that was but he was evidently a man of some importance.

'We can go if you want,' his companion said. 'But I don't think Mister Walsh will be very happy. He seemed pretty insistent that we see the prisoner.'

The guard glanced round at his partner and whispers floated down towards Thomas as they discussed what to do, although he couldn't make out any words. After a couple of minutes, the first guard turned round and nodded.

'Okay, you can come up, but just you.'

'We both need to be there,' Brother Jerome said as he began walking up towards the guards, Thomas following at his back. 'But if that's a problem, I can go and let Mister Walsh know.'

By the time they reached the top of the gangplank, the guard had decided against risking any prospect of the two priests leaving without seeing the prisoner, so he stood aside as both men stepped onto the ship. The other guard muttered at them and began walking back across the deck. They followed him, with the first guard bringing up the rear. They clambered down the stairs that led to the hold, which was black as night, and Thomas bumped into his companion. They stopped and waited for the first guard who was now approaching down the stairs with a candle that cast a gloomy but welcome light over their surroundings.

Thomas saw him immediately, a sagging figure bound to a chair at the far end. He resisted the urge to make a dash for his brother, waiting instead for the two guards to lead the way. Soon, all four men stood in front of Mick, who remained sitting, head bowed and oblivious to what was happening in front of him.

'Right, there you are,' the first guard said. 'Do what you have to do and then you can be away.'

'You can't stay here,' Brother Jerome said.

'I'm not leaving you alone with him.'

'I'm a priest and I'm here to hear this man's confession. That's a private thing between him and God, so you'll have to wait up on deck.'

The guard hesitated again and Jerome sighed.

'I've had enough of this,' he said, turning away from Mick and walking towards the stairs.

'Okay, okay,' the guard said, 'but you've got ten minutes. No more.'

The two guards disappeared back up to the deck, having left their candle sitting on the floor in front of Mick. As soon as they were out of sight, Thomas rushed to his brother, kneeling down and grabbing his shoulders.

'Mick . . . Mick!'

Thomas shook him and Mick groaned.

'Mick, it's me. Thomas. Your brother.'

He pulled back his hood as Mick mustered enough strength to raise his head slightly and open his eyes. It took him a few seconds before his mind registered who it was and he smiled weakly.

'We're going to get you out,' Thomas said. 'We're here to rescue you.'

Mick groaned again. Thomas wanted to hug him but he feared that he would only end up crushing him. He kept trying to look away from Mick's left arm, which appeared even worse since the last time he'd seen him.

'We need to hurry up, Father,' Brother Jerome said. 'We've not got much time.'

Thomas stood up and began pulling the robe over his body as the other man untied the rope binding Mick to the chair. He then started undressing Mick, ignoring the groans of pain from the broken figure and handing each item of wet clothing to Thomas who bundled them together before hiding them in a dark corner of the hold. When his brother was dressed in the Marist robe they stood him up, holding either arm to keep him steady.

'This isn't going to work,' Thomas said, looking at his brother.

'We've got no other choice,' Jerome said. 'Mick! Listen to me. You've got to be strong now. We're going to get you out, but you need to help us. Can you do that?'

Thomas wasn't sure if Mick's head nodded in agreement or whether he just wasn't able to control it, but he knew his companion was right. It was this or nothing. He let go of Mick's arm and his brother swayed slightly, but he remained on his feet.

'You better tie me up,' Thomas said, sitting down on the chair.

'I'm afraid it's not as easy as that, Father.'

'What do you mean?'

'Well, to make it look like I've attacked you and stripped you and tied you to the chair, then there'll have to be some sign of a struggle.'

'I don't understand.'

'I need to hit you, Father.'

'What?'

'Just to make it look real.'

Thomas knew it made sense and started to nod in agreement, though just as he did the man's forehead suddenly came into contact with the bridge of his nose, and he collapsed on the ground, holding his face and moaning, in shock and in pain.

'Sorry, Father,' Brother Jerome said.

'I thought you were just going to punch me,' Thomas said, taking his hands away from his nose and staring at the blood on his palms. He felt sick.

'Now I'll tie you up,' he said, letting go of Mick, who remained as unsteady on his feet as a drunk at closing time. He grabbed Thomas under the arm and helped him up.

'I thought you were just going to punch me,' he said again, blinking furiously.

'It looks more realistic this way,' Jerome said as he tightened the rope, binding Thomas to the chair. Thomas' nose throbbed – he was sure the man had broken it – and a vicious pain was beginning to spread out across his skull.

'Once they realise what's happened, they'll let you go. You'll be fine.'

Thomas nodded, knowing that the most difficult part of the plan was still to come when Jerome attempted to get Mick off the ship.

'Good luck,' he whispered, then winced. It was even sore to talk.

'Thanks, Father,' Brother Jerome said as he picked up the candle and steered Mick towards the stairs. Thomas watched them as they got further away, leaving him in increasing darkness, and he tried to muster up enough effort to blank out the pain so that he could say a prayer for his brother, who remained an unsteady figure, hidden behind the hood. Thomas wasn't concerned for his own safety, broken nose aside. At least that part of Padraig's plan had made sense. He would know soon enough whether the rest of it was a success.

# 20

# THE QUIET ASSASSIN

Mick felt like he was walking with someone else's legs and he needed the steady grip of the hooded man to keep him upright. The ship swayed unpredictably but it was a gentle rocking. The Clyde was relatively calm tonight and he was glad of that at least. He felt himself being pulled along and his feet seemed to slide on the floor without ever really managing to lift themselves. When they reached the stairs, he was propped against the side of them as the man peered up towards the deck, taking off his hood to get a better look.

'Right, Mick, can you hear me?' the man said.

Mick nodded.

'I'll help you up the stairs but once we get to the top, you have to try walking on your own. If I help you, the guards will notice right away and then we'll be in trouble. Can you try and do that?'

Mick nodded again but he knew that it wasn't convincing. It would be a miracle if they made it off the ship safely, but he guessed that was his companion's problem more than his since he didn't have the strength to punch a hole in a cloud. He glanced back to where Thomas sat watching them. He was worried for his brother and only hoped that they believed he was an innocent victim in the escape. Neither of them knew what had happened with the barrel and Mick realised that if it could break him, then Thomas didn't have a chance.

'Are you ready?'

Mick tried to reply but only a grunt came out. It was enough for the man, however, and he tugged him forward. Together they began climbing the stairs until their heads appeared through the hole and Mick spotted the two guards standing at the top of the gangplank, staring down at the dock. The hooded man scrambled up onto the deck first and pulled Mick up. He was on his knees and he groaned as the man grabbed him under the arms and stood him up.

The noise was enough to alert the two guards who spun round at the same time. One of the men strode forward while the other scurried along behind him. Mick could feel a steadying hand on his arm and he tried to stop himself from swaying.

'Is that you finished?' the first guard asked.

'Our work here is done,' the hooded man said and gently nudged Mick's arm as they began moving towards the gangplank. Mick was still shuffling, even though he tried to lift his feet and every step that he did manage to complete only seemed to shoot a sharp pain through his ribs. After the third one in quick succession, he breathed in sharply.

'What's wrong with him?' the guard asked.

They stopped but it was too sudden for Mick whose feet seemed to get tangled up with each other and he began toppling over. His companion tried to keep him upright but his grip wasn't strong enough and Mick's fall had taken him by surprise. He crashed to the ground, cracking his head noisily off the wooden deck and he lay, one side of his face pressed painfully into the harsh wood, the other side woefully exposed to the watching guards.

'What the hell's going on?' the guard said. The man had barely managed to get the words out before a knife had glided across his bare neck. He immediately clutched it, gargling like a drowning man – the same sound that Mick had made in the barrel – and he sunk to his knees as blood began pouring out from the invisible wound, seeping through his fingers.

The hooded man turned his attention to the other guard, who was rooted to the spot, shocked at the suddenness of the attack on his partner. Seeing the man approaching with a knife, however, snapped him out of his daze. He stumbled back and then turned and ran, falling blindly into the gap that led to the hold below. Mick heard the crash as the body bounced down the stairs and landed on the floor, and there was a moment of silence before the man began to cry out in pain. Mick's companion disappeared down the same hole and within a few seconds there was silence again.

Mick began trying to push himself up using only his right arm, all the time keeping an eye on the gurgling guard who had now slumped to the ground, unable to stem the flow of blood and probably aware that it was only a matter of minutes before he'd be dead. Mick managed to get back on his feet at the same time as the final sound eased out of the man's mouth and he stood, trying to calm his own breath, staring at the dead body on the deck.

The hooded man had acted with impressive and chilling swiftness and Mick didn't know whether to be relieved or scared. He was both, but the man had done it to save his life, so he was grateful for that at least. He felt no remorse for the guard lying at his feet, not after what had happened with the barrel. He watched as a pool of thick, purple liquid spread out across the deck and he took a couple of steps back so that his feet wouldn't become immersed in the blood. He knew the other guard was lying at the bottom of the stairs in the hold, his throat cut just as swiftly and silently, and he briefly thought about blessing himself – old habits die hard – but then he remembered the barrel of water again and he decided against it.

Thomas was the first to emerge from the hold, followed by his hooded companion. His brother's nose seemed to have spread out across his face and his eyes were screwed up, like he was staring intently at something – a Bible with extremely small print. The two brothers embraced, gently, while the guard's body was dragged across the deck and pushed down into the hold where its fall was cushioned by the other dead guard. There was nothing any of them could do about the pool of blood in front of them or the trail that led to the hold.

'Come on, we need to hurry,' the hooded man said. 'I don't know who else is about.'

Mick and Thomas looked round and then nodded in perfect synchronicity. They followed the man until all three of them were safely on the dock. When they were back in the shadows, Mick found himself almost smothered by Kate's embraces, while the hooded man quickly explained to Padraig what happened. He had barely finished speaking before he slipped away in the darkness without a word of goodbye, leaving his robe crumpled in a heap on the ground. Mick would have liked to thank him but he sensed it would have been an inappropriate gesture.

Kate hadn't let go of Mick and he was grateful for her presence. It was too dark to stare into her eyes, both of which he noticed were now open, but every now and then, it seemed like they sparkled when a trace of moonlight drifted across them. She clung to his arm, trying to offer both support and comfort as Padraig led the way, slipping out of their hiding place and scurrying along the dock, quickly followed by Thomas with Mick and Kate lagging behind. Mick was forcing himself to keep going, though every step forward was a painful one. He knew, however, that they had to get away from the ship as quickly as possible, before the dead guards were discovered and the alarm was raised.

He thought they were heading back to the chapel house, and he was already imagining being in the same bed as before, with Kate snuggled in alongside him. Instead, they headed in a different direction until they came to a stop outside a tenement close.

'Make sure he doesn't go out again, Father,' Padraig said. 'They'll be tearing down the city looking for him and I'm not sure they'll waste any time sending him back to Ireland now.'

'Thank you, Padraig,' Thomas said, holding out his hand, which the other man clasped briefly but firmly. 'Thanks for everything.'

'Don't mention it, Father,' he said. 'Just mind what I said.'

Padraig walked away down the street without any acknowledgement of Kate or Mick, and Mick watched the dark figure until it seemed to melt into the night and he was gone.

'This'll be safe for just now,' Thomas said, regaining Mick's attention and he turned to look at his brother. 'Kate's been staying here so it'll be fine.'

'I didn't think anyone would find me,' Mick mumbled, trying desperately to find the right words of gratitude.

Thomas nodded. 'It must be that guardian angel of yours again,' he said and Mick smiled.

'I don't care who it was,' said Kate. 'I'm just glad you're safe.'

She stood up on tiptoes and gently kissed Mick. Thomas looked away.

'You heard what Padraig said,' he eventually muttered, and Mick and Kate broke off their lingering kiss.

'I'll not be going anywhere,' Mick said. 'I promise.'

'You'll be a wanted man in Glasgow now,' the priest said. 'And there will be a proper price on your head, what with two dead men to account for.'

Mick nodded, grateful for the comforting squeeze of his hand that Kate offered by way of support.

'I told you, Thomas, I'm not going anywhere.'

'Well, make sure you don't. I think you've used up enough luck to last a hundred lifetimes.'

Mick nodded again and he began to inch back towards the mouth of the close, Kate still attached to his right arm.

'I'm sure we'll find something to occupy our time,' he said with a wink to his brother and Kate let out a giggle.

'Remember you're staying under somebody else's roof,' Thomas said. 'And it's only a short-term arrangement, just as long as it takes for me to organise everything for you to get out of the city.'

'What?'

'You can't stay here now, Mick, not after tonight. There are two dead men lying on that ship and someone will have to account for them. If you stay here, then that will surely be you.'

Mick gave a final nod as he and Kate climbed up the stairs and into the close. He heard his brother's brisk footsteps growing fainter as he strode down the road and he knew that Thomas was right. To stay in Glasgow now would be madness. It would be like signing his own death warrant. Now all he had to do was persuade Kate to go with him, wherever that might be. He leant into her and kissed her roughly and frantically.

'Did no one ever tell you that patience is a virtue, Mick Costello?' she said with a laugh, and he didn't want to tell her that he'd done it because he was scared – scared of what might happen to him, to them, and he was going to savour every single second of their time together. He also knew that if she wouldn't leave Glasgow, then neither would he.

# 21

# AN INSPECTOR CALLS

There was a gentle knock on his bedroom door which Thomas knew was Mrs Breslin but he lay back on the bed, feigning deafness and hoping the housekeeper would presume he was still sleeping and leave him be. It was a daily struggle to get up now and it seemed to only get harder with each passing day.

The Christmas celebrations in the parish had gone smoothly and Monsignor Dolan seemed to be in good spirits. Thomas had tried to avoid him as best he could even though it was difficult with them sharing the same house and, on occasion, the same altar, but even when they were together the conversation never once mentioned Mick or Kate. Thomas was permanently on edge, waiting for the older priest to enquire as to what had happened but he didn't say anything. Thomas presumed that he was studiously avoiding the subject but occasionally he would pretend that the Monsignor had completely forgotten about it all. He knew that wasn't the case, and he wasn't fooling himself for a second, but he was still grateful that his boss had so far decided against quizzing him because he didn't know what he would say.

He hadn't seen Padraig again since the night of Mick's rescue. There hadn't been another meeting in the hall, or indeed any other activity from the men of the Brotherhood as far as he was aware, and Thomas was grateful for that as well, though he was resolved to thank Padraig again next time he saw him. Mick owed his life to the man and Thomas wouldn't forget it. He presumed that they'd put everything on hold, perhaps because of what had happened on the ship, though he hoped that it had ended permanently now that the crates had been taken away. He'd had enough deception to last a lifetime and he felt that the longer the Brotherhood used the hall, the more chance there was of Monsignor Dolan finding out about them.

Mrs Breslin knocked on the door again, this time slightly louder and with just a hint of urgency, which was entirely out of character. Thomas groaned and pushed himself up, swinging his legs across the bed until they hung over the side. He ran his hand through his hair and yawned. It had been another restless sleep and he wished he could crawl back under the covers, close his eyes and not wake up for a day at least. There was another knock on the door. Mrs Breslin was probably just going to ask him what he wanted for breakfast and he was tempted to shout, 'Porridge!' and see if that would send her scurrying back to the kitchen.

Thomas had also avoided going to see his brother. He was worried that he might lead the authorities straight to him and he'd never forgive himself if that happened. He knew, however, that there was another reason for staying away. Every time he imagined Kate with Mick, it was like a hand reached into his chest and grasped his heart, squeezing it until the pain became so unbearable that he wished he was dead. It would be a million times worse if he actually saw them together. The frustration was enough to make him want to cry, but he knew there was nothing he could do about it. Never mind that Mick was his brother and it would be a terrible thing if he suddenly declared his love for Kate. He was also a priest and that just wasn't allowed. He kept reminding himself of that fact, though it had little effect on how he felt and he had a sense of not being in control of his own emotions, which left him feeling uneasy.

He knew the two of them were safe – he'd have heard news if Mick had been tracked down and captured – but he also knew that it wouldn't last forever. He'd already made some discreet inquiries and he was hopeful that a priest friend in Liverpool would be able to help. That wouldn't be a permanent arrangement either, since the hunt for Mick would eventually spread further afield when they couldn't find him in Glasgow, but at least it might give him enough respite to recover physically from his ordeal. He didn't know if Kate would go too – he presumed she would – and the thought of never seeing her again brought a fresh surge of pain that seemed to grip his whole body now.

The guilt that haunted him came in unexpected waves. He'd avoided any mention of it when Monsignor Dolan had heard his confession. The old man wouldn't be able to say anything, the confessional seal making sure of that, but Thomas didn't even like the idea of anyone else knowing his deepest thoughts and darkest secrets – well, apart from God and there was nothing he could do about that.

It actually made him smile when he tried to imagine what he'd have said to the Monsignor, knowing that whatever it was would leave both men embarrassed. The parish priest might have heard more confessions than he ever cared to remember in all the years since his ordination, but it was unlikely he'd ever have heard anything so scandalous from a fellow priest. God only knows what his penance would be for that confession, but he suspected it would be a lengthy one.

Yet, his sin was all in his mind. He had not actually done anything wrong. That was a mere technicality, of course, and Monsignor Dolan would be unlikely to be any more lenient just because he hadn't committed any physical discretion.

Mrs Breslin knocked on the door again, three quick, angry thuds and Thomas stood up, shuffling across the room. He opened the door a fraction and popped his head round the frame – he didn't want Mrs Breslin to see him in his nightshirt. The embarrassment would be too much for both of them.

'Sorry to bother you, Father,' she said, staring down at her feet.

'It's alright, Mrs Breslin. I was already awake.'

'It's just that Monsignor Dolan wants to see you.'

Thomas nodded. So this was the old man's plan. Wait until he least expected it and then summon him for an interrogation. Well, let him wait, Thomas thought, though he could already feel his stomach beginning to churn. He'd not had to face the wrath of the Monsignor before, though he had witnessed it once or twice when it had been unleashed on other victims and it wasn't a pleasant sight. He nodded at Mrs Breslin and began to close the door, but the housekeeper didn't move.

'It's just that . . . well, Father. He says you've to come straight away.'

'Why, what's the matter?'

'I don't know, Father, but there's a gentleman in with the Monsignor who's waiting for you.'

'A gentleman?'

'Yes. I think his name is Mister Walsh. A small man, dressed all in black. He's got a squinty nose. Do you know him?'

Thomas shook his head.

'Tell Monsignor Dolan I'll be down in two minutes,' he said, shutting the door without waiting to see if the housekeeper left with his message.

He quickly slipped off his nightshirt and began grabbing the various items of clothing he needed, not even taking the time to wash, which was usually always an essential part of his daily routine. His mind was racing. He'd heard that name and he felt sick, worse than any time he tried to imagine Monsignor Dolan's possible anger. It was the name his hooded companion had used to get them on the ship and now he was here in the chapel house. As he slipped his jacket on, Thomas tried to figure out what he would say, though without knowing what the questions would be it was near impossible. Stay calm, he told himself as he bounded down the stairs, stopping outside the drawing room and quickly blessing himself before opening the door.

Mister Walsh was sitting in the armchair Thomas normally used, a black hat lying at his feet, while Monsignor Dolan stood at the window, hands clasped behind his back. As soon as he saw Thomas, he moved forward and made the formal introductions, with the visitor standing up and holding out a hand that Thomas shook. The man had a weak grip and his palm was sweaty. His eyes, however, displayed a steely resolve and Thomas had to look away from the unblinking stare, turning his attention to the Monsignor.

'Mister Walsh would like to ask you a few questions, Thomas,' Monsignor Dolan said. 'If that's okay with you?'

'That's fine,' Thomas said in what he hoped was a steady voice. 'What about?'

'Well, that's my cue to leave,' the Monsignor said. 'I believe this is a private matter, Mister Walsh?'

The visitor nodded.

'I'll be in my room if you need me for anything.'

'Thank you, Monsignor,' Mister Walsh said as the parish priest slipped quietly out of the room.

'Sit down, Father,' Mister Walsh said, dropping back onto the chair and nodding towards Monsignor Dolan's armchair near the fire. Thomas perched himself nervously on the edge of the seat.

'So how can I help you, Mister Walsh?'

'I'm looking for your brother.'

'My brother?'

'Your brother is Michael Costello?'

Thomas nodded.

'I'm sorry to tell you this, Father, but he is a wanted man.'

'He is?'

'Here and in Ireland.'

Thomas sat back in the chair, trying to look more relaxed even though his heart was racing and he felt Mister Walsh could smell the nervousness seeping out of every pore.

'Why, what's he done?'

Mister Walsh sighed. 'I am here to take him back to Ireland for the crimes he committed there, crimes for which, I'm afraid to tell you, he will pay for with his life. I had him already but he has escaped, helped by friends he has in this city. Unfortunately, that came at a cost, Father, and two of my men are now dead. And someone will have to pay for that as well.'

'You think my brother . . . you think he killed them?'

'I don't know,' he said. 'There are already lives he has to account for back in Ireland. These will merely be added to the charges.'

'I can't believe it, Mister Walsh. I know my brother and I know he's not a killer,' Thomas said, hoping his face hadn't started to glow.

Mister Walsh stood up and walked purposefully over to the window, staring out and shaking his head.

'How many of us really know our own family, Father?' he said, turning round to face the priest. Thomas shrugged.

'Your brother is a tricky character. I thought I had him in Ireland and he slipped through my grasp. Then I did have him here and, again, he's gone. But I need to find him, and I will.'

Thomas watched Mister Walsh, who had resumed his gaze out of the window, clocking every passer-by with casual interest. He was dressed all in black and he knew for sure this was the man who'd been offering money to find Mick. From his questions, however, it was obvious that he didn't suspect Thomas' involvement in Mick's escape or worse, any part in the killings, and why would he? He was a Catholic priest after all, a man of the cloth, a respected member of the community, and he would not have been a part of any rescue which resulted in the murder of two men.

Yet, whenever Thomas closed his eyes, he saw the two dead guards. It had looked at first as though they were just sleeping but both of them wore slim wounds across their throats like crimson necklaces from which continued to seep blood even though both of them had long since breathed their last. Thomas had watched from his chair in the hold of the ship as Brother Jerome dispatched the guard to meet his maker.

The man had plunged suddenly through the hole, startling Thomas, but he'd barely time to gather his thoughts, or for the guard to groan out in pain before Jerome was upon him, a brief flash of moonlight on steel enough to let Thomas know the man had a blade, which he used swiftly and to deadly effect. And even when he was being led, stumbling, towards the stairs, he couldn't resist a ghoulish glance at the dead man, or his companion when they emerged on deck, though he wished he hadn't succumbed to the temptation since their empty faces continued to haunt him.

'Your brother is a traitor,' Mister Walsh suddenly declared, though he did not look round. 'A traitor to the Crown and it is my responsibility to ensure he pays for his treachery.'

'Those are strong accusations to be making, Mister Walsh,' Thomas said. 'I presume you have the evidence to back it up?'

Mister Walsh walked back to his chair and sat down, a lazy smile breaking out across his face.

'I have the proof. I have the witnesses and I have the confession of one of his fellow traitors.'

'What did he do?'

'It is a long story, Father, and one that is not for the faint-hearted. It is enough for you to know that what he did was serious enough for me to hunt him down to this God-forsaken city, if you'll excuse me for saying.'

Thomas nodded to show he wasn't offended, though his mind was racing as he tried to imagine what it was that Mick had done. He would have to ask his brother yet again, and he wasn't going to be put off with an answer as vague as Mister Walsh's. It would mean having to go and see Mick, of course, which suddenly seemed an even riskier option, and Thomas was now convinced that someone would be following him if he left the chapel house. Not for the first time, he wished that O'Connor was still alive.

'So how can I be of help, Mister Walsh?'

'If he contacts you I want you to let me know.'

'You want me to turn in my own brother?'

Mister Walsh nodded. 'There are lives which have to be accounted for and horrors that your brother and his friends in the Brotherhood are responsible for . . . things beyond your imagination.'

Thomas could feel his face burning and his heart suddenly start racing at the mention of that word, which Walsh had spat out venomously. He hoped the other man hadn't noticed the surprise that was now masking his face.

'The Brotherhood?' Thomas croaked.

'I'm afraid your brother's involved with some very bad people,' said Walsh. 'I can see you don't believe me, but don't be fooled by the romantic stories you might have heard about these people. I've seen what they're capable of, and trust me, Father, it would change your opinion. You might think differently about your brother too.'

'What are you saying?'

'Too much, Father. Too much. I will leave it at that and bid you a good morning.'

Both men stood up and Mister Walsh held out his hand again for another limp handshake. This time Thomas held the gaze of his visitor, though he still realised he had been the first to blink. It was as if the man had glass eyes.

'Thank you for your time, Father. And, remember, if your brother gets in touch . . .'

Thomas nodded as he ushered the man out the room, walking ahead of him until they reached the front door. Mister Walsh pushed his black hat firmly back on his head as he stepped outside, striding towards the carriage that had been waiting patiently for him while he'd been inside. Thomas didn't wait for him to leave but immediately shut the door, turning round and coming face-to-face with Monsignor Dolan.

'I think it's time you and I had a chat, Thomas, don't you think?'

# 22

# THE NAME GAME

Mick was worried that his presence might spark resentment amongst the other men, who would glare at him with silent fury, their own arms aching with the strain of work, backs bent painfully out of shape at the end of a long day's toil. He knew he'd avoid all eye contact, embarrassed and slightly shameful that he could do so little when they did so much.

'Don't be an eejit,' Thomas said when he voiced his reservations. 'It's not like you're getting paid anyway.'

'But they'll think I'm just a waster.'

Thomas laughed and shook his head.

'Look at your arm,' he said. 'Everyone will see it and they'll know what you can do and what you can't . . . and I'll have a word with the foreman as well, just to be on the safe side.'

Kate was sitting beside Mick and squeezed his hand reassuringly as he frowned.

'See, I told you Thomas would sort it out.'

Mick kissed her, wanting to let his lips linger on hers, knowing he'd never tire of them no matter how many times he tasted them, but Kate pulled away, conscious of Thomas' silent presence in the room.

'Well, I suppose that's okay then,' he said with a shrug and now it was Thomas' turn to frown.

It had been his brother's idea to find him work. He needed to get out of this house before his mind began to go or, more likely, his temper snapped. Mrs Breslin's sister – Eileen - had been kind enough to put them up and for that he was grateful, but with only one room and kitchen for three adults and two children, it felt claustrophobic. Mick had whispered on more than one occasion to Kate that they needed to find somewhere else to stay.

For one thing, there was little opportunity for the sort of intimacy they'd enjoyed in the chapel house. At times there, it had been possible to forget where they were and imagine instead they were living in their own house, where they could lie naked alongside each other every minute of every day if they wanted. In Eileen's house, however, even their clumsy fumblings in the dark seemed out of place. They both imagined they were making enough noise to wake the dead and they sensed curious eyes trained on their mattress in the small alcove beside the kitchen, watching every movement.

Mick wanted to be able to sit back in bed, his head resting against the wall, the cover pulled up to his waist, rogue specks of ash from his cigarette floating onto his bare chest and watch Kate glide towards him, his eyes taking in every inch of her body in all its glorious nakedness.

'Working will help get your strength back up,' Thomas had said. 'And it's just till I get word back from Liverpool that it's safe for you to go there.'

'But should I be out at all?' Mick asked. 'What if they're waiting for me to show my face?'

'They won't expect you to work, especially not on a building site. They saw the state of your arm.'

Mick had to admit that his brother made sense and the prospect of some fresh air amidst wide, open spaces was appealing enough. Kate would walk him there every morning and she'd be waiting for him when it was time to finish for the day.

Thomas had also tried to press him for more information on what had happened in Ireland, but Mick would only smoke silently and sullenly until his brother eventually gave up with a frustrated sigh.

★ ★ ★

192

Mick wasn't sure whether it was his physical condition – he still felt weak and fragile – or his mental anguish, but he was sure he was walking even slower than normal on the first day he was to report for work. He'd taken his time getting ready that morning, though his washing had only consisted of a cursory splash of water on his face. Before his imprisonment on the ship, he'd liked nothing better than to rest his face in a bowl of water – hot or cold – for a few minutes while it felt like the clear liquid seeped through his skin and he was ready to tackle the new day. Now, even the sight of water left him shuddering and he had to force himself into contact with it.

His subtle reluctance to get to work wasn't detected by Kate, however, who led the way with an enthusiasm Mick felt was out of place in the early morning haze they shuffled through along with other silent figures, most of whom were heading for their own place of work.

'You'll be fine,' she whispered as they drew closer to where he would be working. Already he could see bodies gathering in front of a man waving a sheet of paper in the air.

'Just ask for Donnelly. He's the foreman,' Thomas had said. 'He'll see you alright.'

Mick presumed the man with the paper was Donnelly. He was suddenly conscious of his injured limb concealed inside his coat, the left arm of the garment hanging limply at his side. He stopped and spun Kate round till she faced him. Leaning forward, he kissed her frantically and she responded in a similar fashion, only breaking free after a couple of minutes.

'Let's go back home,' he said. 'We'll spend the day in bed.'

'But Eileen and the kids will be there.'

'What about the chapel house? We could go there. Thomas would let us.'

'Indeed he would not. Your brother's probably in enough trouble already for letting us stay in the first place without the two of us turning up on his doorstep again.'

Mick sighed and Kate gently kissed his cheek.

'Everything's going to be fine,' she said. 'Thomas said he'd have a word for you.'

'But what if he didn't?'

She kissed him again.

'I trust your brother,' she said. 'He's a man of his word. If he says he'll help then that's what he'll do.'

There was nothing else Mick could do or say. He would have to go to work.

Work turned out to be a giant field of dirt and rubble and timber and shrubbery and every sort of debris imaginable.

'We're going to clear it all,' Donnelly had explained to him after Mick had introduced himself, 'every last bit of it, and then we'll flatten it down so they can put the pitch on it.'

Mick glanced over Donnelly's shoulder.

'I know what you're thinking,' the foreman said. 'We've already got a football ground. You're right there, Mick, but the thieving landlords have hiked the rent up – ten times as much is what I've heard. Landlords are Ireland's bloody curse and they've followed us here to Glasgow. So we're going to build a new ground for the team to play at, one that we can call our own.'

Mick remembered his visit to the other ground to watch a game of football and it made him shudder as he immediately thought of Duffy, picturing him holding court in the middle of the crowd.

'So what do you want me to do?' he asked Donnelly, glancing down at his arm with a shrug.

'Well, you can start by handing out the shovels and we'll take it from there.'

Donnelly was a Kerry man, of that Mick would have bet his life on. He had hands that looked bigger than the shovels Mick stood beside, and his ears stuck out from the side of his head like a pair of wings. Mick couldn't stop staring at them, even though he kept trying to look away, glancing up and down or left and right, but still his gaze returned to the ears. He presumed Donnelly was used to it because he never said anything or gave any indication that he was aware of Mick's attention.

There were already men at work, piling the dirt into barrows which, when filled to the brim, would be pushed slowly over to the carts at the far end of the field. The heavy load would then be guided carefully up a plank of wood and the contents tipped into the cart. Occasionally, a barrow would topple over before it reached the top, the air suddenly filled with a hundred angry curses as the unlucky worker began reloading the barrow with the spilled earth. When the cart was full, and Mick reckoned it took about twenty barrows to do so, a driver would snap the reins and the Shire horse would begin its slow and laborious journey to wherever the final resting place of the dirt would be before returning, ready to be filled again. There were three carts that were constantly being filled up, emptied and filled up again.

As more men arrived to work, having first checked in with Donnelly, they were directed over to where Mick stood, smoking a cigarette and idly watching the exertions of everyone around him. He would hand each man a shovel, usually to be greeted with a nod or a grunt, and then they would join in the monotonous work. Thomas had explained to him that it was all volunteers who were helping, the word having spread quickly round the various East End parishes.

'They all seem to like the Celtic,' Thomas had said with a shrug, showing as much interest in the sport as his brother.

'They must do if they're working for nothing,' Mick said. Normally he would have laughed off such an idea but in his physical state he didn't think anyone would pay for his services.

Once the pile of shovels had disappeared, Mick shuffled over to Donnelly who was scribbling furiously in a little black notebook.

'Is there anything else to be done, Mister Donnelly?' he asked.

'I'll have something for you in five minutes,' Donnelly muttered without glancing up from his notebook. Mick lit a cigarette and stood smoking, feeling awkward and useless at the same time, wishing that he was back home with Kate, even if it was in Eileen's house.

Eventually, Donnelly snapped his notebook shut, placed the pencil behind his ear and lit his own cigarette, blowing smoke in Mick's direction.

'Do you follow the football, son?' he asked.

'No,' said Mick.

'You should now. It's a grand game, so it is, and Celtic are a grand team. Do you not even like the Celtic?'

'I watched them once, over there,' Mick said, nodding towards the old ground.

'This place will be something special when it's finished,' Donnelly said as they tramped across the field. Mick didn't say anything and avoided looking at the foreman in case he could see the doubt in Mick's eyes. The Kerry man was in full flight now, pointing out where the goalposts would be, and the pavilion, and where he would stand with his son for the first game after the ground was opened. Donnelly had a fine imagination, Mick thought, because whenever he looked around, he couldn't picture any of the things the foreman was describing. They stopped beside two men who were on their knees digging furiously at the soil to loosen the bushes that were randomly dotted all over the field.

'You think you can manage this?' Donnelly asked and Mick immediately nodded, knowing that anything would be better than just handing out shovels. At least now, if the other men looked round, they would just see another worker on his hands and knees. Soon he was digging alongside the other two men, happy to be working at last and able to forget, for a few moments at least, that he was doing so with only one arm.

'Denis Meehan,' the older of the two men said with a nod after Mick had introduced himself. He looked at the other man, who kept his head bowed and was burrowing like a rabbit, puffing and panting in time with each thrust of his trowel.

'That's my brother, Joe,' Denis said. 'He doesn't say much . . . Joe! JOE!'

Joe looked up, startled.

'This is Mick,' Denis said and Joe stared vacantly for a moment at Mick before bowing his head again and resuming his work. Mick glanced at Denis, who shrugged.

'He's harmless,' he said in a Donegal accent. 'And he'll do the work of two men, so he will.'

'What happened to – ' Mick said, immediately stopping himself. 'Sorry,' he mumbled.

'Don't be worrying about it, Mick. That's just the way God made him, but he's a good boy,' Denis said, giving his brother an affectionate punch on the arm which Joe didn't appear to notice.

Mick nodded and began digging, the three men now working silently, and he could see that Denis was right. Joe dug faster and deeper than the two of them and they seemed to be clearing the bushes with an impressive swiftness that Mick found invigorating. He realised after about fifteen minutes that he hadn't thought about anything in particular – not his injured arm, nor the man in black or even Duffy. He smiled, seemingly content, though he immediately felt slightly guilty that this list included Kate.

As he continued digging he tried to picture her, imagining what she would be doing at this very moment and hoping that she had him in her mind. They had spoken of Liverpool – she was set on going with him, and though he had explained the dangers it was without conviction and with a secret joy in his heart.

'There's nothing to keep me here anyway,' she said when he asked her if she'd miss the city. 'And I've got as much reason to go as you.'

He knew she was talking about Duffy and the name made him shudder again. He'd been lucky enough to escape with his life the last time he'd clashed with him, but Mick knew Duffy wasn't the sort of man to accept defeat graciously and he still seemed to think he had some sort of claim on Kate.

At half past ten, Donnelly blew a whistle, the sound of which floated shrilly out across the field, signalling a temporary halt to all the work. Shovels were dropped gratefully and noisily to the ground and the air was suddenly filled with a million tiny clouds as men sucked hungrily on their cigarettes. Mick stood up, stretching himself with a groan and Denis did the same. Joe remained kneeling, though he too had stopped digging. Denis lit two cigarettes and handed one to his brother, who snatched it and thrust it clumsily into his mouth. Denis nodded to Mick and they began walking over to where a group of men had gathered in front of a barrel of water.

Mick gulped, feeling his heart begin to race, but he tried to quell the rising fear as they got closer to the barrel, realising that he'd look foolish if he said or did anything. He remained at arm's length from the barrel, however, taking the cup quickly from the man who was doling out the water and then stepping away and turning his back on it. Denis had already finished his water and was on to his second cigarette, and he shuffled to the side to allow Mick to join the circle of men who were smoking and drinking.

'They were back in the pub again last night,' one of the men was saying in a gravely Belfast voice.

'What for?' asked another man.

'I told you before,' the Belfast man said.

'No, you didn't.'

'I did so, O'Brien, you big daft Dublin eejit. We were talking about it yesterday.'

'No, we weren't,' O'Brien muttered, but the nodding heads from the rest of the group indicated that he was wrong.

'It must be serious then,' said Denis, 'if they're still searching.'

'Well, there were two men killed,' the Belfast man said, 'and a prisoner's on the run. They say it was the boys who did it, to rescue one of their own.'

'The boys?' O'Brien asked.

'Bloody hell, O'Brien,' the Belfast man said, flicking what was left of his cigarette at his companion. 'I told you all this before. The boys. . .' he glanced round and then whispered, 'the Brotherhood.'

O'Brien nodded. Mick was desperate to ask his own questions but he knew he was still a stranger and didn't want to risk raising any suspicions. Denis had introduced him, but the rest of the men took little notice of him, not even acknowledging his injured arm. He was grateful for that at least, but he wanted to know who was doing the searching and what questions they were asking. More than that, he realised that he would have to get away from Glasgow soon because it was only a matter of time before someone provided a piece of useful information, and now that he was out of the house, it only increased the chances of detection.

The Belfast man seemed most upset that his drinking time the night before had been disrupted and soon the conversation drifted towards football and Celtic, at which point Mick stopped listening, though he studied each man in the group, wondering if any of them would betray him if they knew he was the prisoner on the run.

Ten minutes came and went in the blink of an eye, and Mick and Denis returned to where Joe remained kneeling. As soon as the whistle sounded again, he began digging with the same ferocity as before, though it took the other two men a bit longer to get back into their rhythm. Mick kept thinking about what the Belfast man had said, and he imagined Walsh barging into the pub, demanding information on where Mick was. The thought actually made him smile. He knew Walsh would probably have hidden behind other men. He might have been asking the questions but it would take a brave man to interrupt an Irishman when he was drinking, and Walsh certainly wasn't that.

Mick didn't hear the whistle sound again at first, his mind still full of thoughts of his pursuer, but when it blew a second time he looked up.

'It's not lunchtime yet,' said Denis, glancing over with a puzzled look to where Donnelly stood. Six men stood beside him, arms folded, while another man sat on a horse. He was dressed all in black. It was Walsh. Donnelly was shouting instructions to the men, telling them all to gather together in front of him. Denis stood up and dragged Joe up as well, while Mick pushed himself onto his feet reluctantly.

'I wonder what's wrong,' Denis said as the three men headed towards Donnelly, soon merging with the other workers, who were all muttering and mumbling. As they gathered together, Donnelly instructed them to spread out in a straight line and disgruntled shouts from men who liked to moan about everything filled the air until the foreman told them to shut up. Mick snatched Joe's cap, the poor soul immediately clasping his bare head. Denis looked round as Mick pushed the cap tightly on his own head, hoping its brim would hide his face and he shrugged apologetically. Denis put a comforting arm round his brother and began muttering into his ear, though Mick couldn't make out what was being said.

Donnelly now explained what was happening, introducing Mister Walsh, who remained on his horse. The man in black edged the beast forward until he was directly in front of the men.

'I am looking for Mick Costello,' Walsh said, his Mayo accent piercing the morning air. 'Once I have him, I will leave, but understand this. Anyone who does not help me will be helping a criminal – a murderer – and you will be an enemy of the Crown.'

Walsh nodded to the six men he'd brought with him and they spread out along the line of men. He manoeuvred his horse backwards to give the men room, and they all stood, arms folded, staring at the workers in front of them. Mick kept his eyes lowered, though he had noticed each of them had a rifle slung over their right shoulders.

'Remember, I only want Mick Costello,' Walsh shouted. 'So if he is man enough to step forward, the rest of you can return peacefully to work.'

No one moved and it seemed to Mick like absolute silence had descended on them, apart from his pounding heart which he was sure would alert the guards to his identity.

'So he's a coward after all,' Walsh said. 'You,' he said, pointing towards a stocky, ginger-haired man in the centre of the crowd. 'Step forward.'

The man shuffled out of the line, glancing over at Donnelly who shrugged his shoulders.

'Do you know Mick Costello?' Walsh asked.

'No, sir. Never heard of him.'

Walsh nodded and one of the guards stepped forward, slipping the rifle off his shoulder and in the same movement smashing the butt of the weapon into the man's face. He collapsed on the ground with a stunned cry and he lay motionless on the ground as blood began to pour out of his head wound. A couple of men moved to help him but Walsh barked orders for them to remain where they were. He gestured to another worker – a tall, skinny man with arms that seemed to stretch down to his kneecaps. He was even more reluctant to step forward but did so after Walsh repeated his instructions.

'Do you know Mick Costello?' he asked.

The skinny man shook his head and braced himself for the blow, though it didn't come from the guard in front of him. As he stepped back into line under instruction from Walsh, another guard who had slipped round behind the men smashed his rifle into the man's skull and he toppled forward like a fir tree that had just been felled. He crashed to the ground, sending clouds of dust spiralling into the air. Walsh looked further down the line and gestured to another man, who did not move. Two guards grabbed his arms and dragged his screaming body out of the line.

'Do you know Mick Costello?' Walsh asked.

The man kept squirming, trying to break free of his captors as a third guard stepped forward.

'I'm Mick Costello,' Mick said, stepping forward just as the guard had grasped his rifle, ready to strike. Everyone stopped. The guards released their grip of the worker, who stopped his howls of protest and slipped meekly back into line. Mick stood, head bowed, breathing heaving, and ready for the rifle blow that would surely knock him out. He could hear the horse moving closer to him and he wondered if there would be any chance of a final attack on Walsh before the six guards overpowered him.

'I'm Mick Costello.'

Another voice shouted out and Mick looked up. Denis stood beside him. He winked. Walsh's horse stopped.

'I'm Mick Costello,' a voice at the far end of the line declared and another man strode forward from the line. The guards looked up and down, not knowing whom to go for and waiting for Walsh to issue his instructions.

'I'm Mick Costello.' Another man stepped forward, and soon a dozen of them had declared their identity and joined the group of Mick Costellos.

'Enough!' screamed Walsh, as the six guards stepped back, one or two with their rifles now poised and pointing at the men. They were nervous and confused, and they wanted Walsh to take control.

'I am going to shoot someone in a minute,' Walsh said as he steered his horse towards Mick and Denis. 'Take off his hat,' he shouted at one of the guards, nodding towards Mick. 'That's him, you bloody fools. Look at his arm.'

'You've got about ten seconds,' Denis whispered out the corner of his mouth. 'You better be a fast runner.'

As the guard moved towards Mick, Denis looked round.

'Joe! Bad man! Bad man going to hurt Denis.'

Joe moved forward like he'd been fired out of a cannon, crashing into the guard and toppling him over. He immediately began pounding on the man's face with his fists as other guards rushed to help their colleague.

'Run, you bloody eejit,' Denis shouted as he jumped in to help his brother and suddenly it was a brawl as guards and men battled on the dusty ground. Mick began running towards the exit, not bothering to look back at the chaos he'd helped to spark.

'He's getting away!' Walsh shouted, as Mick jumped onto one of the dirt carts, lashed the horse with the reins and began steering the cart out of the field, the sound of Walsh shouting to his men echoing in his wake. He managed the briefest of glances over his shoulder, catching sight of Walsh who had turned his horse round and was heading towards him in quick pursuit, followed by a couple of guards who had managed to break free of the melee. Mick urged the horse on with greater urgency, hoping that once they were on the cobbled streets it might speed up, though knowing that the work horse would be no match for Walsh's beast.

# 23

# THE HUNTER AND THE HUNTED

The cart suddenly hit the cobbles and Mick could hardly hear himself think over the clatter of the wheels and the hooves of the horse. He kept a tight hold of the reins, continuing to thrash the horse that moved with unaccustomed urgency. He still worried that it would never be able to keep up the frantic pace, particularly pulling a cart that was half full of dirt. Mick didn't want to look back though he knew that Walsh would be on his trail. Instead, he kept one eye on the road while checking to see if there was any way he could loosen the reins that attached cart and beast.

When he steered the animal round the first corner, he could feel the cart lurching over and for a moment he was hanging grimly onto it as it tipped over on two wheels, but it managed to correct itself and he lashed the horse again. This time, he did glance back up the street towards the field and Walsh was indeed chasing him, his horse galloping towards him while the other two carts were also in pursuit, driven by the guards who'd managed to escape the fighting which Mick presumed was still going on.

He had no idea where he was going, only that he had to get away from Walsh. He knew his hasty escape was being watched with curiosity by passers-by, who instinctively took a step away from the road as he noisily clattered by. If he could at least put a couple of streets between him and Walsh he might be able to detach the cart, which would speed him up, but he was sure it was his pursuer who was gaining ground on him.

He turned another corner, this time edging over to the left, but the sudden movement did not panic him and he was now on his feet, driving the horse on with shouts as well as encouragement from the reins. He was automatically heading in the direction of Eileen's house, though he also realised that he wouldn't be able to stop there or hide out. For one thing he didn't want Kate to become involved.

Just as he reached the end of the street, another cart suddenly appeared round the corner and Mick yanked the reins hard to steer the horse away from a collision, though while the beasts missed each other, his cart smashed into the other horse. The impact sent Mick flying through the air as the injured animal screamed in pain, though Mick's only concern was where he would land.

'You feckin' maniac!' the other cart driver screamed as Mick crashed onto the pavement, landing heavily on his right shoulder. He immediately sprung up, realising there wasn't enough time to consider the pain or even apologise to the man who had jumped down from his cart. He seemed to be caught in a dilemma between wanting to tend to his horse and shout at Mick, who had begun sprinting away as Walsh's horse came into view.

He skidded round the corner, glad to have avoided any further collisions with anyone on the pavement and he was running now as fast as he could, quickly realising it was better to stick to the road which was less crowded. It reminded him of his initial escape from Walsh when he'd turned up with the soldiers at their cottage to arrest him. Would he still be alive now if he'd been caught? It certainly seemed like Walsh was determined to see him hang.

The clatter of hooves was following him, getting louder with each step he took, though it could well have just been other horses and carts innocently going about their daily business. He wasn't taking any chances, however, particularly when he knew Walsh's determination to catch him was as strong as his own desire to evade capture. As he kept running he was aware of a growing pain in his right shoulder that provided an irritating balance for his body; though his left arm was in constant pain, he was so used to it now that, more often than not, he barely even noticed its presence.

There was shouting further back down the street and he imagined it was Walsh screaming for someone to grab Mick. He knew that no one would step in and help, not until they found out what it was they were going to becoming involved in.

A cart and horse sat idly outside a tenement about ten yards ahead of him and Mick decided he was going to steal it before he even reached it. He'd already got the horse moving when the owner came strolling out of the close. He stood, momentarily stunned, his mind taking a few seconds to register what was happening before he began shouting. He bolted out into the street, chasing after his prized possession. He'd just about managed to catch up with Mick, his fingertips touching the end of the cart when it veered round a corner and the man toppled over, sprawling across the cobbles and cutting his chin. He looked up, unconcerned at the blood pouring from his wound, as his horse and cart sped away from him. He began banging his head off the ground and groaning just as a thunderous noise approached him and Walsh and his horse leapt over the man as they continued their pursuit.

Mick had turned left and then left again, speeding down a street that was full of carts heading in the opposite direction, and it took what little skill he possessed as a driver – and a one-armed one at that – to avoid any collisions. When he made his third left turn in succession, he suddenly realised he was heading back to where he'd run away from in the first place.

He knew he'd have to turn right at the next junction, shifting his body across the seat to help compensate for the tilt in the cart when he did so. It all seemed to be going so well until he looked up and realised he was heading straight for the two carts from the field that were being driven towards him by the guards. They didn't see him at first – it was only for a split second, though, and then they recognised him. There was nowhere for Mick to turn now. If he veered to the left or right he'd hit one of them so he kept driving straight ahead. At the last second both guards, who'd also appeared so resolute, steered their carts to the side.

The one that headed left managed to stay on the road and the guard was able to bring it to a halt. The wheels of the other one, however, hit the kerb, sending piles of dirt scattering into the air and showering anyone nearby, while the cart tipped over, catapulting the guard out of the seat and onto the hard surface of the road, where he lay groaning.

Mick reached the end of the street, glancing back as he turned left. Walsh had stopped briefly to check on the injured guard, who was now being tended to by his companion. He snapped to attention, however, no doubt commanded by Walsh, and headed back to his cart, leaving his colleague on the ground. Once out of sight, Mick drew to a halt halfway up the street and jumped out, landing in front of a startled man.

'I'll give you a shilling to drive this cart round the block for ten minutes.'

'What?' the man said, taking a step backwards.

'Alright. Two then,' Mick said, delving into his pocket and fishing out the two pieces of silver. They were immediately snatched out of his hand and the man leapt onto the front of the cart.

'Ten minutes, you say?'

'Yes,' said Mick. 'Just keep going round the block.'

The man nodded and cracked the whip, and the tired horse, which had welcomed the unexpected rest, now broke into a canter again. Mick stepped back from the pavement and into the mouth of the close just as Walsh came thundering into the street, followed by the guard driving the dirt cart, and they raced past Mick's hiding place, their eyes firmly focused on what they thought was Mick in the cart further down the street. He grinned as he peered out, watching them get smaller and smaller.

He started walking in the other direction, keeping his head bowed and wishing he'd managed to hold onto Joe's cap, which had long since blown off. He wondered if the fighting was still going on in the field. He still couldn't believe what Denis had done and he hoped there might be some time in the future when he could thank him and his brother. He owed Denis much – perhaps even his life – and he wanted to show his gratitude. Mick also realised he was running out of luck as far as his own life was concerned and he knew he wasn't safe quite yet.

He pressed his chin down on his chest and strode firmly away from where he presumed the search for him would continue and he wondered how long the man would be able to lead Walsh on a fruitless chase before he was caught. Mick was two streets away by now and began to relax slightly, though he still kept his head bowed as a precaution. He was heading back to Eileen's house. Now that he wasn't being followed, it would be safe enough – well, for today at least – but they would have to leave Glasgow, and soon, perhaps without waiting for Thomas' friend to send any word. Walsh had somehow known where he was working today, and if he knew that, he might well also know where he was hiding out.

Mick's mind was racing now, trying to figure out who might have betrayed him, or was it just a lucky break Walsh had enjoyed, turning up on the off chance Mick would be working there? He frowned, knowing there had been nothing lucky about it. Someone had tipped Walsh off. Now he realised that nowhere was safe. It would be best just to get Kate and they could be on their way.

His head still bowed and his mind filled with potential traitors, Mick didn't see the woman coming towards him pushing a pram. He collided with it, immediately looking up and apologising as soon as he saw what he'd run into.

'You clumsy fool,' the woman shouted as her baby began crying. She leant into the pram, offering some soothing words of comfort to her baby, and then glanced up with a scowl.

'An hour it took me to get her to sleep and you go and bloody wake her up,' she shouted.

'I'm really sorry.'

'Sorry? So you bloody should be,' the woman said, leaning into the pram again. Whatever she said had no effect on the baby, who was crying bitterly. Mick started to back away.

'That's right,' the woman shouted. 'Run away now you've made a bloody nuisance of yourself. Typical man.'

'Look, I said I was sorry.'

'I've been walking these streets for an hour . . . an hour!'

'I know,' said Mick, suddenly aware of clomping hooves that were slowing down on the street behind him. He knew who it was without having to glance up and he thrust his head in the pram, hoping Walsh would think it was just an angry couple arguing over a crying baby.

'What the hell do you think you're doing?' the woman screamed, grabbing his right shoulder to pull him away, her grip, which was surprisingly strong, sending a bolt of pain shooting through his body.

'That's my baby, so get your ugly head out of there.'

Mick looked up. Walsh sat on his horse, wearing the grin of a man who had finally got what he wanted. He glanced down the road and Mick followed his gaze, spying three guards approaching on foot. He looked along the other end of the road though he knew he'd never outrun Walsh and his horse.

'I guess it's all over now, Mick,' he said, leaning forward. Mick shrugged as the woman looked round at Walsh, who was inching his horse ever closer to the pavement.

'And keep that bloody beast away from my baby,' she shouted, slapping the horse's nose hard with the palm of her hand. The beast reared up on its hind legs and Walsh battled to calm it and remain in the saddle. Mick didn't need a second invitation to start running, a stream of abuse from the woman ringing in his ears, along with the distressed braying of Walsh's horse. Walsh was also shouting to the guards and Mick knew they'd already be chasing after him.

It didn't take long before Mick could feel himself tiring. He was amazed he'd managed to keep going this long, and he knew it was only his determination to escape that had given him the strength to continue. But the beatings and torture his body had already endured was now beginning to tell and he was getting slower. It felt like he was running into a gale, even though there wasn't a hint of wind in the air.

He sensed that the guards were gaining ground on him, and no doubt Walsh had regained control of his horse and had either rejoined the chase or was leading it again. He ran through groups of people, provoking angry shouts after barging into them, and raced across busy junctions without bothering to check for any oncoming traffic, thanking God whenever he managed to reach the other side of the road safely. He hurtled round a corner, almost losing his balance in the process, and headed for the first tenement, taking the stairs two at a time and disappearing into the mouth of the close. He kept bounding up the stairs until he'd reached the top landing, where he stopped, bending over, hands on his knees as he tried to regain his breath.

He'd run up a dead end but at least he'd given himself a few moments of respite and when his breathing started to calm down, he glanced out the window and into the back court where two small boys chased each other round and round the small patch of grass, dancing in and out of the bed sheets which someone in the building had hung up in the hope of drying them, though that would be a long process in the winter chill of the day.

Mick now started to walk slowly down the stairs, stopping just above the second landing and sitting down when he heard voices echoing up from the ground floor. It was the guards and they were searching for him. Someone must have pointed out where Mick had gone. They were knocking on the doors of each house, asking the same question each time – 'Have you seen a man running into this close?' – before barging into the house to search it, ignoring the angry protests of the occupants. Mick scurried back up to the top floor and looked out the window again. If he jumped out now, he'd be dead for sure. He glanced up at the attic hatch and realised it was his only hope.

Jumping onto the flimsy banister, he pushed at the hatch, which sprung open straight away, though it fell back down with a

209

clatter. He did it again, managing to keep it open this time and, clutching the side of the hole with his hand, he slowly pulled himself up with his right arm and into the attic, quickly closing the hatch behind him, leaving himself in absolute darkness. He stood for a few seconds, trying to get a sense of where he was and hoping that his eyes would become accustomed to the gloominess, but there was not even a sliver of light to help him.

Slowly, he began inching his way across a wooden beam, stretching out his arm in the hope it would come into contact with something solid he could grip onto. After a few more nervous steps, his fingertips hit another beam, this one snaking down the side of the roof and Mick smiled as he grasped onto it, not caring if his hand picked up any skelves.

Feeling slightly more secure, he took another step forward and his foot missed the beam, plunging through the soft roof. There was a split second when it seemed like he was frozen to the spot and then his whole body plunged through the roof, landing with a deafening thud on the floor below, though he was momentarily hidden amidst the dust and debris which had followed his fall. As the cloud of dust cleared, Mick opened his eyes.

Standing in a steel bath in front of a fire, which looked warm and inviting, was a young woman. She was naked and Mick allowed his eyes a couple of seconds to take in the sight, appreciating every curve and smooth contour of her body before she started screaming, splashing frantically in the tub as her arms and legs tried desperately to offer some privacy, though they failed miserably. She was in her twenties and wore a scar across her belly that Mick guessed was done by a knife and he figured she was lucky to be alive after a wound like that.

'I'm sorry,' he said with a groan as the woman kept screaming. He could hear the heavy footsteps of the guards bounding up the wooden stairs towards the source of the noise and he tried to move. Nothing happened. He waited a few seconds and then tried again, slowly beginning to push himself onto his knees. He was still kneeling in front of the naked women when the guards burst into the room. There were worse sights he could feast his eyes on in his last few seconds as a free man, Mick thought with a smile as one of the guards strode towards him, swinging an arm in his direction and cracking his head with the butt of his rifle. Where before there had been breasts, now there was only darkness.

# 24

## MURKY WATERS

Thomas needed to go to confession. It was a last resort but he hoped that absolution might bring him some relief from the guilt that was eating away at his heart and soul. He had woken even earlier than usual, and even with his eyes barely open and his body still languishing in that limbo between sleep and being fully awake, his first thought was of Kate. Her face danced before his eyes. He saw her smile and heard her laugh; when he breathed in deeply he could swear he smelt her. He smothered a pillow over his face and groaned. There was no respite from this.

At one point, his heart would soar whenever she came into his thoughts but it was beyond that stage. Now he tortured himself with the fact that he couldn't have her. More than that, he just wanted to tell her how he felt. He knew, when he wasn't trying to delude himself, that his feelings wouldn't be reciprocated. She looked on him as Mick's brother and, just as importantly, as a priest. The thought of having feelings for a priest would, he was sure, be horrifying to her. God knows how she'd react if she knew what feelings he harboured for her.

He held little hope that confession would provide the peace of mind he was looking for but in his desperate mental and emotional state, he was prepared to try anything. They hadn't warned him about this at seminary. Stern priests had spoken of evil women, trying to tempt them as Eve had tempted Adam, warning them that they must resist the temptations of the flesh at all costs. How that was to be done was another matter, and one that was left unexplained, and Thomas was discovering to his cost that the power of prayer was having little effect. He was now pinning his hopes on the prospect of a fellow priest offering some words of wisdom, if not comfort, in the confessional box. More likely, it would be words of condemnation, but he was prepared to accept that as well.

He'd eventually decided against going to Monsignor Dolan. Regardless of the parish priest's discretion, and he had been gratefully surprised at the manner in which the Monsignor had handled everything so far, every man has his limits and Thomas suspected his confession would be well beyond that. So he'd decided to go to St. Mary's. He knew the priests there, but he didn't think they'd recognise his voice. For one thing, they wouldn't be expecting him to make a confession, though just to be sure, he'd decided to hide his dog collar to avoid attracting any attention from priests or parishioners.

As he got dressed, he went over in his head what he was going to say, though he couldn't quite find the words that properly explained how he felt. The truth was, he was in love with Kate, but his face burned brightly when he said it out loud. What would his confessor say? Thomas would have to offer some sort of explanation as to why this was a problem that needed to be unburdened, but he wasn't going to admit to being a priest, so there was another lie straight off. Eventually, he decided he would just wait and see how he felt when he was there, putting his trust in God that he'd find the right words at the right time.

Thomas recognised the carriage straight away and instinctively slowed down. He stopped across the road from St Mary's, standing at the corner of a tenement where he could watch the front of the church without detection. Suddenly he wasn't sure whether it was a good idea to go to confession. Not that he wasn't desperate to unburden his conscience, but he feared now that he might be identified.

Father Angus McNeill's carriage sat outside the chapel house, the driver patting down the horse but continuing to glance every few minutes towards the front door, ready to spring into action if it should suddenly open. The Archbishop's Chancellor was obviously on his parish visits, though the way the carriage was facing suggested that he would be heading back to the Cathedral. He hadn't called in at St Alphonsus' for a few weeks now, not since the meetings in the church hall had stopped, though Thomas knew that once they resumed the Highland priest would once again be on his doorstep, looking for more information to scurry back to the Archbishop with.

There would be no obvious explanation Thomas could offer if he was spotted now. He fingered the dog collar in his coat pocket and thought about slipping it back on, though he decided to wait and watch for Father McNeill's departure before finally deciding what to do. He could imagine the discomfort among the priests of St Mary's. It was the same in every parish of the diocese whenever Father McNeill paid a visit. His position brought with it obvious unpopularity. He had to do the Archbishop's bidding and that could be an unpleasant task, while the Chancellor's own personality, which was cold and aloof, did nothing to endear him to his colleagues. Finally, there was his nationality. He was Scottish, a minority within the teeming mass of Irish men, women and children who populated the city and its parishes. Just as significantly, he was a minority among his fellow priests, who were mostly from across the water.

Yet, even given all this, he still exuded an air of superiority that was silently tolerated by the rest of the clergy, the power of his office and the patronage of the Archbishop enough to protect him.

That wouldn't last forever, thought Thomas, and he hoped he was there to see the day when Father McNeill finally got what was coming to him. He knew thoughts like that should also be confessed, but if he did make it as far as the confessional box, he would concentrate on the one sin – and the most serious one at that.

The door of the chapel house began to open and the driver immediately rushed over to the door of the carriage to hold it for the Chancellor. Thomas took a step back just to be sure no one could see him from the front of the church and almost bumped into an old man who was shuffling along the street, his hands gripping the lapels of his flimsy jacket to try and protect his body from the worst excesses of the bitter cold. He nodded at Thomas as he reached the corner and then headed down the street in the same direction as the church or, more likely, a pub. Thomas thought briefly of going after the man and offering him a few pennies but he decided against it as he looked over to the carriage.

Father McNeill was talking with another man who had his back to the priest. At one point whatever the man said was enough to amuse the Chancellor who threw back his head and let out a laugh that could have been heard six feet under. The other man nodded and held out his hand, which Father McNeill grasped, and they stood vigorously shaking hands before the priest stepped into his carriage.

The driver immediately closed the door and scuttled to the front of the carriage, jumping up and setting the horse on its way. The other man stood watching the carriage until it reached the end of the street then, clasping his hands behind his back, he turned and strode across the road, heading straight towards Thomas.

Thomas couldn't believe what he was seeing and he blinked a couple of times. He also realised he had a choice to make because he didn't want to be discovered. He began stepping back, glancing over either shoulder so as to avoid colliding with any other passers-by, while his mind was racing, even though there was really just once question to answer. Why was Father McNeill meeting with Mister Walsh?

Thomas made it to the other end of the street and had just stepped round the corner, his mind still in turmoil at what he'd witnessed, when he saw Kate walking towards him. She didn't notice him at first but when she looked up and realised, she raced towards him. She was crying. Thomas stood as she ran straight into him, burying her head in his chest and wrapping her thin arms round his waist. He glanced around him, checking to see if anyone was watching and glad at the same time that he wasn't wearing his dog collar. Slowly he moved his arms and embraced her, gently at first and then holding her tighter, his touch provoking more tears from Kate.

His chin was almost resting on the top of her head and every time he breathed in, he could savour the scent of fresh apples that seemed to follow him everywhere. God, what are you doing to me, he thought, even though he made no attempt to let her go or find out why she was crying. It was enough that she had turned to him for comfort, though at the back of his mind he was worried that someone would spot him and report back to Monsignor Dolan, leaving Thomas with a lot of explaining to do. He'd already tried to reassure him that the business with his brother would be resolved and wouldn't land on his doorstep again, but trying to explain why he was embracing a woman, and in public, might be more difficult.

'What's wrong?' he eventually asked, though Kate didn't hear him at first. He took a small step back but still kept hold of her.

'Kate, what's happened?'

'It's Mick. He's gone.'

Now Thomas did release her and in between sobs, she told him about Mick's escape. Word of the fight had quickly spread through the East End and Kate had immediately headed out onto the streets, though she had no idea where she was going or what she was looking for. She just knew that she couldn't have sat in Eileen's house doing nothing.

Thomas glanced back round the corner, expecting to see Walsh almost upon them, but the street was empty. The man in black had disappeared. Kate's sobs had subsided and though Thomas wanted to hold her again, he sensed the moment had passed. She was looking at him, waiting for him to say something, confident that he would have the right answers. He had helped find Mick before so why couldn't he do so again? There was so much for him to take in, with his brother missing again and the man who had been hunting him now meeting up with the Chancellor of the diocese.

He hardly dare imagine what Mick was involved in, yet he knew it was serious because Walsh had pursued him from Ireland. So what did he want with Father McNeill? More than that, he needed to know exactly why they'd asked him to spy on the Brotherhood. That would mean confronting the Chancellor and he knew that would be a more difficult proposition, and one that would require some thought and planning. The Chancellor would be a difficult adversary. Thomas' only advantage was that of surprise, since he'd stumbled upon the two men together, and he'd have to use that well when the time came.

Kate didn't speak all the way back to the church, though he sensed she was desperate to ask him what he was going to do next. Perhaps she guessed that he didn't actually know and it was better to harbour false hopes than to suffer the disappointment of his own admission of failure. The truth was, he had absolutely no idea what to do. Mick had enjoyed more luck than any man could fairly claim, and there would come a time when that luck would finally run out. Maybe it already had? He should have sent the two of them off to Liverpool right away without waiting for news that it was safe. It would have been easier for the two of them to hide out in a city where no one was looking for them. Glasgow had proved to be too small for them to remain there safely, but that realisation appeared to have come too late for Mick.

Thomas was angry with himself, though he tried not to let it show. He had suggested that Mick go out to work when he was sure his brother would rather have stayed at home, and that had obviously put him directly in the path of danger. He'd have to speak to Padraig and ask him to help again. He seemed to know a lot about what was going on in the city and Thomas hoped he was still grateful for using the hall. Or was it just that Padraig wanted to look after one of his own? Thomas' fear, and it was one that he was never going to voice to Kate, was that Mick was already on a ship halfway across the Irish Sea to meet the hangman's noose.

As they reached the chapel house, Thomas thought of Monsignor Dolan's reaction to seeing Kate again. Ideally, he would have liked to leave her at Eileen's but he knew that she would have refused if he had even suggested it. He was also secretly glad to have her alongside him and every now and then his thoughts drifted back to those few moments when they'd held each other, even if her motives were entirely different from his.

Standing outside the door, he suddenly realised that Kate's hand had slipped into his. It was tiny and totally lost in his palm. He glanced at her but she stared ahead at the front door. He squeezed her hand and was sure he saw the faint traces of a nervous smile beginning to crack at the edges of her mouth.

Thomas opened the door and stepped inside the house, almost having to tug Kate to follow him. There were voices coming from the front room and he automatically began creeping along the corridor, though when Kate closed the door noisily he stopped, knowing that it had announced their presence. He decided to take the initiative by opening the door and walking into the room. Monsignor Dolan sat in his usual chair while Mister Walsh sat opposite him. He stood up when he saw Thomas and Kate.

'It's good to see you again, Father Costello,' he said, holding out a hand, which Thomas took reluctantly, having let go of Kate when he stepped into the room.

'And you must introduce me to your . . . companion.'

Everyone looked round at Kate, who blushed and stared down at her feet.

'This is . . .' Thomas began.

'Miss Riordan is one of our parishioners,' Monsignor Dolan said, now standing up. Walsh bowed slightly.

'So what brings you're here this time, Mister Walsh?' Thomas asked, hoping his voice didn't sound too nervous.

'Your brother, Father Costello. As always.'

'My brother? What's he done now?'

'Just being a nuisance as usual,' said Walsh with a smile.

'Well, that's Mick for you.'

'It certainly is. But I was just wondering, Father Costello, whether you'd like to see him?'

# 25

## REVELATIONS

Kate felt like they were re-tracing the footsteps that she and Thomas had just left behind when they'd headed back despondently to St Alphonsus'. Walsh led the way while Thomas followed at his shoulder. Kate had to keep breaking into a jog to catch up with him and a couple of times she tugged his sleeve to make him slow down. He would do so for a few steps, usually muttering an apology at the same time before speeding up again. Eventually she grabbed hold of his hand and allowed him to almost pull her along. She was sure a few curious eyes watched them. Anyone who recognised the priest would be surprised to see him walking hand in hand with a girl. Anyone who knew her, and knew her past, would be shocked.

At some point on their journey, a couple of men had joined them without her noticing, and they remained a few steps behind. They were obviously with Walsh and Kate suddenly felt like she and Thomas were prisoners being led off to jail, even though they had done nothing wrong.

'Where are we going?' Thomas shouted at Walsh, but he either didn't hear or pretended not to because he didn't answer. Kate squeezed Thomas' hand and when he glanced round at her she mouthed the same question to him. He whispered something in reply but she couldn't make out what he said.

She was nervous about seeing Mick. More than that, she was worried. After what had happened the last time Walsh had captured him, she wondered what would greet her when she saw him again. Whatever Walsh had done on the ship had scared Mick so much that he wouldn't talk about it. She tried to persuade him, encourage him – she even threatened not to have sex with him unless he told her – but she could tell that, no matter what she tried, he was going to remain silent. The temptation was to let her imagination run wild, but that would only upset her. She'd seen enough terrible deeds herself to know exactly how wicked people could be and she couldn't bear the thought of Mick suffering. Why did he have to keep getting himself caught?

Kate mentally blessed herself as she remembered what had happened to some of the other girls she used to work with. She didn't want to let go of Thomas' hand, which was comforting at the same time as being useful in pulling her along.

They arrived outside St Mary's and Walsh strode confidently to the chapel house, knocking loudly on the door, which was opened almost immediately as if he'd been expected. It wasn't a priest who stood aside, holding the door open while they all walked in, and Kate presumed it was another one of Walsh's men.

He led the way up the stairs, taking them two at a time, and stopped outside one of the bedrooms. He knocked on the door – two quick knocks which were greeted by two from the other side, and then he knocked a further three times. A key clicked in the lock and the door opened. Soon they were all inside the bedroom – Walsh, Thomas, Kate, the two men who'd walked with them from St Alphonsus' and two guards who'd already been in the room. And then there was Mick.

He sat up in bed, arms folded, smoking a cigarette that nearly fell out of his mouth when he saw Kate and Thomas. Kate wanted to rush over and tend the wound on the side of his head – a large bump covered in dried blood – but she thought the guards would have tried to stop her, so instead she began to inch her way towards him, hoping they wouldn't notice so quickly. Even if they did pull her away from him, at least she'd have time to leave the imprint of her lips on his. She had let go of Thomas' hand and he stood at the foot of the bed. He nodded at his brother, who nodded back, slowly and painfully. Kate was at the side of the bed now, facing Walsh who stood with his arms folded and grinning.

'I brought you some visitors,' he said as Mick took a deep draw on his cigarette. 'Just so that you can say goodbye.'

He turned to face Thomas, still wearing the same grin that Kate knew would always haunt her.

'And I've taken no chances, Father Costello, as you can see,' he said, nodding towards the guards. 'We don't want any fake priests turning up and trying to rescue this man, do we? Even the Brotherhood wouldn't shed blood here, in this place of God.'

Kate was now at Mick's side and discreetly placed her hand on top of his, smiling when she caught his grateful eye.

'How romantic,' Walsh said. 'You certainly have a way with the ladies, Mick. I'll give you that at least.'

Kate wondered why they hadn't bothered tying Mick up if he was their prisoner. He'd escaped so many times before she thought Walsh would be worried it would happen again but he didn't seem at all concerned. Perhaps it was the fact there were four guards in the room that gave him the necessary sense of security. Still, she was grateful if only because it meant they were able to hold hands, which Walsh and the guards were happy to ignore.

'I just want to know why,' Thomas said. 'What's he done that's so bad you've hunted him all the way from Galway to Glasgow?'

'You really want to know?' Walsh asked.

Thomas nodded and Walsh laughed.

'Forget about it, Thomas,' Mick said as he flicked his cigarette onto the floor. 'It doesn't matter.'

'Of course it matters,' said Thomas. 'They tried to get you in Ireland and they burned our family out of our home. He's followed you here and hunted you down, no matter how many times you've managed to get away. So, yes, it does matter and I want to know.'

'Just leave it,' Mick muttered as he let go of Kate's hand and folded his arms. He was chewing his bottom lip nervously.

'Well, I think your brother has a right to know,' said Walsh. 'And your young lady, too.'

'Leave her out of it,' Mick snapped. 'She's got nothing to do with any of this.'

'Why don't you tell them, Mick?' Walsh said.

All eyes were on Mick now, who shook his head angrily. Kate tried to take his hand again, but he snatched it away.

'Sorry,' he immediately said.

'I love you,' she whispered, surprised at her own words, but he shook his head, which was not the reaction she'd been expecting.

'So are you going to tell them or shall I?' Walsh said.

Mick shrugged. 'I'm sorry,' he said again to Kate.

Walsh walked slowly over to the window and stared out for a few minutes. Kate's eyes darted between him and Mick, who was glaring at Walsh's back, throwing imaginary daggers at it. Walsh turned round and folded his arms.

'Now, where should I start?'

'Just get it over with, Walsh,' Mick said with a sigh.

'Okay. Her name was Agnes . . .'

Walsh began telling his tale while everyone watched him except Kate who kept her eyes on Mick the whole time, knowing she'd be able to tell instantly from his reaction whether what was being said was true or not.

'You'll know who I'm talking about,' Walsh said to Thomas. 'You remember Agnes Flaherty?'

Thomas nodded.

'And of course you'll have heard what happened – the heroic lovers who gave their lives for Ircland.'

Kate glanced at Thomas who nodded again while Mick looked away, not wanting to catch his brother's eye.

Walsh explained for Kate's benefit that Agnes Flaherty lived in the next village from Mick and Thomas. She was a girl who could turn heads from a mile away and many a young man found himself drawn towards her cottage, only to be chased away by her father, who issued threats as to what would happen to them if they were ever to re-appear. Charlie Flaherty was a giant who could flatten a man with a single punch, so his words carried some weight. More than that, he was a big man in the Irish Republican Brotherhood, so you crossed him at your peril.

Agnes was a good girl, so far as her father knew, a daughter not to be promised to any young heifer on heat that turned up. It would only be an Irishman of good, upstanding republican credentials who would be considered and even then there was still no guarantee that Charlie would approve. What Charlie didn't know, however, was that Agnes had fallen in love. James Lyons had been in her class at primary school, and while they had lost contact when their schooling finished, a chance meeting at the Galway City Fair had sparked a romance that, though secret, was fired by their youthful passions.

'James Lyons was my nephew,' Walsh said. 'He was my sister's only child.'

It seemed like no one knew about the secret romance, Walsh explained, apart from him. His nephew had confided in him, asking for advice. James knew there was no chance that Charlie Flaherty would give his daughter's hand to a man whose uncle took the Queen's shilling. So they were faced with two choices – never see each other again or leave Ireland forever. Since the first choice was unbearable to both of them, they began planning their escape to America, with Walsh helping them.

It was also around this time that the Brotherhood suffered a number of setbacks, Walsh told them. An ambush on an army patrol had gone wrong, and three of their men had been killed in a shoot-out with soldiers, while a number of others had been arrested. The Brotherhood suspected an informer and suspicion gripped the organisation.

'And my nephew just happened to be in the wrong place at the wrong time,' Walsh said. 'He was caught near Flaherty's croft, hiding in the hills. They thought he was spying on the cottage while he was only waiting for Agnes.'

'But he was your informer,' Mick said and Walsh held up his hands in mock surrender.

'Everything has its price,' he said in an almost confessional tone. 'And the price James had to pay for my help in arranging passage for him and Agnes to America was some information. She would tell him who'd been visiting, anything she saw or heard at the cottage, and he would pass it on to me. I thought it would work – it was working – for the time it took to help them get to America, but then James had to go and get caught.'

There was a hint of remorse in Walsh's voice and Kate studied him as he composed himself before continuing his story. James was not a strong character – 'He had the soft heart of a mammy's boy,' Walsh said – and it did not take the Brotherhood long to find out the source of his information. Then they told Charlie Flaherty.

'I don't know exactly what was said,' Walsh said. 'All I know is that Charlie warned that there would be much blood spilt between former comrades if anyone tried to take his daughter. The Brotherhood was anxious to avoid a civil war and so a compromise was reached. Charlie Flaherty and his family were to be banished from Ireland, and never allowed to return. And this is where our very own Michael Costello enters the story.'

Kate stared at Mick who held his head in his hands.

'I need a cigarette,' he muttered and she was surprised when it was Walsh who offered one from the small silver case he produced from his coat pocket, before striking a match off the wall behind Mick's head and holding it close to his face until the cigarette was lit. Mick drew deeply and then filled the room with smoke.

'I didn't know,' he said to Kate, stretching over and taking her hand. 'I swear to you, Kate. I didn't know what they were going to do.'

'It's a bit late to be claiming innocence,' Walsh laughed. 'Let me tell the rest of the story and leave your pleading for God. He's the only one you'll really need forgiveness from and I wouldn't hold my breath as far as that's concerned.'

Kate kept hold of Mick's hand but now she was desperate to hear what Walsh had to say. There was a sick feeling in her stomach, but still she gave Mick's hand a reassuring squeeze, which he quickly returned.

Charlie Flaherty's family had been given fourteen days to leave Ireland, Walsh explained, and as the family tried to make plans for where they would go, selling what they could to raise money, they remained virtual prisoners in their own home. Charlie didn't want to let any of them out of his sight, especially Agnes who he knew was still in danger. They already had James and he knew what they'd do to him.

The day before they were due to leave, there was a visitor to the Flaherty's house. It was someone they trusted, the son of one of Charlie's oldest friends, who had since passed away. Not only that, but it was someone who grew up with Agnes, who had gone to school with her, sitting in the same classroom as her and James Lyons. At one point, Charlie and his father had spoken, only half in jest, of the great and proud union that the two would make in years to come when they grew up. So Charlie Flaherty opened the door and let Michael Costello into his cottage.

'You were only there to say goodbye. Is that not right, Mick? Isn't that what you told Charlie?' asked Walsh.

Mick said nothing.

'So after having made those final farewells to the family, he asked to speak to Agnes. Charlie hadn't let her across the door since he'd found out what she'd done, but now he relented. After all, it was Mick Costello, someone he could trust. He warned them not to go far and then closed the door on his daughter for the last time.'

There was silence in the room for a few moments. Kate snatched her hand away as Mick shook his head while Walsh stood grinning. Kate wanted to slap Mick. She wanted to run away and plunge into the Clyde to cleanse herself of his smell and touch and taste on her body. But she didn't move, though she couldn't meet his eyes, which she knew were fixed on her.

'But I don't understand,' Thomas said, breaking the tension in the room. 'It was the army that shot them both when they attacked Galway Barracks. So how could that be the case when he was working for you and she . . . well, when Mick had . . .' Thomas couldn't bring himself to complete the sentence.

'I didn't bloody kill her,' Mick said.

'But you're not exactly innocent either, are you, Mick?' Walsh said.

Mick had delivered Agnes to the Brotherhood, Walsh explained. Just yards from the cottage they were waiting for her and then she was gone.

'We searched everywhere,' he said. 'Every safe house or farm that Charlie knew about, but there was no trace of her or James. It was like they'd vanished off the face of the earth. And then, about a week later, came the first package, one to Charlie and one to my sister. You've heard of the three wise monkeys, Father?' Walsh asked. Thomas nodded but Kate looked puzzled.

'Hear no evil, see no evil, speak no evil,' Thomas mumbled.

'Exactly,' said Walsh. 'And that was the message the Brotherhood wanted to deliver just in case anyone else was thinking of betraying them. So in a little box that was delivered to my sister was her son's ear. The same thing was sent to Charlie, a bloody reminder of his daughter. My sister was shocked – we needed to get the doctor for her – and she couldn't understand why anyone would do such a thing, but Charlie Flaherty knew. He got the message loud and clear and he waited for the other packages to arrive.'

'Oh my God,' Thomas said, blessing himself and staring in horror at his brother.

'I didn't do it,' Mick said.

'Do what?' Kate asked, tugging on Thomas' arm. The priest looked at Walsh, almost pleading with him to finish the story, not wanting to be the one to explain to Kate what had happened.

'One week after the ears were sent, my sister and Charlie Flaherty each received a bloodied eye. See no evil. And seven days later came the final package. Charlie knew without opening it that it contained his daughter's tongue. I made sure that my sister never got to see the other two deliveries, sparing her at least some of the horror.'

Kate couldn't speak. She stared at Mick. The thought that he might have killed the girl had been shocking enough but to have been part of this butchery was too much to bear. She couldn't comprehend how this man who had lain naked on top of her, under her, beside her, at times a gentle lover, at other times powerful and strong, yet never selfish or inconsiderate and certainly never violent, could be capable of such a thing. Hadn't she told him just minutes before that she loved him?

'I didn't do it,' Mick said, almost pleading now.

'But the shooting?' Thomas asked at last.

'Now that was genius,' said Walsh. He explained how the two of them had been tied to a cart. Then the Brotherhood drove it as near to the barracks as they could before thrashing the horse, which bolted straight for the front gate. They'd also fastened pieces of wood to their hands that the soldiers had mistakenly believed were guns. Thinking they were under attack, the soldiers opened fire, and since neither James nor Agnes could cry out for help or shout a warning, they drove straight to their deaths.

'Not only did the Brotherhood get two traitors killed but they also got themselves a couple of martyrs at the same time. As I said, Father, it was genius.'

There was silence in the room now except for Kate's gentle sobs. She had backed away from the bed and stood beside Thomas, who stared at his brother. Mick's head remained bowed.

'I didn't do it,' he kept muttering until Thomas turned away and walked over to the window.

'That's true, Mick,' said Walsh. 'You didn't actually slice off their ears or take out their eyes or cut out their tongues . . .'

'I think I'm going to be sick,' said Kate.

'. . . But you've still got their blood on your hands. The minute you lured Agnes out of that cottage you became as guilty as the monsters who did carry out the attack.'

'But if he didn't actually do anything to them, why do you want him so badly?' Thomas asked.

'Charlie Flaherty is a broken man,' Walsh said. 'Can you imagine what that must be like to lose your daughter, and know that it was people you considered to be friends who mutilated her like that? No, I don't suppose you could ever know, Father. But trust me when I tell you she was a beautiful girl, as fair as any girl in Ireland. God only knows the mess that pretty face was in when they'd finished with her.'

Walsh sighed. 'But Charlie is also a vengeful man. What money he'd gathered for his escape he has given me to find the person who betrayed his daughter and delivered her to his former comrades. He wants to see Mick Costello swing for what he did and he's made it worth my while to make sure he gets his wish.'

'What about the men who actually carried out this . . . this horror?'

'Two of them are already dead,' Walsh said, 'shot in another attack, while another is in a Galway jail counting down the hours to his own death. Now I have your brother and after that, I just need the man who was in charge.'

Kate moved forward and Mick flinched, anticipating the blow. When it didn't come he looked up nervously. She spat at him, a silent and venomous attack.

'I didn't do it,' Mick said, not bothering to wipe the spit away. 'I swear to you, Kate. I didn't know what they were going to do. I only thought they'd scare her, shave her hair off at worse. I didn't know they were going to do that to her.'

'But why? Why did you help them?'

'You don't say no to the Brotherhood, Kate. You just don't.'

Kate was crying now, silent tears running down her cheeks.

'He is right,' Walsh said. 'They can be difficult to turn down. Is that not so, Father?' he said, looking at Thomas, who blushed. 'So now that I have your brother, I just have one more man to find and I already have a name, so that should be helpful,' he added, patting Mick's cheek playfully.

'Who are you looking for?' Thomas asked.

'Dan Foley. He was the man in charge. He killed my nephew and Agnes Flaherty, and he is going to pay for that.'

# 26

## POWERS OF PERSUASION

Thomas and Kate stood outside St Mary's. Neither of them had said anything when they were led out of the chapel house by one of Walsh's men. Thomas had said a prayer in the room, telling his brother that he would pray for his soul while Kate had stood silently at the door, avoiding all eye contact with Mick, even though he kept pleading with her, muttering her name over and over again. It felt like the final goodbye and Mick had the look of a man resigned to his fate. The fight had finally gone out of him and all he could say as they left the room was, 'Sorry.'

'I think you should go back to Eileen's,' Thomas said without looking at Kate.

'What's the point?'

'He's still looking for you – Duffy.'

Kate shrugged but made no attempt to move.

'I'll come round and see you later,' Thomas said. 'I've got someone I need to speak to right now.'

Kate started to walk away while Thomas stood with his hands in his pocket, watching her, still wanting to shout her name and stop her. Then he'd run to her and hold her and tell her how he really felt and see what the consequences of that would be. He shook his head, knowing it probably wouldn't end well for him, certainly not the way he imagined or hoped it would. He kept watching her until she disappeared out of sight and then he headed off in the opposite direction towards the city centre, taking no more than ten minutes to reach the Cathedral.

The Chancellor's office was a small room beside the sacristy and Thomas walked in without knocking. Father McNeill looked up, startled at the unexpected intrusion and started to speak but Thomas strode over to his desk and punched him in the face, sending him sprawling across the floor. The blow stunned the priest, who slowly began pushing himself up onto his knees, but Thomas stepped forward and planted a kick in his ribs, knocking him back to the floor.

Father McNeill groaned but remained lying on the ground, apparently sensing very quickly that any attempt to move would provoke further attack.

'You told Walsh about my brother,' Thomas said, standing over him.

'Are you going to let me up?' Father McNeill mumbled.

Thomas took a step back and slowly the Chancellor dragged himself to his feet. His nose was bleeding and he wiped it with a handkerchief from his pocket. He sat on his chair and patted down his hair instinctively.

'You betrayed my brother,' Thomas said and Father McNeill smiled.

'I'll wipe that grin off your face,' Thomas snapped, stepping forward. The Chancellor flinched. 'So what have you got to say for yourself?'

'You have no idea what's going on, do you?' Father McNeill said with a sigh.

'I know why Walsh wants my brother and he's got him too, thanks to you.'

'Do you think I care about your brother? This is about the future of the Church, you fool, and if one thick Irishman has to pay with his life, then it's a price worth paying.'

Thomas punched him again and the Chancellor was back on the floor. He lay there and groaned. There was a strange exhilaration flowing through Thomas' body and he was slightly shocked at how much he enjoyed hitting Father McNeill. Once again, the other priest dragged himself to his feet and then dropped onto his chair.

'You're finished,' he said, examining the handkerchief now saturated with blood.

'So I've nothing to lose,' Thomas said. 'I'm not leaving until you explain yourself.'

Father McNeill shrugged and his shoulders were still moving when Thomas hit him again, his hardest punch yet. The priest seemed to fly off his seat and he crashed off the wall at the back of the room, his skull cracking off the stone façade. He lay perfectly still as Thomas knelt over him, quickly checking that the other man was still alive.

'God forgive you,' Father McNeill muttered.

'I'm sure he will,' Thomas said, leaning over until he was close to the other man's face. 'This isn't going to stop unless you talk,' he whispered. 'That's a promise.'

He grabbed the Chancellor roughly and dragged him to his feet where he stood unsteadily, looking dazed. Thomas guided him to the seat while he sat on the desk directly in front of the other man, slapping his face a few times to get his attention, making sure that each blow carried more force than the previous one to remind the other man what awaited him should he remain silent.

Father McNeill kept trying to move his head out of reach of the blows but he wasn't able to and soon a bright red glow began to appear on either cheek.

'Enough,' he muttered, but Thomas kept slapping him. The Chancellor held up his right hand, nodding weakly.

'This had better be the truth,' Thomas said.

'You will regret this, Thomas. I swear,' Father McNeill said.

Thomas slapped him again, hard and the other man cried out.

'Hurry up, Angus.'

'This is bigger than you or me, or even your stupid brother.' The Chancellor braced himself for the expected blow but it never came. 'This is about the future of the Church.'

Thomas shook his head dismissively.

'There are people who do not like our presence in this city or

232

indeed this country,' Father McNeill said. 'And they would like nothing better than to wipe us off the face of the earth.'

'A bit over-dramatic, don't you think?'

The Chancellor raised his eyebrows and shook his head.

'So imagine that someone comes to the Archbishop and says that a group of Irish republicans are living in the city, plotting and planning against the government. They want the Archbishop's help to find out who these men are and what they're up to. Now the Church does not get involved in politics, and Irish politics is a murky world full of people you'd cross the road to avoid, so the Archbishop politely declines . . . which turns out to be the wrong answer.'

'What do you mean, the wrong answer?' Thomas asked.

'Just to make sure the Archbishop knows how important it is to help, he's told that if he doesn't, he'll be arrested on charges of plotting with these men, the Church's property will be seized and the credibility of the clergy destroyed forever when he's found guilty of treason and hung for his crime.'

'Walsh said this to the Archbishop?'

Father McNeill laughed and then began choking, spitting a mouthful of blood on the floor before wiping his mouth on his sleeve.

'Walsh has got nothing to do with this. He just happened to be in the city at the same time and helping him was a good way for the Archbishop to show his willingness to do the right thing. No, this goes much higher than Walsh. Much, much higher.'

The two priests stared at each other, and Thomas could sense that Father McNeill suddenly felt in a stronger position, even though he'd still realise that a wrong word could lead to another fist in his face. The Chancellor had always believed that information was power and he certainly gave the impression of knowing more than Thomas. He could have wasted time thinking about who had approached the Archbishop – how 'high' did it go – but it would only distract him from what he'd come for in the first place, and time was running out.

'I need you to help my brother,' he said.

Father McNeill looked at him with amazement, leaning back slightly and trying to put himself out of range of Thomas' arm.

'I have something Walsh wants and I can help him get it, but the price is Mick.'

'You're a fool, Thomas. You are well in over your head as it is. Get out while you still can.'

'Well, here's the deal, Angus. I'm going to go home now and I will do one of two things. I will either get Mister Walsh what he wants or I will let it be known what you've been up to. By my reckoning, you'll have about two or three hours at most to get out of the city after that. And trust me when I say that what these people will do to you won't be pleasant.'

'You're making a big mistake, Thomas,' Father McNeill said.

'Just do it, Angus. Go and speak to Walsh now. If you don't, you'll regret it.'

There was silence for a few minutes and Thomas could feel his heart racing. What if the Chancellor said no? He had nothing left to offer and nothing else to threaten him with. The Church wouldn't care whether Mick lived or died. He knew that and he also realised that they might call his bluff. Would anyone believe him if he revealed what the Church had been up to? He was just one voice and might not be heard. He could tell Padraig Clarke but then he'd have to admit his own role and the fact he'd been spying on the meetings and he knew the Brotherhood were an unforgiving group.

It didn't help that he had to plead with Father McNeill. The simmering animosity that had always existed between the two men loitered in the room and the fact that Thomas had also attacked the Chancellor didn't help his argument. Part of him was now cursing the fact that they had never got on and that he had made little or no effort to be friendly, but he didn't think it would have made any difference.

'Okay,' Father McNeill said at last.

'Thank you,' said Thomas, trying not to sound surprised.

'I will speak to Mister Walsh and I'll tell him you'll help him, but that's as much as I can do. I can't promise you that he'll agree.'

'Just tell him I can help him find what he's looking for.'

Thomas started to walk towards the door when Father McNeill spoke up.

'Since you know just about everything now, you may as well know this too. It was Monsignor Dolan who kept me informed about your brother. I knew where he was all the time.'

Thomas stared at the Chancellor, who grinned, revealing bloodstained teeth. Then he rushed forward and punched him one final time.

# 27

## TEA AND SYMPATHY

Kate felt like she'd been stuck in Eileen's house forever. It had only been four days since she'd seen Mick and found out what he'd done but it felt like an eternity. Minutes dragged towards each hour and every new day seemed to take an age to arrive. Thomas had visited her that same night and made her promise to stay in the house until he was sure it would be safe for her to leave the city. After what had happened to his brother, being chased and captured on his first day at work, he didn't want to take any chances with her. Kate appreciated the fact that he seemed to care, but she noticed he blushed when she thanked him. He did that a lot, she realised, presuming he wasn't used to daily contact with women.

She kept hoping he would visit again, if only to break the monotony of each day, but no one ever appeared at the door. Eileen's time was occupied with her kids, though once or twice she had nervously asked if everything was okay. Kate didn't know how she even could begin to tell her story and she wasn't sure that Eileen would either care or understand anyway, but since it did not have a happy ending, she didn't want to speak about it. She told Eileen she was fine and that seemed to be enough reassurance for the other woman to go back to what she had been doing before.

Thomas had told her it would take about a week to arrange everything. He wanted to be sure that when she did go, he would not be left with the burden of worrying whether or not she was safe. Kate realised that she would miss the priest. She'd always presumed all of them would judge, condemn and keep their distance from her, but he had done none of those things and she was glad. She knew it was because of his brother that Thomas had been like that, but it still felt nice to be treated as a normal person. She would thank him again before she left and she didn't care how red his face turned when she did.

Mick still occupied most of her thoughts, however. It didn't matter that she couldn't forget what had happened to Agnes Flaherty, it wasn't easy just to change her feelings for him. She wanted to fill her head with happy memories of everything they did together but instead all she seemed to feel was a gnawing pain in her stomach. She was never going to see him again. He was probably dead already, she realised. Walsh wouldn't have wasted any time in getting him back to Ireland and she kept trying to picture him lying in bed, a cigarette in his mouth and laughing, to try and push out the image of him swinging from a rope.

Kate blessed herself as she thought of Agnes. The girl was probably the same age as her and Walsh had said she was beautiful. What must she have felt as they took a knife to her face? Kate shuddered at the thought. Maybe they started on James and she had been forced to watch, suffering as the love of her life had his ear cut off, his screams as painful to her as any physical blow they might have delivered to her. Yet, even as she saw what they did to James, could she have realised they were going to do the same to her? She was a girl, after all, and Charlie Flaherty's daughter, too. She had known these men, had seen them many times in her home plotting and planning with her father, or even just drinking tea and smoking and telling jokes that were probably too rude for a young girl to hear.

Kate stood up and busied herself making a pot of tea, even though she was the only one in the house. She needed to do something, otherwise the thoughts swirling in her head would drive her crazy.

Yet Agnes Flaherty was never far from her mind. She guessed that the couple would have been barely alive by the time it came to taking their tongues out; Kate swallowed hard at the thought. They'd probably have been out of their minds as well, horribly mutilated and in constant pain, all of which was compounded by the fact they'd seen the other suffer as well. They would have both prayed for death to come and ease their pain. He would have asked God to take her and she would have done the same for him. It would have been their last act of love, to have pleaded that the other's suffering would be over. At least that's how Kate imagined it would have been, though she realised they would most likely have used up any prayers for themselves.

'Mick couldn't have known.' Kate kept telling herself that over and over again, her voice rising in anger to fill the whole house, because she could see him walking side by side with Agnes, the sound of the cottage door closing ringing in his ear, and she imagined the girl's voice, excited and relieved to be outside, at least for a few minutes and she would have filled the air with hopes and regrets and thanks to Mick for this small act of kindness. All the while he would have pretended to be listening, knowing he was leading her towards something terrible.

'Mick couldn't have known,' she said again. It still didn't mean he wasn't guilty, she decided, and she could understand why Charlie Flaherty had wanted his revenge. Wouldn't her father have done the same? Though, she wasn't actually sure what the answer to that really was since he had no idea of her life in Glasgow and had never shown any inclination to find out.

Kate thought back to the first time she had met Mick, closing her eyes and picturing the scar on his shoulder that looked like a map of Ireland. She had loved that scar and she would miss it, just as she would miss the rest of him as well. It did matter what he had done and she just couldn't forget what she'd been told, but how do you stop loving someone just like that? The feeling had crept up on her so unexpectedly. She had never thought she'd find it in this city, and she'd resigned herself to the life she led, her main concern trying to stay alive from day to day, but he had offered her hope. Perhaps there was a life out there for her that would let her escape, and for a couple of months at least she'd been able to pretend that this was the case. Every day they had made love or slept beside each other, or talked of everything and nothing, making grand plans or just talking nonsense, had seemed to her like the life she deserved to have. Now, that hope was swinging from the end of a rope in Galway and it still left her heart feeling crushed.

'Mick couldn't have known,' she whispered as a stray tear escaped from the corner of her eye and crawled down her cheek.

She knew she wasn't going back to her old life, however. That was gone for good and she was determined that a new city would mean a new start. She also realised that if she did go back, Duffy would kill her. He'd done it to plenty of girls in the past – she didn't even remember all their names – and he'd think nothing of doing it to her. Duffy always warned that she couldn't hide from him, but she still hoped that he wouldn't come after her.

'You'll be safe in Liverpool,' Thomas had told her. 'My friend has arranged a job as a maid for you, with somewhere to stay as well, and as far as anyone knows, you've just arrived from Donegal. There will be no mention of Glasgow to anyone.'

Kate had finished her tea – it seemed like that's all she did these days. The only other times she'd drunk that much tea was whenever someone had died back home. The house was as tidy as it could possibly get, yet she unmade her mattress and then began slowly to smooth out the cover and fold it across the bed again.

She'd just finished patting down the pillow when there was a knock on the door. Perhaps this was the day when she was to leave and Thomas was here to take her safely to the train station? Now that it had finally arrived, she realised she was glad to be leaving Glasgow. There was nothing to keep her here anymore and the city just seemed to be crammed full of unhappy memories for her. It was time for a new beginning and there was a spring in her step as she headed for the door, looking forward to seeing Thomas again and now eager to be on her way. What belongings she did own were already packed into a small case that

Mrs Breslin had given to her, so she was ready to go now. She wouldn't even bother waiting to say goodbye to Eileen. Thomas could do that later, along with her gratitude for having given her a safe place to stay.

Kate opened the door and saw a ghost.

'Hello, Kate.'

She stumbled back, still hanging onto the door handle and Mick gripped her free arm to steady her. She knew it was Mick from the fresh cut on his temple and the arm which still hung loosely at his side, though he did not smile the way he always had before whenever he saw her. His pupils darted nervously in their sockets, not keen to catch her own gaze, where before he'd always stared into her eyes and told her they were so beautiful he would gladly have died a happy man at that very moment.

'Can I come in?' he said and she nodded, still trying to find her voice.

He guided her over to the table and she sat down. He took the seat opposite her and lit a cigarette with trembling fingers. She ran her hands through her hair and stared at him through the cloud of smoke that now enveloped him. Was he really here in this room with her or was it a dream? She'd heard stories of people being visited by their loved ones just after they'd passed away, the dead returning to bid their final farewells before continuing their journey to wherever it was they ended up – heaven, though in Mick's case, she doubted that's where he'd go.

'How are you?' he said.

She stretched out a hand and touched his arm, running her fingers up and down it before nipping the skin. He flinched but there was also the flicker of a grin that appeared on his face. He was real. He felt real. She wouldn't have been able to touch a ghost, and could ghosts smoke? Still, she couldn't find her voice and just shook her head a few times.

'I'm so sorry,' he said.

She looked at him again, more closely this time, almost demanding that he meet her gaze and hold it. Eventually, she blinked and looked away.

'What for?' she whispered.

'What do you mean?'

'What are you sorry for?'

'For everything. For not telling you the whole story, for getting you involved.'

'For Agnes?'

'Of course, for Agnes.'

Kate sighed and sat back. How could someone she'd pictured dangling from the gallows now be sitting here beside her, so close that she could almost kiss him without even having to lean in? There was part of her that wanted to do just that and her heart felt like it was doing somersaults. Yet, he might think everything was okay then and that he'd been forgiven and that wasn't the case either.

'How . . . how did you escape?'

'I didn't. They let me go.'

'What?'

'Well, sort of,' Mick said with a shrug. 'I've got about a week before they come after me again.'

'Who?'

'Walsh.'

'But he already had you. Why did he let you go?'

'They caught Dan Foley,' he said. 'Thomas helped them.'

'Is he okay?'

'Who?'

'Thomas?'

'He's fine,' said Mick. 'God knows how many times he's saved my life now, but I know I'll never be able to pay him back.'

'I thought that was him just now, at the door,' said Kate. 'He's got me a job and a room in Liverpool.'

'I know.'

'So why did they let you go?' Kate asked, tugging his arm and then keeping her hand on it.

'Thomas made a deal with them that if they let me go, he'd tell them where Dan Foley was.'

'So you're free now? It's all over?'

'Not quite,' Mick said. 'Walsh was paid to bring me back to Ireland, remember? And that's what he's still planning to do. So he's given me a few days' head start. He's in Ireland now with Foley, and when that's all finished, he's coming back over here to get me.'

'Oh God.'

'Don't worry. I'll be long gone from here by then. He'll not find me again.'

Kate sat back and for a few minutes there was silence in the room. Mick had finished one cigarette and immediately lit another one and she found the smell of the smoke strangely comforting, breathing it in deeply as it swirled around her head. There were a million and one questions dancing in her head though she couldn't get any of them out, and all the time she kept thinking of Agnes and James, which would make her angry at Mick. Then she'd remember how he made her feel and how she longed to kiss that map of Ireland just one more time, and it pushed her mind into turmoil.

It was like she was thinking about two different men, though if was as easy as that, then she'd be able to forget about the Mick who had delivered Agnes Flaherty to her inevitable death, and just concentrate on the Mick who made her laugh and smile and feel like the most beautiful girl in the world. She wanted to go back to when it was just the two of them in the chapel house, lying in bed. She'd be resting her head on his chest as it rose and fell; he was in a contented sleep while she was glad to be awake, knowing that her dreams would not make her as happy as the way she felt right at that very minute.

Would she ever be that happy again? Would anyone love her the way Mick did, and could she bear to go through all that just to find out that, at the end of it all, there was only pain?

'I want you to come with me,' he said at last.

She stared at him, but couldn't think of anything to say.

'I'm going back to Ireland,' he said.

'Ireland? Are you crazy? They'll catch you for sure if you do that.'

Mick grinned and Kate felt another somersault in her heart.

'Well, I figure Walsh will come back here and then, when he can't find me, he'll head for Liverpool and then London. He'll never think to look for me in Ireland. As you say, who'd be crazy enough to go back there?'

'You're not going home, though?'

'I have a cousin who's a farmer in Cork. There'll be work for me there.'

Kate shook her head, but she couldn't help smiling. He was a daft Galway boy but his plan just about made sense. As long as she knew he was safe, then she'd feel better, even if the Irish Sea continued to separate them.

'So will you come with me then?'

She shrugged.

'I know I don't deserve another chance, Kate,' he said. 'And I won't blame you for saying no but I love you and I don't want to spend another minute without you, never mind the rest of my life.'

'But what you did . . .'

'I know, and I'll never forgive myself, so I don't blame you not forgiving me either. But I want you to come with me. I need you to come with me.'

'I don't know . . .'

'Please, Kate.'

She looked at him again, and there was a tiny spark in his eyes that she locked onto, knowing it was something to treasure. Thomas had arranged a new life for her in Liverpool and that was the sensible choice to make, but it would be a lonely life with little or no prospect of that ever changing. She didn't think she'd ever forget what Mick had done, and she wasn't sure she'd ever really forgive him, but she also knew that she'd never be able to get that map of Ireland out of her mind.

'So will you come with me then?' he asked.

She sighed. 'I'll put the kettle on and we'll have a cup of tea and talk about it some more.'

# 28

## HEART AND SOUL

Thomas knew in his mind that this was going to be a day like no other, even though it had started with him waking at seven o'clock in the morning as usual. He lay in bed for ten minutes before pushing himself out from under the covers into the chilly early morning temperature that filled his room. His feet touched the cold wooden floor but he found it strangely invigorating as he almost danced towards the door, heading for the bathroom at the other end of the corridor.

He was always first to get up on Sundays, and that wasn't just because he said eight o'clock Mass. He found it impossible to sleep any longer than his body normally allowed and by the time he had returned from the bathroom, cleansed by the cold water he splashed on his face, he was ready for the day ahead. Still, on both journeys to and from his room, he crept past Monsignor Dolan's door, anxious to avoid provoking the parish priest's anger by waking him before he was ready to get up of his own accord.

Back in his bedroom, Thomas quickly dressed, realising that he only had two more days at St Alphonsus' before he had to leave. It still hadn't quite sunk in yet that he was being sent away to Benbecula. It meant nothing to him. The Archbishop could have as well said Botany Bay or Ellis Island for all the difference it would make. As far as Thomas was concerned, it sounded like the end of the world and he felt like his banishment was taking him away from everything and everyone he cared about.

It was why he knew that today was going to be different, because he had decided to speak up. Now that he was leaving, what was the point of holding everything in? That hadn't done him any good thus far and he was tormented at what could be or even what probably would never be. No more, he had decided while lying in bed last night. Today was a day for finding out. The thought was enough to make him feel sick and his mind continued to wrestle with the positives and negatives of his course of action, even after he'd finished getting dressed and headed down to prepare the church for Mass. He decided against eating anything, fearing that it would only make him sick, though he knew at some point later in the day he might regret it. Then again, he would probably have other things on his mind.

Thomas prepared the altar methodically, laying out the cloths and the candles like it was second nature to him. There were never too many people at the first Mass of the day but whether it was one person or a congregation of a thousand, they all deserved the same effort. He stood behind the altar and looked out into the empty church. Most of the time he had his back to the people as he performed the rituals of holy Mass, ones he'd followed as a boy, taking comfort from the pomp and ceremony of the occasion. That feeling had never left him, even after his ordination, and celebrating Mass remained the highlight of his vocation.

Yet, he couldn't shake off the guilt that now seemed to cling to his body like an unwelcome cloak of stale smoke. For, even as he celebrated Mass and read the Gospel and preached to the people and consecrated the body and blood of Christ, he was thinking of Kate.

Those thoughts slid up and down the scale of impurity, depending, it seemed to Thomas, on how many garments of clothing she wore in his fantasies. The first time he had imagined what it was like to kiss her, he should have immediately headed to the confessional box in the hope that Monsignor Dolan would give him absolution, or at least offer some advice or hope that the feelings would eventually evaporate.

The parish priest had asked for his own absolution for betraying Mick, but Thomas had told him there was no need. The old man was crying as he tried to explain what had happened. He'd been faced with the prospect of his own banishment if he didn't help Father McNeill and, at his age, such a move was a virtual death sentence.

'I'm so sorry, Thomas,' he said.

'Don't be,' Thomas said. 'You've been a good friend and I know you did what you felt you had to do.'

He'd handed Monsignor Dolan a handkerchief to dry his eyes and there was an awkward silence between the two men before Thomas held out his hand.

'I'm going to miss you,' he said, and the Monsignor grasped his hand gratefully, nodding as more tears poured down his cheeks.

Thomas wasn't surprised at his own punishment. He'd been summoned to the Cathedral just a couple of days after his confrontation with Father McNeill and he half expected that he'd be sacked. That would have been a messy option, however, and the Archbishop was much cleverer than that.

Even as he'd strode out of the Chancellor's office, having left him bloodied and battered on the floor of his office, Thomas knew there would be a price to pay. There was no way he would be allowed to challenge the authority of the Church, threaten it even, and then expect to get away with it. So he was leaving Glasgow for good, banished to some God-forsaken place that he'd never heard of.

'You'll like the Western Isles,' the Archbishop had said without looking up at him as he stood before his desk. 'I spent many enjoyable times there before I came to this city. And Father McNeill will put in a good word for you, I'm sure.'

'Yes, Your Grace,' Thomas muttered.

'It can be good to take some time to reflect on life, Thomas,' the Archbishop said. 'Everything seems to move so quickly these days, don't you think? How often do we get the chance to actually sit down and examine our consciences, asking ourselves whether what we did was right or wrong? Benbecula will give you that opportunity.'

'Thank you, Your Grace.'

'Our Church has been around for nearly nineteen hundred years now, Thomas. We endure, sustained by the truth of God's word. It would be a foolish man who'd think he could challenge God's power on earth and that there would be no repercussions for that.'

Thomas nodded. It was just the two of them in the room. There was no sign of Father McNeill, who was normally never too far away from his boss. Perhaps they both feared more violence if Thomas saw the Chancellor again, but he knew that angry moment had long since passed. The Archbishop looked up, tapping the Bible that sat on the desk in front of him.

'Saint Paul, as you know, can be so perceptive,' he said. 'And it was his letter to the Romans which came to mind today . . . "That is why you must not let sin reign in your mortal bodies or command your obedience to bodily passions, why you must not let any part of your body turn into an unholy weapon fighting on the side of sin; you should, instead, offer yourself to God, and consider yourselves dead men brought back to life; you should make every part of your body into a weapon fighting on the side of God, and then sin will no longer dominate your life, since you are living by grace and not by law." '

'Quite appropriate, don't you think?' The Archbishop closed the Bible over and slowly stood up. 'I doubt we'll meet again, Thomas,' holding out his hand. Thomas bowed slowly and then leant forward to kiss the large gold ring on the Archbishop's index finger. 'But you will be in my prayers.'

'Thank you, Your Grace,' Thomas said, even though he didn't believe it.

Thomas was heading for Eileen's house now, feeling nervous and excited and sick all at once. Several times he stopped, trying to calm his breathing, and once he actually turned round and started walking back to St Alphonsus', telling himself that what he'd been about to do was crazy. Yet, he turned back after a few steps and began walking towards the house again. He had to tell her. He knew that in his mind. Whatever else he would do in his life he had to be sure that she knew how he felt. He didn't want to be tortured with regrets, and even though his heart and his head were telling him that it would be a painful experience, he was still charging blindly towards it.

At least he knew his brother was safe, or as safe as he could be. By the time Walsh returned to Glasgow, Mick would be far-gone, back to the one place he'd probably never think of looking for him. Thomas had joked that he should go home to Ireland, but while Mick had laughed at the idea, they both realised that it made sense. Walsh seemed to relish the chase and was confident that he'd catch up with Mick again. He'd not be looking in Cork for a while, thought Thomas with a smile, hoping his brother would be able to keep his head down and out of trouble.

Now there was just Kate. She was going to Liverpool and once she'd boarded that train, he knew he would never see her again. Would he go with her? He hadn't really thought about the future, beyond the next fifteen minutes when he would speak to her, but occasionally he would allow just a hint of optimism to creep into his thoughts, a picture of the two of them together flashing briefly in his mind before it evaporated.

He gently knocked on the door and waited. Kate seemed surprised to see him but stood aside to let him into the room. She walked over to the table and sat down but Thomas paced the room, trying to form the right words in his head before he blurted them out. His nervousness was obvious, and there was still part of his mind telling him just to speak about her imminent departure and then make his excuses and leave.

'Will you not sit down?' Kate said and he nodded, though as he sat, she stood up. 'Are you okay?'

'I'm fine,' he said, almost stumbling over the words.

'You seem a bit on edge.'

'I'm fine.'

'I'll get you a wee cup of tea. That always helps.'

He watched her as she danced round the stove, wondering if this was how it would be if they were together, perhaps with a baby sleeping in the corner or one crying in his arms. It was a picture of a happy family that he knew he shouldn't dare imagine, yet the only alternative for him was a remote Scottish island with about a hundred people and a thousand sheep, where he would count down the years till he died, lonely and unloved.

Kate brought the tea-pot over to the table and then filled two mugs with hot brown liquid, blowing the steam off the top of her own mug and then handing the other one to Thomas, who smiled gratefully. He took a gulp, not even bothering with the fact the tea was still boiling and it burned his mouth and throat. At least the physical pain would take his mind off the mental one he was suffering at this moment.

'I love you,' he mouthed, unable to find his voice but fearing that he would start crying in frustration if he didn't. Kate glanced up at him.

'I love you,' he said, this time out loud. He knew that it was audible and that he'd heard it himself. The look on Kate's face told him she'd heard it too.

'What?' she said, embarrassment creeping over her face like a bright red veil had been drawn across her.

Now was the moment to laugh it off, perhaps offer a lame excuse or try to pretend that he hadn't said anything at all and she had just imagined it. It might make Kate feel less scared than she looked at that moment.

'I love you,' he said again, staring into Kate's eyes as she held his gaze, her eyes piercing his, looking for clues as to whether he was serious or not. She knew, however, within seconds of studying his face, that this was not a joke.

'What did you say?' she mumbled and Thomas presumed she was playing for time or still trying to register the enormity of what he'd just said. He took another gulp of tea. It was still boiling.

'I love you, Kate.'

'But . . . but you're a priest.'

'I know, and I wish I didn't feel like this, God forgive me, but I can't help it.'

'I don't know what to say.'

'I'm leaving Glasgow in a couple of days,' he said.

'Why? Where are you going?'

'It's a long story, but I'm going up north – one of the islands.'

Kate frowned.

'I'm sorry, I shouldn't have said anything,' Thomas mumbled.

'No, it's not that.'

He took a deep breath, knowing that this was the moment.

'When I go to bed every night, you are the last thing I think about before I fall asleep and then when I wake up the next morning, you are the first thing on my mind. I feel sick all the time because I want to see you and hear you speak and make you laugh, and then when I do see you, my heart feels like it's going to explode.'

'But you're a priest.'

Thomas laughed. 'And right now, I wish I wasn't.'

'But Mick . . .'

'He's safe,' said Thomas. 'I managed to get him freed and he's now somewhere they'll never think of looking for him.'

Kate groaned and buried her head in her hands.

'I know it's strange,' said Thomas. 'I'm a priest and then there's you and Mick. He's my brother and I know I shouldn't feel this way about you because you were with him. I shouldn't feel this way about anyone, I know, but I can't help it, Kate. I wish I could but I can't.'

Kate groaned again.

'I love you, Kate.'

'But Mick's still here,' she said.

'No, he's not.'

'Yes, he is.'

'But he's on his way back to Ireland. I left him at the dock with money for a ticket home.'

Kate took Thomas' hand but he pulled it away, seeing the pity in her eyes.

'He came back here . . . for me.'

'What?'

'I'm sorry, Thomas. I'm going home with him.'

Thomas stood up and backed away towards the door, not sure whether to feel angry or embarrassed; he felt like he was going to be sick.

'I love him, Thomas. I'm sorry, but I really do, even after everything he's done.'

Thomas nodded and stood in the middle of the room, head bowed, the colour draining from his face. He closed his eyes and prayed that the ground would open up at that very moment and swallow him. He heard a chair scrape and gentle footsteps approaching him. A hand was on his neck and his head was being pulled down. Still, he kept his eyes closed. Then her lips were on his and they were kissing. At first he wasn't sure what to do, but then he responded and it seemed like the most natural thing in the world. He didn't want to open his eyes and spoil the moment but it felt perfect, better than anything he had ever imagined. It could only have lasted ten seconds at most and then she let him go.

'I'm sorry,' she whispered.

He opened his eyes and looked at her. She was crying.

'So am I,' he said and turned towards the door.

'Thomas, wait!' she said.

'He makes you happy and you make him happy, I know that for sure,' he said. 'It's for the best.'

'I'm so sorry.'

Thomas shook his head. 'It's fine,' he whispered before walking out of the room, resisting the urge to sprint as fast as he could. Instead he walked slowly back to St Mary's, and every few minutes he would touch his lips with his fingertips.

# 29

## PARTING OF THE WAYS

Mick and Kate were already at the train station when they saw Thomas walking towards them. He was carrying a black case, and he would tip his hat every few minutes when he passed someone who offered him a greeting. They watched as the priest approached. Kate hadn't wanted to come to the station but Mick had insisted.

'It's your brother,' she said. 'You don't need me there.'

'But you're practically family,' he laughed, dragging her back into bed as she tried to slip out from under the covers, squeezing her waist until she started giggling.

Still, as they walked towards the city centre, she was quiet and muttered a couple of times about not wanting to be there but Mick just ignored her. They strolled arm in arm, and it seemed to Mick like the sun was tracking them as they made their way to the station. It wasn't a warm day and most people they passed were still wrapped up with hats and scarves and heavy winter coats, but Mick didn't feel any winter chill. He would just glance to his right and catch sight of Kate's black hair, shimmering in the gentle breeze, and he felt as happy as he had ever done in his life.

Even the aches and pains which wracked his body seemed to have eased up ever since Kate said she'd go back to Ireland with him. He didn't know what he would have done if she'd said no but he felt like the luckiest man in the world when she agreed. He had wanted to carry her onto the mattress that very moment, rip off all her clothes and make love to her until they both collapsed with exhaustion, but while she had been happy enough to kiss him, she said she wasn't quite ready for anything else, not after all that she'd heard. He told her he'd wait forever as long as she was with him, though he'd only had to be patient until the following day when Eileen and the kids had left the house. Kate pushed the table up against the door so that no one could burst in unexpectedly and he was almost falling out of his clothes in his eagerness as she led him to bed.

If there were moments when he felt he couldn't be any happier – and he knew it would still be a long time before Kate never mentioned the name of Agnes Flaherty again – there was still sadness that he was having to say goodbye to his brother. Thomas hadn't said anything beyond telling him where he was being sent but Mick guessed it wasn't a request but a punishment. He would miss him. They'd become closer these past couple of months and it now seemed like they were heading to the opposite ends of the world.

Mick knew that they weren't likely to see each other too often in the future, if at all, and it felt strange to think that this might be the last time they'd ever stand face to face. Thomas reached them and automatically tipped his hat.

'Travelling light?' Mick said, nodding at the case.

'I don't think I'll need much where I'm going,' Thomas said.

Mick had never heard of Benbecula before – 'I thought it was a mountain,' he said – and when Thomas described the journey he'd have to make, it did seem like he was heading for another continent. There was a six-hour train journey to Oban, followed by a ten-hour boat trip to get to the island. Even if at some point in the future Mick had any inclination to visit his brother, the length of that journey made it unlikely he'd ever act on it.

'When's the train leaving?' Mick asked as Thomas glanced up at the clock.

'Eleven o'clock,' he said. 'About ten minutes.'

Mick lit up a cigarette in the silence that followed, offering one to Kate and Thomas, though it was only his brother who took one, accepting a light with a grateful nod. They'd both started smoking with roll-ups stolen from their dad's tin when he was lying drunk on the bed, and even when he'd sobered up, he never realised any were missing. Mick smiled at the memory and wondered whether Thomas would remember it too.

'When are you leaving?' Thomas asked Mick, though he looked at Kate.

'Tomorrow morning,' said Mick. 'We'll get the train to Liverpool and then the boat home the next day. I can't wait to get back to Ireland. I've had my fill of this place.'

'I don't think this city will see us again,' Thomas said.

'Will they never let you come back?' Kate asked nervously.

'I don't think so,' Thomas said, shaking his head.

'So why go then?' said Mick 'Just say no. What can they do?'

'I'm a priest. I have to do what I'm told. And there's nothing for me anywhere else, anyway. This is all I know.'

The three of them stood watching the large clock hanging down from the ceiling of the station as the hands slowly crept towards eleven o'clock. With about three minutes to go, Thomas picked up the case at his feet and held out his hand.

'What's that for?' Mick asked.

'Goodbye?'

'We're brothers,' he said. 'Come on,' and he hugged his brother who dropped the case and returned the hug.

'Look after yourself,' Mick said and Thomas nodded.

The priest looked at Kate and then moved forward, giving her a gentle but brief hug.

'Take care,' she whispered.

'And you look after my brother for me,' he said.

Mick and Kate held hands as Thomas moved up the platform, only briefly stopping to look round and wave before he opened the door of one of the carriages and stepped inside, closing it behind him.

They began walking back to Eileen's house in silence. A whistle sounded in the distance and Mick thought that was probably the signal for Thomas' train to pull out from the platform, taking him to a new life in a strange land. He would miss his brother, he realised, and any prayers that he was ever likely to say in the future, even if they were to be few and far between, would be for him. There was not much they could have said to each other on the platform. Irishmen weren't like that, he knew, whether they were brothers or not, but he hoped that his brother knew how he felt.

'If we ever have a son, we'll call him Thomas,' he said as they walked through George Square.

'Is that right?' Kate said. 'So who says you get to choose the name?'

'And if it's a girl, she'll be Kathleen, and she'll turn out as beautiful as her mother.' Mick grinned as he leant over and kissed her. 'But I'll let no Irishman near her,' he said. 'Certainly not one like me.'

'God forbid,' laughed Kate.

He wanted to take his time walking back to the house, soaking in every inch of this city. He didn't think he would ever return but it would always be the place where he met Kate so he knew he'd remember it fondly. It also felt like a weight had been lifted off his shoulders, even though Walsh would continue to hunt for him. He'd probably never truly be free and it might even be when he was an old man, sitting on a mound of earth outside his cottage in Cork, that Walsh would finally catch up with him. Still, as long as Kate was with him, he knew he'd be happy wherever he was and whatever happened. He stopped walking and stood facing her.

'I think we should get married,' he said.

'What, right now?'

'As soon as we get home. I want to lie in bed beside Mrs Kate Costello and when we meet people, I want to say, "This is my wife, Kate."'

'I think maybe that bump on the head's affected you,' she said, but she smiled and he knew that she was thinking about it now, if she hadn't been already.

They had now passed through Glasgow Cross, standing for almost five minutes until there was a gap in the traffic and they could race across, Mick pulling Kate by the hand. The air was filled with a thousand city noises – men selling pots and pans from hastily assembled stalls, babies crying, mother's shouting at badly behaved toddlers, carts rattling up and down the street, and the occasional song from a drunken man staggering to or from the pub. Mick looked forward to the tranquillity of home.

He imagined being out on a summer's afternoon in Cork, the smell of freshly cut grass hanging in the air and tingling his nose. He would be driving the cart, his left arm hopefully mended enough so that he'd be able use it, while Kate sat beside him, snuggling in so close her own aroma fought for attention with the grass. In her arms was a baby – it would be their son, Thomas. He was sleeping contently, resting against his mother's swollen belly that was carrying their second child, the daughter he would love and protect forever.

People would shout greetings to them – Mr and Mrs Costello – as they drove out into the countryside, not really knowing where they were going, but just enjoying being together as one happy family. He sighed contentedly and squeezed Kate's hand. They were going to get married as soon as they got to Cork. A visit to the priest would be the first thing he'd do after they'd got settled. He liked the sound of that – Mrs Kate Costello. It fitted together perfectly, like it had always meant to be.

A sudden pain shot through his back and he could feel the air being sucked out of him like someone had reached a hand in and ripped out his lungs. He was instantly breathless and he tried to squeeze out a sound from his mouth but there was nothing. He was gargling now as his throat quickly filled up with blood and it felt like he was back in the barrel of water again, a drowning man counting down the last seconds of his life, thrashing about in a desperate attempt to save himself. Only this time there was no one to pull him out with seconds to spare.

His legs began to buckle and he was pulling Kate down with him, though as he got nearer the ground he could feel her hand slipping away from his. He tried to hold on but there was no strength in his arm. He didn't know why that would be the case since it was his good arm but the more he grasped, the more it felt like he was trying to get a firm hold of water. His mouth was filling up with blood now and it was pouring down his chin. He kept trying to take deep breaths to fill up his lungs but nothing seemed to help.

He was on his knees, and his arm thrashed around blindly looking for Kate. Where was she? Why had she let him go? He felt cold, like the winter air had rushed into his body through his back and he tried shouting out her name, 'Kate! Kate!' though he knew nothing made sense when his mouth was overflowing with blood.

Then the voice of the devil was at his ear and he knew that this was what had sent the chill through his body.

'You can run but you can't hide.'

There were dull screams as he toppled over onto the ground and he saw Kate. Her mouth was open and he presumed she was screaming but the noise was getting fainter and fainter. He held up his arm again and a hand grasped his as he began choking. I'm drowning, he wanted to shout. Help me! But he knew there would be no words now.

He was rolled over onto his side and it felt for a moment that everything would be okay as the liquid ran clear of his throat, but it was only a temporary respite. He wanted to keep his eyes open to see Kate but they were blurring over and he rolled them to try and stay focused on her face. He could hear nothing now but he knew she was close to him, the smell of freshly picked apples drifting up through his nostrils and he smiled. The dull pain in his back was now throbbing and he felt like his whole body had been plunged into an icy river.

Hold me, Kate Costello, he tried to say and she must have read his mind because her arms dragged his body up off the ground and she was hugging him. It seemed like it was raining now, salty drops of water splashing onto his face. His eyes were closing over and there was nothing he could do about it. His head felt light, like he'd stood up too quickly and got dizzy and he could only take tiny breaths, which fought for space in his throat alongside the torrent of blood which now spilled onto the pavement, mixing with the liquid pouring from the wound in his back and turning the cobbles an ominous black colour.

His eyes flickered and when he saw her face he realised that she was the most beautiful girl he had ever seen in his life. He smiled again as his eyes closed for the last time.

# 30

# NO NEWS IS GOOD NEWS

Thomas could hear the roar of the sea which built to a crescendo as it crashed against the shore, then there would be a lull for a few moments until the next wave came rolling in, and it never seemed to end. It had taken him weeks to become accustomed to the noise and even now it would startle him when he wasn't expecting it. He looked out the window of his cottage, his eyes gazing beyond the endless fields which surrounded him on all sides and focusing on the angry waters of the Atlantic Ocean. They looked chilly and uninviting and he knew that they had devoured many bodies down through the years.

There was nothing on the horizon but he kept staring at it, knowing that somewhere out there, beyond the vast body of water that seemed to stretch into infinity, lay America. Many people must have stood on this island and thought the same thing, only they viewed it as a means of escape. There was no escape for Thomas. This was his prison and here he would see out the rest of his days amidst the crashing waves and howling winds and desolate nothingness.

Slipping his coat on and grabbing his hat, he ventured outside. Immediately the wind rushed in from the ocean, sensing a fresh victim, and it began its relentless onslaught. He stuck his hat tightly on his head, still keeping one hand pressed firmly down on it, and stepped away from the front door. The cottage had given him some measure of protection from the elements but now, as he struggled down the path, he was cruelly exposed and it took all his strength to make it the two hundred yards to the church, where he quickly pulled the door open and scurried inside, slamming it shut behind him and grateful for a moment of peace.

He patted his breast pocket just to check that the letter was still there. It had arrived that morning. Roddy the postman had delivered it almost as soon as the boat had dropped off the weekly mail.

'It's from the city,' he'd said, hovering in the kitchen in the hope that Thomas would open it. He recognised the handwriting straight away. It was from Monsignor Dolan. Normally he would have opened it there and then but he liked the idea of keeping Roddy waiting. Eventually, when there was no movement on the letter and no offer of a cup of tea, the postman left, though Thomas knew he'd be back tomorrow, hoping to satisfy his curiosity.

Thomas wanted to read the letter alone and thought he'd have more chance of some solitude in the chapel. He was tempted to bolt the door but if anyone tried to get in and discovered they couldn't, the news that the church was locked would race round the island faster than the vicious Atlantic wind that kept him feeling permanently cold. He had been an object of curiosity since his arrival, some of it friendly and some of it hostile. It helped that he spoke Gaelic; his Irish version was close enough to what they spoke on the island that he was able to communicate, and he was picking up their language with each passing day. He knew that, eventually, they would become used to him and he to them. After all, he was going to be here for a long, long time.

It was probably the safest place for him to be, far from people who would want him to answer for what he'd done. He knew Dan Foley had been caught – that had always been the deal – though the bonus for Walsh was that he also found the guns. Thomas had presumed the crates were already safely hidden in Ireland rather than stacked untidily in the kitchen of a flat just a few streets from St Alphonsus'. It was Padraig who'd set up the meeting. He'd been suspicious but Thomas had managed to convince him he had information that only he could tell Foley. Padraig gave him a time and a place when his comrade would be expecting him and Thomas passed it on in return for his brother's release.

The Brotherhood didn't forget. Thomas knew that and he only hoped when it came time for him to answer for all his words and deeds, it would be to his maker rather than facing the barrel of an unforgiving gun.

Padraig Clarke would never forget either. He'd fled to Ireland, just managing to evade capture, which would probably have resulted in him suffering the same fate as Dan Foley. It would be a while before he'd venture back to Glasgow, even though his family remained there. Thomas was glad of the distance between him and Padraig, thankful of the isolated protection his island home offered him.

Thomas knew that reading Monsignor Dolan's letter would probably make him feel homesick and he feared it might take him days to shake it off, but at the same time, it would be nice to hear from his old parish priest. No doubt there would be more apologies for what had happened back in Glasgow but Thomas did not hold a grudge against the old man. He walked to the front of the chapel, genuflecting before the altar and then sitting down in the first row. He slipped off his jacket, draping it over the back of the chair and placed his hat on the seat beside him. Then he reached into the coat pocket and took out the letter, opening the envelope and sliding out a single sheet of white paper, smiling as he saw the familiar handwriting that covered most of the sheet.

*Dear Thomas,*

*I had to get Monsignor Dolan to write this for me since I'm not very good at writing and I will probably have to get him to read your reply if you send one, even though I won't be in Glasgow if you do.*

*I thought you should know that Mick is dead. I'm sorry to be the one to tell you and I wish it could have been to your face. Duffy killed him. I always thought that he'd kill me but this is worse and maybe that's what he wanted. I miss him all the time and it hurts so much that sometimes I wish I could go to sleep and never wake up. I'm glad*

*Monsignor Dolan is writing this letter otherwise the paper would be covered in tears by now.*

*I know this news will hurt you because he was your brother, but he was going to be my husband. He had asked me to marry him, just after we said goodbye to you at the train station.*

*The funeral was a lovely service. There weren't many people at the church but Monsignor Dolan said some really nice things about Mick and I'm sure you would have been pleased.*

*By the time you read this, I'll be back in Donegal. I can't bear the thought of staying in Glasgow because I see him round every corner and hear his voice on every street.*

*I know you'll say a prayer for Mick but will you say one for me too, even though I don't really deserve it after I chose your brother. I loved him and I miss him all the time.*

*You are in my prayers, Thomas, even though I'm not sure if God ever listens to me, and I hope that you will find some happiness in your life.*

*All my love,*

*Kate*

Thomas sat for a long time inside the chapel, ignoring the howling wind that swooped and swirled round the building. He knew he should say a prayer for his brother's soul and in the fullness of time he would, but for just now his head was filled with images of Mick, fresh ones rushing into his mind every few seconds, some of them from when they were boys in Galway, running and shouting and laughing through the green fields that seemed to stretch forever, or ones of the two of them together in Glasgow. Each memory seemed to make him smile.

When he had stepped onto the train, he had resigned himself to the fact that he might never see his brother again, but he hadn't imagined it would be because Mick was dead. The news was taking some time to sink in and he read the letter again.

Slowly he stood up and walked to the little altar at the side of the main one. It sat unobtrusively below a picture of Our Lady holding the baby Jesus. He took out a packet of matches from his statue and lit one of the candles, and when the flame began to dance nervously, he pushed the paper close to it until it caught fire. Then he held it delicately at one of the edges until the flame raced across the page, devouring all in its path. He dropped the crumbling remnants of the letter on the floor and quickly stamped on it.

There was no point replying to Kate since she would now be in Ireland, and he'd never know how to find her, while there was nothing he wanted to say to Monsignor Dolan. He looked up at the crucifix on the wall behind the altar and made the sign of the cross, offering a quick prayer for his brother. Then he picked up his coat and hat and prepared himself for another battle with the elements to get back to the cottage.

# 31

# A SORT OF HOMECOMING

The woman shuffled up past a couple of men who stood leaning on the side of the boat, looking out at the choppy waters and silently smoking, then dropped onto the wooden seat next to Kate. Kate didn't glance round at the woman, who was now hauling a bag onto her lap and rummaging in it, muttering to herself and occasionally clearing her throat and spitting out the contents at her feet.

The boat had broken out into the open sea now and the spray from the waves which buffeted the vessel would occasionally shower them. Kate found it strangely refreshing though she heard other people complaining every time it happened. The boat was busy, though not as full as the ones that headed in the opposite direction and she was grateful for the welcome space on the deck. She didn't know whether she'd be able to cope if she'd been packed onto one of the cattle ships. Her case was jammed between her legs and she would rip the hand off anyone who dared try and touch it since it contained the few mementos she had of Mick. There wasn't much. His bloodstained shirt, with the hole in the back; a few coins that were in his pocket; his cigarettes and a holy medal that Thomas must have given to him before he left – St Michael the Archangel. It hadn't done him much good, and it seemed he'd been abandoned by his guardian angel as well, Kate thought, but those few things were more precious to her than just about anything else in the world.

Occasionally she had lit one of his cigarettes just so that the smoke would remind her of him but she didn't want to use them all up. Once they were gone, that smell would be lost forever, and she wasn't sure her memories would be enough to sustain her. She could still smell him on the shirt, which she clutched every night when she slept. It didn't matter to her that it was covered in his blood, because that was still part of him. When she couldn't sleep, haunted by pictures of him dying in her arms on the street, she would spread the shirt out and run her fingers round the hole where Duffy's knife had sliced through the material and then his flesh, trying to imagine how he had felt in those last few seconds, and she'd do that until her eyes stung from the tears which were falling onto the shirt and she finally fell into an exhausted but restless sleep.

'I'm Molly Flannigan,' the woman beside her said, holding out a silver canister. Kate shook her head. She could smell the whiskey, from the canister and the woman's breath, and she felt like she was going to be sick; there had been more than enough of that already.

'Suit yourself,' Molly said and took a deep gulp before wiping her mouth on her sleeve. 'It makes the journey shorter, darling.'

Kate knew her parents would be surprised when she turned up on their doorstep but she didn't know what else to do or where to go. She just wanted her mammy to hug her, letting her cry into her bosom, while her daddy would stand awkwardly in the room before muttering something by way of welcome and then heading off to the pub. Secretly he'd be delighted that his little Kathleen was home again. There'd probably be a few drinks bought that night.

Would they even recognise her? It had been a long time since she'd left Donegal and she had changed. For one thing, she felt old now, weary, and her face already wore the tell-tale signs of a hard life. Would they still be alive? For all she knew they could have both passed away and she'd be none the wiser. She shook her head. It was better not to think like that. And she felt sure that her mammy would recognise her in the middle of a snow storm, so she knew she wouldn't be a stranger to them.

'And what's your name?' Molly asked.

'Kate.'

'Just Kate.'

Kate looked at her and smiled. 'Kate Costello.'

'Nice to meet you, Kate Costello,' said Molly, holding out a dirty hand, which Kate shook. 'Are you going home then?'

Kate nodded.

'So am I. It's always nice to go home, so it is.'

Kate stared ahead of her, though only the clear and vast sea was visible, but she had resolved not to look back. She didn't want to set eyes on Scotland ever again. She bit her tongue to stop a tear escaping. She didn't want Molly to see her crying because she knew it would only bring more unwelcome questions. There had been too many tears already anyway, enough to fill up the Irish Sea ten times over, and they never made her feel better or change what had happened.

Her hands rested on her belly. She knew it was too early for her to be showing and it would be another few months before she'd be able to feel it kicking, but there was a baby growing inside of her at this very moment. She knew it would be a boy – a son who would grow up and look after her in her old age. He would remind her of his father and sometimes that would make her happy. Other times it would make her sad. And he would have the name she chose for him just so that he would always know where he came from. Thomas Michael Costello would be born and raised in Ireland, and she'd make sure he never set foot in the country that had taken his father from her.

Everything happens for a reason, her mammy used to tell her, and she had to believe that was true.